Billionaire's Marriage Bargain

LEANNE BANKS

Rich Man's Fake Fiancée

CATHERINE MANN

MILLS & BOON

Pure reading pleasure™

First published in Great Britain 2009
by Harlequin Mills & Boon Limited,
Eton House, 18-24 Paradise Road, Richmond, Surrey TW9 1SR

The publisher acknowledges the copyright holders of the individual works as follows:

Billionaire's Marriage Bargain © Leanne Banks 2008
Rich Man's Fake Fiancée © Catherine Mann 2008

ISBN: 978 0 263 87104 3

51-0709

Printed and bound in Spain
by Litografia Rosés S.A., Barcelona

BILLIONAIRE'S
MARRIAGE BARGAIN

by
Leanne Banks

Dear Reader,

You first met wealthy, charming and heartless Alex Megalos in *Bedded by the Billionaire*. Ever met a man with so much charm and good looks he should wear a caution sign? That's our Alex.

You can't blame our heroine, heiress Mallory James, for falling under his spell on sight. Who wouldn't? After she embarrasses herself with him, however, she pulls herself together and declares him out of her league.

When Alex comes around again, she's forced to reject him repeatedly. Alex is determined, though, and with each repeated exposure, Mallory becomes more susceptible to his seductive charms. There's more to him than she'd originally thought. With a man like Alex, it's easy for a woman to lose her head and her heart. But what are his real motives?

Danger: shocking scandals ahead.

Don't you love a delicious, shocking scandal… as long as you're not in the middle of it? Enjoy this newest BILLIONAIRE'S CLUB story. After you read this story, visit me at www. leannebanks.com and tell me who you think our next hero will be.

Until next time…

Warmly,

Leanne

LEANNE BANKS

is a *New York Times* and *USA TODAY* bestselling author who is surprised every time she realises how many books she has written. Leanne loves chocolate, the beach and new adventures. To name a few, Leanne has ridden on an elephant, stood on an ostrich egg (no, it didn't break), gone parasailing and indoor skydiving. Leanne loves writing romance because she believes in the power and magic of love. She lives in Virginia with her family and her four-and-a-half-pound Pomeranian named Bijou.

This book is dedicated to Tami.
Thank you.

One

"She needs a husband."

Alex Megalos looked at the man who had made the statement, sixty-year-old Edwin James, owner of the extremely successful James Investments and Wealth, Inc. Alex wondered if Edwin was hinting that Alex should take on the job.

Alex had successfully avoided commitment his entire thirty years, although things with his most recent girlfriend had gotten a bit dicey and that relationship was headed for the end. The fact that it didn't bother him made him feel a little heartless, but he knew it was best to end a relationship that was doomed. Plus he'd known enough women to realize that they all wanted something. As far as he was concerned, love was fiction in its purest form.

He swallowed a sip of Scotch and glanced across the ballroom at the woman under discussion. A sweet brunette with ample curves, Mallory James was no man-eater like most of the women Alex dated. She wore a modest deep-blue cocktail dress that cradled her breasts, and featured a hem that swung freely at the tops of her knees. Nice legs, but what appealed most about her was her smile and laughter. So genuine.

"Mallory should have no trouble finding a husband. She's a lovely girl with a lot of charm."

Edwin set his empty squat glass on the bar and frowned. "On the outside. On the inside she's a pistol. Plus, she's picky."

Alex did a double take. "Mallory?" he said in disbelief.

"Her mother and I have tried to match her up with a half-dozen men and she passed on all of them. I had some hope for that Timothy fellow she's with tonight, but it doesn't look good. She says he's a great *friend*."

Alex nodded. "Friend. The kiss of death. Just curious. Why do you want her to get married?"

"She's out of college and she wants to work in my company."

"Is that bad?"

Edwin glanced from side to side and lowered his voice. "I hate to admit it, but I can't handle it. She could be a perfect employee but I can't handle the possibility of having to correct her, or worse yet, fire her. The truth is when it comes to my daughter, I'm a marshmallow. You can't be soft if you want to achieve what I have."

"No, you can't. You think marriage will solve things."

"I want her safe, taken care of. She works with a bunch of charity foundations, but she says she wants more. If she's not kept occupied, I'm terrified she'll end up like some of her peers. In jail, knocked up, on a nude sex tape."

Surprised, Alex looked at Mallory again, a wicked visual of her dressed in skimpy lingerie coming out of nowhere. "You really think she's that kind of girl?"

"No. Of course not. But everyone can have a weak moment," he said. "Everyone. She needs a man who can keep her occupied. She needs a challenge."

Alex was at a rare loss as to how to respond. He had approached Edwin to casually set up a meeting to discuss finding an investor for his pet resort project. "I'd like to help, but—"

"I understand," Edwin quickly said. "I know you're not the right man for Mallory. You're still sampling all the different flowers out there, if you know what I mean," he said, giving Alex a nudge and wink. "Nothing wrong with that. Nothing at all. But," he said, lifting his finger, "you may know someone who would be right for my Mallory. If you know some men with the right combination of drive and character, send them my way and I would be indebted to you."

Alex processed Edwin's request. Having Edwin in his debt would put Alex in a better position of strength in gaining the funding he wanted. One of the first rules of wealth was to use other people's money to achieve your goals.

Alex glanced at Mallory. It wouldn't hurt anyone to help Edwin in this situation. In fact, all parties stood to gain.

He caught Mallory's eye and shot her a smile. She gave a slight smile then her gaze slid away and she waved to her father. "I haven't had a chance to talk with Mallory in a while. I'll go over and get reacquainted. I'll see what I can come up with for you, Edwin."

Over six feet of pure masculine power, with dark brown hair and luminescent green eyes that easily stole a woman's breath, Alex Megalos turned women into soft putty begging for the touch of his hands. His sculpted face and well-toned body could have been cut from marble for display in a museum. He was intelligent, successful and could charm any woman he wanted out of her clothes. His charm belied a sharp and tough businessman. As a hotshot VP for Megalos De Luca Resorts, International he was prized for his dynamic innovative energy and making things happen.

So why was he looking at her? In the past, Mallory had always felt he'd looked through her instead of at her. When she'd first met Alex, she'd turned into a stuttering, clumsy loon every time he'd come close. He was so magnetic she'd instantly developed a horrible crush and flirted with him.

And that awful night when she'd actually tried to seduce him… Mallory cringed. Even though Alex had been chivalrous by catching her so she didn't get a concussion from falling on the floor when she'd blacked out, it had been one of the most mortifying moments of her life. Although Alex had thought her fainting spell had been due to her drinking her cocktails too quickly, the incident had been a wake-up call.

Good sense had finally prevailed. She was over the crush now. She knew good and well he was out of her league. Plus she wasn't sure Alex Megalos had the ability to stay focused on one woman for more than a month. Talk about an invitation to heartbreak.

Mallory exhaled and turned toward some guests of the charity event she'd planned. "Thank you so much for coming, Mr. and Mrs. Trussel."

"You've done a marvelous job," Mrs. Trussel, a popular Las Vegas socialite raved. "The turnout is so much better this year than last year. I'm chairing the heart association's event. I would love to get together with you to hear some of your ideas."

"Give the poor girl a break," Mr. Trussel, a balding attorney said. "She hasn't even finished this project."

"I feel like I need to call dibs." Mrs. Trussel

paused and studied Mallory for a long moment. "You aren't married, are you?"

Mallory shook her head. "No. Too busy lately."

"I have a nephew I would like you to meet. He's earned his law degree and been working for the firm for the last year. He'd be quite a catch. May I give him your number?"

Mallory opened her mouth, trying to form a polite *no*. If she had one more setup, she was going to scream. "I—"

"Mallory, it's been too long," a masculine voice interrupted.

Her heart gave a little jump. She knew that voice. Taking a quick, little breath, determined not to embarrass herself, she turned slowly. "Alex, it has been a while, hasn't it? Have you met Mr. and Mrs. Trussel?"

"As a matter of fact, I have. It's good to see you both. Mrs. Trussel, you look enchanting as ever," he said.

Mrs. Trussel blushed. "Please call me Diane," she said. "We were just saying what a wonderful job Mallory has done with the event tonight."

"I have to agree," Alex said. "Would you mind if I steal her away for a moment?"

"Not at all," Mr. Trussel said, ushering his wife away.

"I'll be in touch," the woman called over her shoulder.

As soon as they left, Mallory turned toward Alex. "If you're being nice to me because my father asked you to, it's not necessary."

Alex narrowed his eyes a millimeter. "Why would you say that?"

Mallory moved a few steps away to keep check on the crowd milling through the giant ballroom. She noticed Alex stayed by her side. "Because you were talking with him just a few minutes ago and I know he's trying to make sure I get more friends so I don't move back to California."

"California?" Alex said. "He didn't mention that. Besides, why wouldn't I want to come say hello to you on my own? We've met before."

"Just a couple of times," she said.

"I can even tell you that the first time we met you spilled wine on me." He lifted his lips in a sexy smile designed to take the sting out of his words.

He would remember that. Mallory tried very hard not to blush. She looked away from the man. He was just too damned devastating. "I didn't spill wine. The server did. Even Lilli De Luca said the server was moving too fast."

"That's right. You're good friends with Lilli. Have you seen her and Max's baby?"

"All the time. Even though she has a mother's helper, she lets me take care of David sometimes. Such a sweetheart. He's sitting up on his own now."

Fearing she wouldn't be able to sustain her airy, you-don't-impress-me act much longer, she took a step away from Alex. "Great seeing you," she said. "Thank you for coming to the event tonight. Your donation and presence will mean a lot to inner-city children and their parents." She lifted her hand in a gesture of goodbye. "Take care."

Alex wrapped his hand around hers. "Not so fast. Aren't you going to thank me for rescuing you?"

Her heart tripping over itself at his touch, she looked at him in confusion. He wasn't talking about the time she'd blacked out, was he? "Rescuing me? How?"

"I've met the Trussels' nephew. Nice guy, but boring as the day is long."

Mallory bit the inside of her lip. "That could just be your opinion. Not everyone has to be Mr. Excitement. Not everyone drives race cars in their spare time. Not everyone keeps three women on the string at one time while looking for number four."

Alex's narrowed his eyes again. "I believe I've just been insulted."

Mallory shook her head, wishing she'd been just a teensy more discreet, but Alex seemed to bring out lots of unedited thoughts and feelings. "I was just stating facts."

"You should get your facts straight. Yes, I've had a few girlfriends, but I generally stick to one at a time unless I make it clear that I'm a free agent and the women should be, too."

A few girlfriends. Mallory resisted the urge to snort. "It's really none of my business. Again, I do appreciate your presence and—"

"You keep trying to dismiss me. Why? Do you dislike me?" he asked, his green gaze delving into hers.

Mallory felt her cheeks heat. "I—I need to watch over the event. The headline entertainer will be appearing in just a few minutes."

"Okay, then let's get together another time."

She stared at him for a full five seconds, almost falling into the depths of his charisma then shook her head. Those were the words she'd dreamed of hearing from him eight months ago. Not now. "I'll check my—"

"Hey, Mallory. You're looking hot tonight," a man said in a loud voice.

Mallory glanced at the man with the bleached-blond shock of hair covering one of his eyes as he sauntered toward her. She braced herself. "Oh, no."

"Who is he?" Alex asked.

"Brady Robbins. He's the son of one of the resort owners. He wants to be a rock star and was hoping my father would underwrite his dream. Bad setup," she whispered. "Very bad setup."

"Hey, babe," Brady said, putting his arm around Mallory and pulling her against him. "We had a great time taking that midnight swim in the pool that night. You were so hot. I couldn't get enough of you. Tell me you've missed me?"

Mallory felt her cheeks heat. She'd worn a swimsuit and nothing hot had happened. She tried to push away from him. "I've been so busy," she said, disconcerted by Brady's ability to hold her captive despite his tipsy state.

"The lady's not interested. Go sober up," Alex said, freeing Mallory in one sure, swift movement.

Brady glanced up at Alex and frowned. "Who are you? Mallory and I have a history," he said and tried to reach for Mallory again. Alex stepped between them.

"She doesn't want to share a future with you," Alex said.

"She didn't say that to me," Brady said in a loud voice. "You don't know it, but she has a thing for me. She likes musicians."

Mallory cringed at the people starting to stare in her direction. She didn't want this kind of situation taking the focus off the purpose of the event. She cleared her throat. "Brady, I don't think we're right for each other," she began.

"Don't say that, baby," he said, lunging for her.

Alex caught him again. "Come on, Brady. It's time for you to leave," he said and escorted the wannabe rock star from the room. Mallory said a silent prayer that she wouldn't have to face either man again.

A week later, Mallory's Realtor friend, Donna Heyer, took her to view a condominium at one of the most exclusive addresses in Vegas. The facility boasted top-notch security, luscious grounds with pools, hot tubs, tennis courts and golf courses.

"I love it. Let me see what I need to do to make it happen," Mallory said after they left the spacious condo available for lease. The truth was she would love a closet at this point, as long as she wasn't under the same roof as her loving, but smothering father.

"Just remember," Mallory said as they walked toward the bank of elevators. "This is top secret. I don't want anyone to know, because if my father figures out that I'm determined to move out, he'll have a cow and find a way to sabotage me."

"No one will hear it from me," said Donna, a discreet forty-something woman whom Mallory had met through charity work. "I'm surprised he doesn't understand that you need your independence."

Mallory sighed. "He's afraid I'll turn all wild and crazy."

Donna gasped. "But you would never—"

"I agree I would never, but within the last year, he has developed high blood pressure and an ulcer. When I told him I wanted to move back to California, he had an episode that sent him to the hospital, so I hate—" The elevator doors whooshed open and Mallory looked straight into the green gaze of Alex Megalos. Her stomach dipped. *No, not now.*

"Mallory," he said.

"Alex," both she and Donna chimed at the same time. So Donna knew Alex, too. That shouldn't surprise her. Didn't everyone in Vegas know who Alex was? He was constantly featured in both the business and social pages. Glancing at Donna as she entered the elevator, she bit her lip.

"Good to see you, Donna," Alex said then turned to Mallory. "If you're considering buying here, it's a great property."

"Just looking," Mallory said.

Donna shot Mallory a weak smile that was more of a wince. "I sold the penthouse to Alex."

"Oh," Mallory said, unable to keep the disappointment from her voice. If Alex mentioned it to her father… The elevator dinged its arrival to the street floor and the doors opened. "Donna, could you give me just a second to talk to Alex?"

"No problem," Donna said. "I'll wander around the lobby."

Dressed in a perfectly cut black suit with a crisp white shirt and designer tie, Alex looked down at her expectantly. "You wanted to apologize for not getting back to me?" he said, more than asked.

"Sorry. I've been busy and I knew you would be, too," she said, catching a whiff of his cologne.

"Shopping for a new condo," he said.

"About that," she said, lifting her index finger. "I would really appreciate it if you could keep that on the down low for me. Please," she added.

"You don't want your father to find out," he said.

"At this rate, I'll be lucky to get out of the house by age thirty."

His lips twitched. "You could always get married."

She rolled her eyes. "Ugh. You sound like him. Besides, think about it, what would you have done if your father insisted you get married at age twenty-five in order to move out of the house?"

"Point taken, but you're female. My father would have done the same if he'd had daughters."

"But you can't really agree with the philosophy?" she asked, unable to believe he would share such a point of view. "You're more modern and liberated than that, aren't you?"

"In business, I am. I have to be. But my father is Greek. I was raised to protect women."

She gave him a double take. "Protecting them? Is that what you call what you do?"

He threw back his head and laughed. "Let's discuss this in the car. I can drop you off at home then go to my dull meeting where I have to deliver a speech."

"If you're the speaker, I'm sure it won't be dull. You don't need to take me home. Donna will drop me off at the mall where I parked my car."

He lifted his eyebrows. "This sounds like a covert OP. I can drop you off at the mall. Before you say no, remember you owe me."

"I don't owe you," she said, scowling.

"I helped you ditch your wannabe rock star ex-boyfriend."

"He was never my boyfriend," she told him. "Just a bad setup."

"Yet you took a midnight swim with him and he describes the evening as very hot."

"Probably because he doesn't remember it. If you must know, he had too much to drink and I had to get home on my own."

"I'm beginning to understand why your father wants to keep you locked up."

Alex helped Mallory into his Tesla Roadster, noticing the diamond anklet dangling from her ankle. She wore sandals with heels and her toenails were painted a wicked frosty red. She had nice ankles and calves. Her hips were lush, her breasts even more lush. Her body was more womanly than that of any woman he'd dated, but there was something about her spirit, the sparkle in her personality that got his attention. Despite the fact that women often described him as charming, he'd been feeling old and cynical lately.

"You must exercise," he said as he slid into the leather driver's seat and nudged the car into gear.

"Yes. Why?"

"You have great legs," he said, accelerating out of the condominium complex.

"Thank you," she said and he heard a twinge of self-consciousness in her voice. "I walk and I've started doing Zumba and Pilates. Now back to the discussion about my father, I really would like your promise that you won't discuss my visit to this complex with him."

"I don't see why he needs to know. You haven't taken any action yet, have you?"

"No, but I hope to." She skimmed her fingertip over the fine leather seat. "I wanted this car. It's sporty and green. Once my father read that it goes from zero to one hundred in four seconds, he freaked out. I should have started out telling him I planned to get a motorcycle. Maybe then he would have agreed."

Alex laughed. "You really are trying to drive him crazy, aren't you?"

"Not at all. I just want to live my life." She looked up at the roof. "Can we lower the top?" She glanced at him. "Or are you afraid of messing up your hair?"

He felt a jerk in his gut at the sexy challenge in her words. "I can handle it if you can," he said and pressed the button to push back the roof.

Mallory lifted her head to the sun and tossed back her hair. The sun glinted on her creamy skin and his gaze slid lower to the hint of cleavage he saw in her V-neck blouse. Alex was beginning to get a peek at the wild streak her father had mentioned. He wondered how deep that streak went.

"What do you do with your time?" he asked.

"Plan charity events, volunteer at the hospital and the women's shelter, visit friends, steal away to the beach when I can." She hesitated. "I'll tell you more if you promise not to tell my father."

"You have my word as a gentleman."

"I don't often hear you described as a gentle-man," she said.

He threw her a sideways glance. "What do you hear?"

"Lady killer," she said. "Player."

"And what do you say?"

"I don't know you well enough," she said. "I just know I'm not in your league."

He shot her another quick glance. "Why not?"

"I'm not a model or a player. I'm just—" She shrugged. "Me. Average."

"You're far from average."

"Yeah, yeah," she said, waving aside his compli-ment.

Her dismissal irritated him. "I gave you my word. Now tell me your secret."

"I'm working on my master's degree online."

"What's so bad about that?"

"My father wants me to get married." She lifted her hand. "Take this exit for the mall, please. Oh, and my other secret is that I'm learning to play golf. Now that's funny."

"I'd like to see it."

She shook her head. "No, no. You probably have a handicap of something outrageously good, like ten."

"Nine, but who's counting," he said.

She laughed and shook her head again. "I'm sure you are." She glanced outside the window. "I'm parked near Saks. The white BMW."

He pulled beside the brand-new model luxury car. "That's not a shabby ride," he said.

Opening the door, Mallory turned to stroke the leather seat. "But it's not a Tesla," she cooed.

Amused by her enthusiasm for his car, he couldn't help wondering about her enthusiasm in bed with the right man who could inspire her.

She leaned toward him. "Now, remember you promised you wouldn't discuss any of this with my father."

"I won't say anything."

Her lips lifted in a broad smile so genuine that it distracted him. "Thanks," she said. "I'll see you around." She got out of the car.

"Wait," he called after her.

Turning back, she leaned into the car. "What?"

"Meet me for lunch," he said.

She met his gaze for several seconds of silence then wrinkled her brow in confusion. "Why?"

Alex's usually glib tongue failed him for a half-beat. "Because I'd like to see you again."

"Aren't you involved with someone?"

"No. I broke up with her."

Mallory's eyes softened. "Poor girl."

"Poor girl? What about me?"

She waved her hand. "You're the heartless player."

"Even players need friends," he said, trying to remember the last time he'd had to work this hard to persuade a woman to join him for lunch, for Pete's sake.

She looked at him thoughtfully. "So you'd like me to be your friend." She sighed. "I'll think about it."

Damn it. Negotiations were over. Time for hardball. "Lunch, Wednesday, one o'clock at the Village Restaurant," he said in a voice that brooked no argument.

Her eyes widened in surprise. Her mouth formed a soft O. "Okay," she said. "See you there."

He watched her whirl around, her hips moving in a mesmerizing rhythm as she sashayed to her white BMW. He hadn't realized that Mallory James could be such a firecracker.

If he was going to help poor Edwin find Mallory a husband, he needed to get some more questions answered. Mentally going through his list of acquaintances, he dismissed the first few men as contenders. Whoever he recommended for Mallory would need to be able to stay one step ahead of her. Otherwise, she would leave him eating her dust.

Two

Alex adjusted his tie as he returned to his office after a series of meetings that had begun at seven this morning. His conscientious assistant, Emma Weatherfield, greeted him with messages. "Three calls from Miss Renfro," she said in a low voice.

He nodded because he'd expected as much after he'd broken off with Chloe last week. "I'll take care of it."

Emma nodded, keeping her expression neutral. That was one of the many qualities he liked about his young assistant. She was a master of discretion.

"Ralph Murphy called. I asked him the purpose for his call and he wanted to know if Megalos-De Luca was still acquiring any additional luxury properties."

Alex's interest inched upward. If Ralph, a minor competitor, was calling him, then maybe he wanted to sell. Alex smelled a bargain. "I'll call him before I take lunch. Anything else?"

Emma flipped through the message slips. "Rita Kendall wants you to attend a benefit with her, and Tabitha Bennet wants to meet you for drinks on Thursday. Chad in marketing wants five minutes with you to get an opinion on a new idea." She paused. "Oh, and Mallory James called because she can't make lunch today. She sends her apologies."

Alex stared at Emma in disbelief. "Mallory ditched our lunch date?" He had women practically crawling over broken glass to be with him and Mallory had blown him off. His temper prickled. "Did she leave an alternate day? Did she offer an excuse?"

Emma gave him a blank look and glanced at the message again, shaking her head. "I'm sorry, sir. She was only on the line for a moment and was very polite, but—"

He waved his hand. "Never mind." He took the messages and turned toward his office then stopped abruptly. "On second thought, get Mallory's cell number and find out what her schedule is for the next few days, day and night."

Mallory had been certain Alex Megalos would forget about her after she canceled their lunch meeting. After all there was always a line of ready and willing females begging for his attention. Mallory knew better than to spend any more time with him. He was too seductive and she was too susceptible. He might as well have been the most decadent chocolate she'd never tasted. Truth told, he was the perfect man for an exciting fling, but he'd said he wanted to be friends. It wouldn't take much time with him for her to turn into a pining sap again.

Stunned when he called and left a message on her cell, she procrastinated in responding, not sure what to say. Between her undercover classwork for her online master's degree, her charity obligations and quest to move out of the house, she was too busy for Alex, anyway. He was the kind of man who would take up a lot of space in a woman's life.

She'd agreed to fill in as head greeter for a charity event organized by one of her friends on Saturday night. As guests entered the ballroom event with music flowing from a popular jazz band, Mallory checked off reservations and directed staff to guide the guests to assigned tables.

As the last of the guests arrived, she tidied up the greeter table and tossed out the trash, still undecided whether she would remain much longer. She was tired and she needed to begin work on a research paper.

Glancing at the crowd of people and the beautiful display of flowers, she wavered in indecision.

"Room for one more?" a smooth male voice asked from behind her.

Fighting the havoc that his all too familiar voice wreaked on her nervous system, she whirled around. "Alex," she said in surprise.

Dressed in a dark suit that turned his eyes a shade of emerald, he pointed to the sheaf of paper on the table. "Isn't my name on the list?"

"Well, yes, but—" She'd noticed his name, but she'd assumed he wouldn't attend. Alex's name was always on the guest lists for these events. He was a high-profile businessman and bachelor. Every hostess wanted him at her party. She swallowed over a nervous lump in her throat and glanced at the seating chart. "There are two reserved seats on a front table just left of center. Will that work?" She waved toward the staff escort.

"As long as you join me," he said.

Surprised, she glanced behind him, searching for a woman. "You don't have a date?"

"I was hoping you would take pity on me," he said, but he reminded her of a sly wolf ready to raid the henhouse.

She gave an involuntary shiver of response. "I hadn't decided if I was going to stay for the entire event."

"Then I'll decide for you," he said and took her hand in his.

Mallory stuttered in response but was so caught off guard she couldn't produce an audible refusal. As Alex led her to the front table, she felt hundreds of eyes trained on her and Alex. Alex may have been accustomed to this kind of attention, but she was not. She quickly took the seat he pulled out for her.

The combination of the rhythm and blues band playing sexy songs of want and longing, the warm flickering candlelight and the close proximity of Alex's chair to hers created a sensual atmosphere. Two glasses of wine appeared for them in no time.

He lifted his glass and tilted it toward her. "To time together," he said. "Finally."

He stretched out his long legs and she felt the brush of his leg against hers underneath the table. He glanced at her again with those lady-killer green eyes of his and her chest tightened. She instinctively rubbed her throat and saw his glance fell to her neck and then to her breasts before he met her gaze again.

"You like this band?" he asked.

Forcing her gaze from his, she looked up at the stage and nodded. "The music is moody and the lyrics are—" She searched for the right description.

"Sexy."

The way he muttered the single word made her whip her head around to look at him. He was staring at her, studying her, considering her. She felt a rush of heat and took a quick sip of wine. "Yes," she said. "Do you like them?"

"Yes. Looks like the dancing has started. Let's go," he said and stood.

She blinked at him and remained seated. "Um."

He bent down and whispered in her ear. "Come on, we can talk better on the dance floor."

Confused, she followed him and slid into his arms. Why did they need to talk? she wondered. For that matter, why did they need to be together at all?

"How is your online class going?"

"Good, so far," she said, catching a whiff of his yummy cologne. "But I need to begin a research paper. That's why I was considering leaving early tonight."

"I'm glad I caught you," he said with a hint of predatory gleam in his eyes. "You're a difficult woman to catch. Do you treat all men like me? Blow off lunch dates, don't return calls…"

Embarrassed and then contrite that she'd been rude, she shook her head. "I'm sorry. I didn't mean to be inconsiderate. I just didn't take your invitation seri—" She broke off as his eyes narrowed and she realized her apology wasn't helping.

"You didn't take me seriously?" he echoed, incredulous. "Don't turn all polite on me now."

She sighed. "Well, you're such a flirt. I just didn't believe you."

"No wonder no man can get close to you. Is that one of your requirements? That whoever you date can't flirt? Sounds boring as hell to me."

"I didn't say that. It's that you flirt with every woman. I wouldn't want someone so important to me flirting with every other woman on the planet."

"Does that mean you want someone with very little sexual drive or appeal?"

"I didn't say that, either. Of course, I want a man with a strong sex drive. I just prefer that his drive be focused on me," she managed to say, but felt her face flaming. "But that's not all. He also needs to be intelligent and liberated enough to encourage me to do what I want to do."

He nodded. "You say you want someone you can walk over, but the truth is you want a challenge. I bet if a man played golf with you and took it easy on you that you'd be furious."

Surprised he'd nailed her personality so easily, she felt another twist of confusion. "This discussion is insane. I'm not looking for a long-term relationship right now, anyway. Just like you aren't," she added for good measure.

"That's where you're wrong. When the right woman comes along, I'll seal the deal immediately in every physical, legal and emotional way imaginable."

A shiver passed through her at his possessive tone and she couldn't help wondering what it would be like to be *the right woman* for Alex. Underneath all his charm, could he ever be truly devoted to one woman?

Mallory caught herself. She was insane to even be thinking about his right woman. Heaven knew, it wasn't *her*. Her thought patterns just proved she needed to create some distance between her and Alex.

She glanced at her watch. "I should help the hostess with the extra collections. You don't mind, do you?"

"If I did?" he said.

"Then because this is for charity, you would be a gracious gentleman and allow me to help the hostess," she said firmly.

"Damn, you're good," he said, admiration and something dangerous flickering in his gaze. Mallory supposed she was imagining both.

She smiled. "Excuse me. Good night."

He caught her before she left. "See me before you leave."

His intensity put her off balance. "I'll try," she conceded because she suspected he wouldn't let her leave until she promised that much. She walked out of his arms in the direction of sanity. She'd manufactured an excuse to get away from him. The hostess probably didn't need help, but Mallory sure did.

Mallory did end up helping the hostess with an assortment of last minute minicrises. Just as she was walking down one of the long halls toward the ballroom from one of her errands, she saw Alex approaching her.

"I had to track you down again," he said. "Why are you so determined to avoid me?"

She swallowed over a nervous lump in her throat. "I'm not—avoid—" She stopped when he lifted an eyebrow in disbelief.

"Oh, Mallory," a woman from the lobby called. "Is that you Mallory? My nephew…"

"Oh, no, it's Mrs. Trussel about her nephew. She's been calling me every other day."

"Come with me," he said, taking her hand and urging her down the hallway.

"Oh, Mallory." The voice grew fainter.

"I should at least respond," Mallory said as Alex tugged her around a corner.

"Did you avoid her, too?" he asked, opening a door and pulling her inside a linen closet.

"No. I called and made my excuses. Besides, you're partly to blame."

"Me? How?"

She pointed her finger at his hard chest. "You're the one who told me he was a total bore."

"I should have let you waste your time with him instead?"

"Well, no, but…" She bit her lip and looked around the small, nearly dark room. "Why are we in this closet?"

"Because this appears to be the only way I can get your undivided attention," he said. "You didn't answer my question. Why are you avoiding me?"

She sighed. "I told you. You're a huge flirt."

"Try again," he said.

She closed her eyes even though it was so dark it wasn't necessary. "Because you have this effect on women. You make women make fools of themselves. I don't want to make a fool of myself again," she whispered.

A heartbeat of silence followed. "Again? When did you make a fool of yourself?"

She bit her lip. "I know you remember that night I fainted," she said. "In the bar."

"You'd just drank your cocktails too quickly. It can happen to anyone," he said.

She took a deep breath. May as well get it all over with, she thought. "When I first met you, I was like everyone else. I thought you were gorgeous, irresistible, breathtaking. I—" She gulped. "I had a crush on you. That evening I was trying to—" She lowered her voice to a whisper. "Seduce you."

Silence followed. "Damn. I wish I'd known that. I would have handled the situation much differently."

"As if it would have mattered," she said. "Stop teasing. You know I'm not your type."

Suddenly she felt his hand on her waist. "I'm getting tired of your assumptions."

Mallory felt as if the room turned sideways.

"I can't tell if you're underestimating me or yourself. Damn, if you haven't made me curious," he said and lowered his mouth to hers.

If the room had been turning sideways before, for Mallory, it was now spinning. His hard chest felt delicious against her breasts, his hands masterful at her waist while his lips plundered hers.

Her heartbeat racing, she couldn't find it in herself to resist this one taste, this one time, this one kiss. With an abandonment she hadn't known she pos-

sessed, she stretched on tiptoe and slid her fingers
through his wavy hair and kissed him back.

She wanted to take in every sensation, his scent,
the surprised sound of his breath, the way his hands
dipped lower at the back of her waist and urged her
closer, his tongue seducing hers.

His kiss was everything and more she'd ever
dreamed all those months ago. Hotter, more seductive, more everything... She drew his tongue into
her mouth, sucking it the same way...

He abruptly pulled his head back and swore,
inhaling heavy breaths. After a second, he swore again.
"Where did that come from? I didn't know you—"

Thankful for the darkness in the closet, she bit her
still-buzzing lips. "You didn't know what?" she
whispered.

"I didn't know you would kiss like that. Hot enough
to singe a man, but keep him coming back for more."

Mallory couldn't help but feel a twinge of gratifi-
cation. After all, Alex was the master seducer.

He lowered his mouth and rubbed it over hers,
making her shiver with want. "You could make a
man do some crazy things. Who would have known
little Mallory—" He broke off and took her mouth
in another mind-blowing openmouth kiss. One of
his hands slid upward just beneath her breast.

He nibbled and ate at her lips. "Can't help wondering what else is cooking underneath that sweet-
girl surface."

A dozen wicked thoughts raced through Mallory's mind. Wouldn't she like to show him what was underneath? Wouldn't she like to feel his bare skin against hers? Wouldn't she like to get as close as she possibly could to him right now?

In a linen closet, some distant corner of her mind reminded her.

And afterward she would have to face the people outside.

She reluctantly pulled back. "I don't think that finding out what's underneath my sweet-girl surface is in the immediate future."

A moment of silence followed. "Why is that?"

"Because I would never want to have a public affair with you."

"This closet is hidden," he said, so seductively he tempted her to leave her objections behind.

"There will be people outside with questions and speculations. I should leave and then you can follow later."

"Later," he echoed.

"It was your idea to pull me in here."

"You would have rather faced Mrs. Trussel?"

She shifted from one foot to the other. "It doesn't matter. I just know I would never want to get involved with you, especially publicly."

"Why the hell not?" he demanded, his voice and body emanating his raw power.

She fortified her defenses. "Because after it's over,

I don't want anyone saying, 'Poor Mallory. Alex took advantage of her.'"

He gave a chuckle that raced through her blood like fire. "What about the poor guy who gets scorched by your kiss?"

She couldn't help feeling flattered, but she pushed it aside. "I should leave."

"I'll be right behind you," he said.

"I don't want to have to answer questions," she said.

"Then grab a towel and say you're cleaning up a mess."

"And you?"

"I'm making plans for the next time you and I get together."

"I don't think that's a good idea."

"I'll change your mind," he promised, and she shivered because she knew if anyone had the ability to change a woman's mind, even her mind, it was Alex.

The following day, Alex's mind kept turning to thoughts of Mallory. She piqued his interest more than any other woman had in ages. Women had come easily to him. The trademark Megalos features had served as both a blessing and a curse for Alex.

With his older brothers committed to medicine for their careers like their father, Alex had always been viewed as the lightweight because he was determined to pursue gaining back influence in the family-named business.

What his father and brothers didn't grasp was that when the tide was rolling against a man, he had to use everything to fight it off—intelligence, charm and power. Alex had used everything he had to rebuild the influence of the family name in Megalos-De Luca Enterprises. He'd butted heads more than once with Max De Luca, but lately the two had become more of a team and less adversarial.

Max had even expressed dismay over the board's decision not to support Alex's plan for a resort in West Virginia near Washington, D.C. Since Alex had secured legal permission to develop the resort on his own, he was determined to make it a success. He would show the board he knew what he was doing, and in the future they wouldn't fight him.

As an investor, Mallory's father could be important to Alex's strategy. Mallory could be the key to unlocking the door to her father.

Funny thing, though, the woman made him damned curious. He pushed the button for his assistant. "Emma, please come into my office."

"Of course, sir."

Seconds later, she appeared, notebook in hand. "Yes, sir."

"I want you to send flowers to Mallory James for me."

Her eyes widened. "Oh. She's lovely," Emma said. "So polite on the phone."

"Not my usual type," he said.

She paused a half-beat. "Much better."

His lips twitched in amusement. Emma was extremely discreet and rarely expressed her opinion unless he asked for it. "How well do you know her?"

"Not well at all. But she's very personable and gracious. You'd never know that her father could pay off the national debt."

"Send her a dozen red roses," he said.

Emma nodded slowly and made a note.

"What's wrong with a dozen red roses?" he asked, reading her expression.

"It's terribly clichéd," she said. "You're dealing with a different quality of woman with Mallory. Something personal might make more of an impression," she said, then rushed to add, "not that you need to impress her."

Alex thought for a moment as several ideas came to mind. "Okay send her a dozen roses in different colors with a Nike SasQuatch driver and a box of Titleist Pro V1 gold balls."

Emma blinked at him.

"She's learning to play golf," he said. "In the note, tell her I'll pick her up for a round of golf on Tuesday at 7:00 a.m."

Three

Tuesday morning at seven-thirty, Mallory was awakened by a knock on her bedroom door. Groggy, she lifted her head and groaned. She'd been up until 4:00 a.m. finishing a paper for her class.

"Miss James," the housekeeper said in a low voice through the door.

Mallory reluctantly rose from bed and opened her door. "Hilda?" she said to the housekeeper.

"There's a man downstairs and he insists on seeing you. Mr. Megalos."

Mallory groaned again. "Oh, no. Not him. I called his assistant to cancel."

"He's determined to talk to you. Shall I tell him you'll be down shortly?" Hilda asked.

"Okay, okay," Mallory said and closed the door. Thank goodness her mother and father were out of town for a business meeting in Salt Lake City, one of the few times her mother left the house. Otherwise, she would be grilled like her favorite fish.

She padded across the soft carpet to her bathroom. Her hair in a ponytail, she washed her face and brushed her teeth. She thought about applying makeup, fixing her hair and dressing up, then nixed the idea. If Alex saw her au naturel, that should really kill his curiosity.

Pulling on a bra and T-shirt and stepping into a pair of shorts, she descended the stairs where he was waiting at the bottom, looking wide-awake and gorgeous.

"Good morning, sleepyhead. Did you forget our date?"

"I called your assistant and gave her my regrets. I had a late night last night."

"Partying?"

"Ha. Finishing my paper until 4:00 a.m.," she corrected and yawned. "I'm sorry if you didn't get my message, but as you can see I'm not ready for a round of golf."

"We may as well squeeze in nine holes," he said. "You won't be able to go back to sleep, anyway."

Frowning at his perceptiveness, she covered another yawn. "How do you know that?"

"I'm just betting you're like me. Once I'm awake, I can't go back to sleep."

She studied him for a long moment. "You have me at a disadvantage. You've obviously had a full night of sleep."

"So I'll give you a few pointers," he said.

A lesson, she thought, her interest piqued. Although she was already taking lessons, it might be interesting to get another approach.

"Nine holes," she said.

"Until you can do the full eighteen," he said, clearly goading her.

She shouldn't give in to his challenge. Although she was tempted, she absolutely shouldn't. "Give me five minutes."

"A woman getting ready in five minutes?" he said. "That would really impress me."

She smiled as she thought about what her finished appearance would look like. No makeup, ponytail, shorts, shirt, socks and golf shoes. "We'll see," she said and headed back upstairs, feeling his gaze on her.

After Mallory took a rinse and spin shower, slapped on sunscreen and got dressed, she joined Alex as he drove to the golf course. She told herself not to focus on her attraction to him. Even though the sight of his tanned, muscular legs revealed by his shorts was incredibly distracting, she tried not to think about how sexy and masculine he was. She tried not to think about how it would feel to be held in his arms, in his bed, taken by him. She tried not to think about how exciting it would be to be the woman who drove him half as crazy as he drove her. Used to drive her, she firmly told herself.

Mallory knew Alex wasn't a forever kind of man, but she'd always thought he would be a great temporary man, amusing, passionate, sexy. If a woman decided to have an affair with him, she would need at all times to remember not to count on him for a long-term relationship. That would be a fatal, heartbreaking mistake.

Not that she was going to have an affair with him, anyway, Mallory told herself as she teed off. She watched her ball fly a respectable distance toward the hole and sighed in relief.

"Not bad," he said. "Just remember to lead with your hips both ways," he said and he swung his club and hit the ball.

His ball soared beyond hers. "What do you mean both ways?" she asked. "How?"

"First get balanced," he said. "Then lead with your hips in the backswing and the downswing. Get behind me and put your hands on my hips," he instructed.

"What?"

"Don't worry. I'm not going to seduce you on the golf course. Unless you want me to," he said and laughed in a voice that made her feel incredibly tempted.

Gingerly placing her hands on his hips, she felt the coil of power as he swiveled his hips and swung the club.

He turned around to face her and glanced down her body. "It's what women have always known. The power comes from the hips."

She felt a heat that threatened to turn her into a puddle of want, but stiffened her defenses and walked toward her next shot. "Thank you for the reminder."

Alex wondered if Mallory was making all those moves deliberately to distract him. After he'd mentioned the tip about hips, she swung her backside before each shot. When she wiggled her shoulders to stay loose, he couldn't help but notice the sway of her breasts.

"Visualize where you want the ball to go," she whispered to herself, and without fail she would bite her lush lower lip, reminding him of how her lips had felt when he'd kissed her.

By the time they reached the ninth hole, he had undressed her a dozen times. He knew she would be in his bed soon, but since she was Edwin's daughter, he figured he may have to play this one a little more carefully.

After she made her last putt, she turned to him with a smile on her face that made the sunny Nevada day seem even brighter. "Thank you for twisting my arm. This was more fun than I'd imagined."

"If you don't enjoy it, then why did you decide to learn to play?"

"The challenge," she said as they walked toward the clubhouse. "I like to learn new things." She laughed to herself. "And my father thought it was a good way to attract a husband."

"But that's not part of your diabolical plan," he said.

"No. But the golf course *is* where a lot of business is conducted," she said.

"Ah. I'm impressed," he said and he was. "The problem with you trying to do business on the golf course is that men will be distracted by your body."

She shot him a sideways glance. "You're not trying to flatter me again, are you?"

He moved in front of her and stopped. "Whatever is between us is more than flattery. I made that clear the other night in the closet. I can make it clear again."

Her eyes widened and she bit her lip. He lifted his finger to her mouth. "Don't do that to your pretty lips," he said. "Let me take you to dinner."

He watched a wave of indecision cross her face. She hesitated an extra beat before she shook her head. "No. I told you I'm not getting involved in a public situation with you where people could misconstrue that we're involved."

He lifted his hand to push back a strand of her hair that had come loose from her ponytail. "We already are involved."

Her eyes widened again. "No, we're not."

"You're not attracted to me," he said.

She opened her mouth then shut it and sighed. "I didn't say that. But I already told you that I don't want to be known as one of your flavors of the month. Wherever you go, you draw attention, so there's no way we could have dinner without people talking about it or it ending up in the paper."

"You really don't want to be seen with me," he mused and shook his head. This was a first. Usually women wanted to parade him in public at every opportunity. Alex switched strategy with ease. "No problem. We'll have dinner at my condo tonight."

Mallory felt a shiver of forbidden anticipation as she stepped inside the elevator that would take her to Alex's penthouse condominium. She shouldn't have agreed, but the more time she spent with him, the more she wanted to know about him.

And who knew? Perhaps Alex could be a resource for helping her get started professionally. As much as she loved her parents, she craved her independence. She needed to succeed on her own.

The elevator dinged her arrival at the penthouse and she took the few steps to Alex's front door. Before she pushed the buzzer, the door opened and Alex appeared, dressed in slacks and a white open-neck shirt. He extended his hand. "Welcome," he said and led her inside the lushly appointed condo.

"This is nice," she said, looking around. Although

Mallory was accustomed to the trappings of wealth, even she was impressed with the architectural design and masculine contemporary furnishings.

"I own a home farther out of town, but this is more convenient during the week," he said as they walked toward a balcony with a stunning view.

"It's gorgeous," she said and closed her eyes for a second. "And quiet."

"I chose it for that reason. After a busy day, I can sit here and let my mind run. It's often my most productive time of the day. I come up with some of my best ideas up here or at my cabin in Tahoe." He waved his hand toward a table set with covered silver platters, fine china and crystal. "I sent my staff away just for you. That means we're on our own except for my full-time housekeeper Jean. She'll take care of cleanup."

Mallory sat down at the patio table and wondered how many other women had sat in this very chair. More beautiful, more sophisticated women determined to capture Alex's heart, perhaps even to marry him.

Her stomach twisted at the thought, so she deliberately pushed it aside. This could very well be the only evening she spent with Alex. She may as well enjoy it.

Alex poured a glass of wine and she studied his hands. His fingers were long, and like everything about him, strong and masculine-looking. She wondered how they would feel on her body. She would bet Alex knew exactly how to touch a woman. A twist of awareness tightened inside her, surprising her with its intensity.

Shaking her head at the direction of her thoughts, she took a sip of wine and latched on to the first subject that came to mind. "You mentioned that your father is Greek," she said. "Your family is obviously part owner of Megalos-De Luca. Do you have other relatives working for the company?"

He shook his head and lifted the silver cover from his plate and motioned for her to do the same. "My grandfather only had one son, my father, who chose to go into medicine. His decision infuriated my grandfather so much that he refused to speak to my father."

"Oh, no. That's terrible," she said. "What does your father think of your career choice?"

He took a bite of the lobster dish the chef had prepared. "He hasn't spoken to me since I dropped out of premed, majored in business and got involved in the family business again. My two older brothers went into medicine and the same was expected of me. Business isn't noble enough. It just pays the bills."

"You and your father don't speak?" she asked in disbelief. "What about your mother?"

"My mother sneaks a call to me every now and then, but she feels her job is to support my father."

"My mother takes a back seat approach to marriage, too. She goes along with my father's whims. I don't think I could do it. I don't want to do it," she said more firmly.

"Maybe if you met the right man…"

Mallory swallowed a bite of dinner and shook her

head vehemently. "The right man will encourage me to follow my own goals and ambitions. Isn't it ironic that your father decided to buck his father's trend? Yet when you did the same thing, he reacted the same way as his father."

"The same thing has crossed my mind more than once," he said in a bitter voice.

Mallory felt a surge of sympathy for him. She never would have dreamed Alex's family had totally cut him off. "That's got to be difficult. What do you do for holidays?"

"Ignore them," he said, his gaze suddenly cool. "What about you? You're an only child, aren't you?"

She nodded, wondering if his estrangement with his family truly bothered him so little. "I begged for a sibling until my eighteenth birthday."

He chuckled. "You finally realized it wasn't going to happen."

She nodded, thinking back to that time in her life when everything had changed. "Everything was different after the accident. My mother changed. My father changed some, too."

Alex met her gaze. "What accident?"

"I was seven at the time. My mother was taking my brother and me with her for a quick trip to a nail salon."

"I didn't know you had a brother," he said.

Her stomach suddenly tightening, she pushed her food around her plate. "Not many people do. It's too painful for either of my parents to talk about. He was two years older than me. His name was Wynn and he was a pistol," she said, smiling in memory. "He was the adventurous one. My father was so proud of him."

"Was," Alex prompted.

"My mother ran a stop sign and we were hit by a pickup truck. All three of us had to be taken to the hospital. My brother took the brunt of the collision. He died in the emergency room. They told me I almost died. They had to remove my spleen and I broke a few bones. I stayed in the hospital for a couple of weeks, ate gelatin and ice cream and got out and wanted everything to go back to normal. But it couldn't. I remember how quiet the house was without Wynn around."

"What happened to your mother?"

"She had a few cuts and bruises. They released her after one night, but she has never been the same. She never drove again and I had to push when it came time for me to get my license. The accident frightened both my parents, and she blamed herself for my injuries. Both of them were, are, terrified of something happening to me."

A thoughtful expression settled on his face. "Now it all makes sense."

"What does?"

"Why your father is so protective," he said. "They almost lost you. They don't want that to happen again."

"But you can't wrap yourself in cotton and climb

into a box because you're afraid something bad will happen," she said.

"*You* can't," he said, his lips twitching in humor.

"I love my mother, but I don't want to live my life that way. I sometimes feel as if every time she looks at me, she remembers losing Wynn."

"That's tough," he said.

She nodded. "It has been. She won't really let me get close to her."

"Maybe she's afraid of losing again," he mused.

"Maybe, but I don't want to make all my decisions based on what could go wrong."

"Caught between being the dutiful, devoted daughter and wild woman hiding underneath it all," he said.

"Parental guilt is a terrible thing," she said with a sigh, taking another sip of wine.

"I don't have that problem," he said.

"What about brotherly guilt?" she asked.

"My brothers followed my father's lead. One of them is a researcher," he said and gave a sly smile. "I donate to his foundation anonymously."

She smiled, feeling as if she'd just been given a rare treat. "You just told me a secret, didn't you?"

"Yes, I did. Don't spread it around," he said, shooting her a warning glance that managed to be sexy, too.

So Alex cared more about his family than he pretended, she realized. He was more complicated than the player she'd thought he was. Mallory wondered what other secrets lay beneath his gorgeous surface.

"I won't tell your secret as long as you don't tell my father about my plan to move out and get a job."

"What will you do if he cuts you off financially?"

She shrugged. "I'm Edwin James's daughter. He's taught me how to invest. I have a cushion. Speaking of employment, do you think Megalos-De Luca could use me on staff?"

He paused for a few seconds, a flicker of surprise darting through his green gaze. He quickly masked it. "I hadn't thought about that. Let me get back to you on it."

"Oooh," she said, shaking her head. "Complete evasion. And I had such hopes."

"You didn't really think I invited you here to interview you for a job, did you?" he asked in a low, velvet voice.

She felt a rush of heat and glanced away.

"Are you blushing?" he asked.

She shook her head. "Of course not," she lied. "Dinner was delicious. Let me take my plate to the—"

"No. My housekeeper will take care of it. You're my guest." He stood and extended his hand. "Let's go up to the second level." He led her up a set of stairs to another terrace. This one featured an outdoor pool, hot tub, bar and chaise lounges.

Sensual music so clear the band could have been

right there on the deck flowed around them. A slight breeze sent warm air whispering over her skin. Looking out into the horizon, she felt as if she could see forever. She drew in a deep breath and felt her burdens and dissatisfaction slip away for just a moment. For just a moment, she felt free.

The moment stretched to two, and because Alex was a man, he didn't feel the need to fill the silence with useless conversation. He hadn't made a sound, but she was aware of him. She knew he stood closer, yet not quite touching her, because his warmth radiated at her back.

"If you sold tickets for this, I would buy a hundred," she said.

"For what? The view?" he asked, sliding his hand down her arm.

"Yes, and the temperature, and the breeze, and the feeling of freedom. Do you feel this way every night?"

"No," he said and closed his other hand over her other shoulder. "But you're not here every night."

"Flattery again," she said, unable to keep from smiling. Even though she knew he was just flirting, she couldn't help but be charmed by him. It had been that way since the first time she'd met him.

"Not flattery," he said. "You need a review." He turned her around and lowered his mouth to hers, taking her lips in a kiss that made her feel as if she were a sumptuous feast.

Sliding his fingers through her hair, he tilted her

head for better access and immediately took advantage. He kissed her like he wanted her, like he had to have her. The possibility threw her into a tailspin.

Her heartbeat racing, she felt a shocking surge of arousal that nearly buckled her knees. She kissed him back and his low groan vibrated throughout her body to all her secret places.

"Say what you want, Mallory, but you make me feel free and hungry at the same time. How do I make you feel?" he asked, dipping his head to press his mouth against her throat.

Another rush of arousal raced through her. She couldn't lie. "The same way," she said, her voice sounding husky to her ears.

"What are you going to do about it?" he asked, but it was more of a dare.

A visual of what she wanted to do scorched her brain. "I don't know," she said. "I thought I had you figured out, but there's more to you than I thought there was."

"It's the same for me," he said, sliding his hand upward to just below her breast.

Mallory sucked in a quick breath. "How am I different?"

"I thought you were a sweet girl, quiet and shy."

"And?"

"And you're sweet, but you're not quiet or shy. You've got a wild streak a mile wide and I want to be there when it comes out."

His fingers grazed the bottom of her breast, making her want him even more. It was a feeling she knew that would roar out of control if she let it. She just wasn't sure she was ready for it.

"So what does Mallory want to do tonight?" he asked.

Her limbs melting like wax, she struggled with her arousal. She wanted to let go, but she didn't want to lose herself to Alex. That would be too dangerous.

She grasped through her brain for something else, something that would give her more time. "Your car," she finally managed to say. "I want to drive your car."

Four

Sweet little Mallory had a lead foot.

She rounded corners and made hairpin turns at breakneck speed. Alex began to understand Edwin's anxiety. If it had been his choice, he would put the woman in a nice, big Buick. Or a Hummer.

"This is wonderful," she said, the wind whipping through her hair. "I love that it only has two gears. I can keep it in second gear all the time. I know there were only seven hundred and fifty models of this car made for this year. Who did you have to bribe to get it?"

"No one. I just had my assistant make a few calls and the deal was done."

"Maybe I could order one and hide it," she mused.

Alex laughed. "Do you really think you could hide a purchase like that from your father? You know he has people watching you 24/7."

She shot him a sideways glance. "He's not supposed to hover," she said. "The agreement is if I keep a low profile on the party scene, then the body-guards must remain invisible to me."

"He'll have my hide when he finds out I let you drive my car like a bat out of hell," he said, but wasn't concerned.

"Bat out of—" She broke off. "And I thought I was taking it easy."

He noticed her skirt flipping around her thighs in the wind and slid his hand over her knee.

She swerved and popped forward. "Oops, sorry," she said, pushing her hair behind her ear. "We should go back."

He slid his hand away, pleased that his touch had flustered her. "I know a place that has a great view not far from here."

"Which way?" she asked. "I have a weakness for a great view."

So did he, Alex thought, looking at her skirt still dancing over her thighs. He gave her the directions and minutes later, she pulled into a clearing on top of a hill that overlooked the Las Vegas strip.

"This is beautiful," she said as she killed the engine and leaned her head back. She inhaled deeply. "I'm surprised you let me drive your car."

"I am, too," he said, reaching for her hand.

She turned her head to look at him. "Why?"

"I haven't let anyone drive that vehicle except me. Sure a Ferrari is more expensive, but I had to wait for that electric roadster for over a year. If you wrecked it—"

"You'd just get another one," she finished for him.

He met her gaze. "True." He sat up in his seat and leaned over her. "So you've driven my Tesla. What do you want to do next?" He dipped his mouth to her luscious, pale neck.

She sighed and he slid his hand over her knee.

"The way you act, I almost think you really want me," she said, turning her lips toward his as he skimmed his mouth across her jaw.

"Almost," he echoed, his voice sounding like a growl to his own ears.

"Like I said, I'm not your usual type," she said, shifting toward him.

"Maybe that's a good thing," he said and rubbed his mouth over her sexy, soft lips. He loved the texture and taste of her. He slid his tongue over her bottom lip.

"But you've dated models, actresses," she protested, at the same time opening her lips to give him better access.

"None of them had a mouth like yours," he said and couldn't put off taking her mouth in a kiss. He slid his tongue inside, tasting her, relishing the silken sensation of her lips and tongue.

She gave a soft sigh and lifted her hands to his head, sliding her fingers through his hair. She massaged his head and welcomed him into her depths. With each stroke of her tongue, he felt himself grow more aroused.

He slipped one of his hands beneath her blouse and pushed upward toward her ample breasts. He touched the side of one of her breasts, stroked underneath. He wanted to touch her all over. He wanted to taste her all over.

He felt her heat and arousal begin to rise. She arched toward him and he knew she wanted more. Giving the lady what she wanted and what he wanted, too, he unfastened her bra and touched her naked breast.

She quivered beneath his touch. Her nipple already stiff, she wiggled against him. Her artless response made him feel as if he would explode.

He continued to kiss her, playing with her nipple and slipping his hand beneath her skirt, closer to her core. Reaching the apex of her thighs, he stroked the damp silk that kept her femininity from him.

"You feel so good," he muttered. "So good." He dipped his fingers beneath the edge of her panties and found the heart of her, swollen and waiting for him.

It was all he could do not to rip off both their clothes and drive into her hot, wet, sweetness. She would feel like a silk glove closing around him.

Groaning, he rubbed her sweet spot until she

bloomed like an exotic flower. She began to pant and it became his mission to take her to the top.

"You're so sexy," he said. "I can't get enough of you." Still rubbing over her swollen pearl, he thrust his finger inside her.

She gasped and he felt her internal shudder of release, her delicious shudder of pleasure. "Oh—Al—" She broke off breathlessly as if she couldn't form another syllable.

She clung to him, dropping her head to his shoulder. Seconds passed where her breath wisped over his throat. Finally she let out a long sigh.

"I don't know whether to be embarrassed or—"

"Not embarrassed," he said, still hard as a steel rod. He closed his arms around her.

"Amazed," she said. "We're not even in bed," she said, awe in her voice.

"We will be," he said. "It's inevitable. I have business at one of our island resorts next weekend. I'm taking you with me."

"Next weekend?" she said, pulling her head from his shoulder to gape at him. "But I have papers and I promised to help at a charitable auction."

"Get your paper done before the weekend and find a substitute, Mallory. I won't take no for an answer."

She opened her mouth to protest then closed it. "It's crazy," she whispered.

"Just the way you like it," he said.

"What if I don't—" She broke off. "What if you

don't—" She frowned. "What if we change our minds and decide we don't want to take this further?"

"We can just treat this like it's an extended date."

"No expectations?" she asked.

"If that's what you want," he said, but he knew what would happen.

Relief crossed her features. "Okay."

He brushed another kiss over her irresistible mouth. "I'll send one of my drivers to pick you up and take you to the airport. My assistant will call with all the details."

She looked at him as if her head was spinning. "That, uh, that might not be a good idea. My father—"

"Don't worry. I'll talk to him," he said.

She blinked. "Talk to him? What will you say?"

"I'll tell him the truth—that we're seeing each other," he said.

"I'm not sure that's a good idea," she said. "He may try to push you to—" She broke off and cleared her throat. "He really wants me to get married and he may try to push you to make a—" She cleared her throat and looked away. "Commitment."

"Mallory," he said, sliding his index finger under her chin. "Do you really think anyone could succeed in pushing me to make a commitment I don't want to make?"

She met his gaze for a long moment. "No. I guess not."

"I can take care of me and anyone else who is important to me. I'll talk to him." The poor woman looked dazed. He took pity on her. "Would you like me to drive back to the condo?"

Relief washed over her face. "Yes. Thank you."

Alex cleared his schedule to meet with Edwin James the following evening. The wily Californian poured Alex and himself a glass of whiskey and stepped away from his desk to a sitting area furnished with burgundy leather chairs and mahogany tables. Edwin's office oozed old wealth, but Alex knew the old man had started with nearly nothing. He'd started his own business, expanded, turned it into a franchise operation and began investing, first for himself then others who paid him handsomely.

Alex knew that he and Edwin had a lot in common. He allowed the older man to start the discussion.

"You told me you wanted to build a resort in West Virginia and you'd like me to find you some backers. Why West Virginia?"

So began the interview. Alex answered all of Edwin's questions with a minimum of spin and an abundance of facts and figures.

"Why did Megalos-De Luca turn this down?" Edwin asked.

"Other than the fact that they're blind as bats, and you can quote both me and Max De Luca on that, they're focusing on expanding in current proven markets."

Edwin nodded. "I would think they wouldn't let you do this on your own. Don't you have some kind of noncompete agreement?"

"I do," Alex said. "But I told them I would walk if they didn't make an exception."

Edwin lifted his bushy gray eyebrows. "So you can play hardball when you want. I like that."

"You're not surprised."

"No," Edwin said. "You don't get as far as I've gotten without being able to read people." He paused for a moment. "I've got three or four investors who would be right for this. I'll get back to you by the end of this week." He rose from his chair and extended his hand. "I look forward to doing business with you."

Alex nodded as he shook Edwin's hand. "Thank you. Same here," he said. "On another subject, you asked me to recommend some men who might interest your daughter."

Edwin's eyes lit up. "You have someone in mind?"

"Yes. Me," Alex said. "Mallory and I are seeing each other."

Edwin stared at him for a long moment. "I already knew that," he said. "I have a couple guys who watch over her. They told me about her driving your car. She lost them on one of the turns." He shook his head. "You're a brave man. Just so you know, I would want to show my gratitude in a substantial way to the man who can get my daughter happily down the aisle."

"That would be down the line," Alex said. "We're

still just getting to know each other. In fact, I have to go to one of our island resorts this weekend and I'm taking her with me."

Edwin nodded slowly. "She loves the beach. Just don't let anything happen to her. She's my little girl."

"She always will be even though she's turned into a smart, adventurous and very capable woman," Alex said. "I wonder where she got that adventurous streak."

Edwin cackled and shook his finger at Alex. "You're a smart one, yourself. Maybe she's finally met her match."

Mallory decided not to join Alex for the long weekend. Staring at her unpacked suitcase, she felt like a wuss. A smart wuss, though, she told herself. Even though Alex was unbelievably hot, had allowed her to drive his car and invited her to go on a weekend adventure with him, she knew he was trouble. She knew she would have a hard time hanging on to her sanity.

Rising from her bed, she paced a path from one end of her room to the other and back again. Biting her lip, she glanced at the small stacks of clothes on the bench next to the suitcase. She'd gathered the items necessary for a trip to an island.

Although deep down, she'd ultimately known that she had no business even thinking about going to a fast food joint with Alex, let alone an island resort, she'd been tempted. How could she not be? She loved the beach.

The fact that she would have Alex's attention away from the glare of Las Vegas shouldn't make her shiver with anticipation. The prospect of walking along a beach with Alex, her hand laced with his, the ocean breeze rippling against their skin. A taunting visual filled her mind of sharing a kiss with Alex under the moonlight with the waves lapping at her toes.

Mallory sighed, looking at the stacks of clothes again. It would take so little. Just a few swift motions to lift and lower them into the designer suitcase. She would be insane to do it. Completely and totally insane.

A knock sounded at her bedroom door, startling her. Her heart jumped into her throat. "Hilda?" she said, knowing it was the housekeeper announcing the arrival of Alex's driver. She went to her door, trying to drum up some mental fortitude. She wouldn't make Hilda do the dirty work. Mallory would calmly tell Alex that she had changed her mind.

Taking a deep breath, she opened the door.

To Alex.

"Ready to go?" he asked.

His eyes met hers and his magnetism hit her like a tidal wave. Her throat closed up and she tried to squeak out the word *no*.

He glanced around the room and his gaze landed on the stacks of clothes and the open suitcase. "Sweetheart, you're running behind," he said, lifting the stacks of clothes in his hands and setting them in the suitcase.

Swallowing over the lump in her throat, she found some semblance of her voice. "I was thinking it would be best if I didn't go."

He searched her face. "You were going to chicken out."

"I was not going to chicken out," she said, automatically lifting her chin. "I was just going to make a wise decision."

He walked toward her and her stomach danced with butterflies of expectation.

"This is your chance to let down your hair. Even your dad has given his okay."

She still considered that miraculous. "Yes, but my mother has freaked out. She said she's too upset to get out of bed."

"It's not as if I'm taking you to some war-torn country."

"Alex," she chided him, but couldn't put a lot of oomph into the emotion because she secretly agreed with him.

"You want me to talk to her?" he offered.

Mallory shook her head vehemently. "No, no, no. You don't have a calming effect on women."

He rested his hands on his hips. "I'm not going to try to push you to do something you don't want to do," he said. "I'll walk down to my car and give you five minutes to join me. But don't blame this one on your parents. Make your own decision," he said and left the room.

Mallory stared after him, her heart hammering against her rib cage. She'd spent most of her life forced to be sensible and ultracareful out of consideration for the most important people in her life.

Alex was right. This was her opportunity to taste a little of the freedom she'd been craving, so why was she stalling? Was it because she was afraid of what he brought out in her? Was it because she was afraid of breaking her hard and fast rule to not fall for him?

Taking a deep breath and telling herself to stop overthinking, she put another stack of clothes in her suitcase. She went to the bathroom and grabbed her travel bag of toiletry items and tossed them into the suitcase. She opened the lowest drawer in her dresser and paused, her hand hovering over the bits of silk and lace that she had *never found the nerve to wear in front of another human being.*

Her door burst open again, startling her. Alex and a big beefy man wearing a chauffeur's uniform stepped inside. "I decided you might need some help," he said and glanced down at her suitcase. "Is it ready?"

"Yes, but—"

"Okay, Todd, you mind closing it up and carrying it downstairs?"

"No, sir," the man said and followed Alex's orders.

Alex met her gaze. "And now for you," he said, moving toward her.

Mallory felt her stomach dance with nerves.

"Where's your passport?" he asked.

"The top left-hand drawer in my bureau, but I can get it," she said.

He opened the drawer, pulled out her passport and flipped through the empty pages. Mallory felt a twist of embarrassment at the lack of places she'd been.

"I don't see a lot of stamps," he said.

"No."

"You don't like to travel?" he asked, turning back toward her.

"I love to travel. I just haven't—" She broke off and squealed as he hauled her over his shoulder and walked out of her bedroom. "What are you doing?"

"Carrying you to my car."

Embarrassed, but oddly thrilled, Mallory bounced against his shoulder as he carried her down the staircase. Hilda stood by the front door wearing an expression of shock and confusion.

"Miss James?" she said, clearly unsure what she should do.

"I'm okay," she said to Hilda. "Just don't tell Mom about this. Alex, I thought you said you weren't going to push me."

"Mallory," he said in a sexy, chiding voice. "This isn't pushing. It's carrying."

When he stopped outside a Bentley and allowed her to slide down the front of him, so that she was acutely aware of his hard, muscular body, Mallory looked into his green gaze and relearned what she'd already known. Alex was trouble.

Five

Mallory flipped through a magazine during the flight to Cabo San Lucas on Alex's private jet. She stole a glance at Alex and tried to push aside her edginess. Alex appeared to be working on a redesign of an existing resort, complete with construction plans and artist's renderings.

"Looks nice," she said.

He glanced up and nodded. "These are for a redevelopment for a resort off the coast of South Carolina. I just bought out a competitor last week. It was a steal."

"And you already have plans?" she asked, surprised because she'd heard so many stories about the drag time associated with construction.

He smiled and at that moment, he reminded her of a shark. "The people I work with know not to drag their feet. Otherwise, they won't be working for me."

She nodded. "I wish I'd brought my laptop. That way I could have done some classwork."

He shook his head and leaned back in his seat. "I want this to be a weekend of total relaxation and ir-responsibility for you."

She couldn't swallow her humor. "That's not exactly equitable. You're working now and you'll be working at the resort."

"Briefly at the resort," he corrected her. "I'm de-livering a keynote because Max De Luca didn't want to go without his lovely wife, Lilli. She wouldn't go because the baby got a cold earlier this week."

Mallory frowned. "I hadn't heard. Poor thing. I know Lilli refuses to leave David when he's sick. She's very protective."

"As is Max," Alex added and glanced down at the drawings again.

"I like that about him," she said thoughtfully.

"What?" he asked.

"I like that Max is protective of David even though David isn't his biological son."

Alex nodded. "Max is tough. Lilli's made him human."

"You like her?" Mallory asked, feeling a twinge of envy.

"She's a lovely woman on the outside and the

inside. She brought cupcakes to the office for Alex's birthday. I thought he was going to fall over, but he loved it. And the cupcakes were damn good. I tried to talk her into making some for my birthday, but Alex told me to call a bakery. SOB."

Mallory laughed. "Are cupcakes your favorite?"

"Anything baked homemade is my favorite," he said. "I like cookies, cupcakes. My favorite is apple pie with ice cream."

She laughed again. "You just don't seem like the all-American apple pie kind of guy."

"Why not?"

"You're too—" She broke off, feeling heat rush to her cheeks.

"Blushing again?"

"I don't blush," she said.

"No?" he said, leaning toward her and lifting his fingers to her cheeks. "Then what is this pretty pink color I see—"

"A gentleman wouldn't make a big deal out of it," she said.

"You've said I'm not a gentleman. And you like that about me," he said, rubbing his index finger over her lips, sliding it inside against her teeth.

Mallory instinctively opened her mouth and he slid his finger onto her tongue. It was an incredibly erotic moment that came out of nowhere. Her gaze held by his, she curled her tongue around his finger and gently suckled.

Alex's eyes blazed with desire and he pushed aside his papers and pulled her onto his lap. "You like to tempt me, don't you?" he asked her. "I think you want to see how far you can push me."

"You started it," she said, her hands resting on his strong chest and loving the sensation of his muscles. He slid his fingers beneath the bottom edge of her blouse and stroked her bare skin.

"Does that mean you want me to stop?" he asked.

Her heart hammering in her chest, she slipped her hands up to his shoulders. "I didn't say that."

"I can't help wondering what you're like when you really cut loose," he said, lowering his mouth to her jaw and kissing.

Craving more, she lifted her head to give him access to her throat. He immediately read her invitation and responded. She sighed at the delicious sensation of his mouth on her bare skin.

"You will be in my bed," he told her. "It's inevitable."

She felt herself sinking under his spell. She wanted him, but she would be a fool to give him her heart.

Five hours later, Alex had delivered one speech and he would give another one during dinner. After that he could attend to his female guest who had followed his advice to make use of all the resort facilities.

As he changed his shirt and tie for dinner, he returned a call to Todd, his chauffeur/bodyguard.

"What's up?" Alex asked, glancing out the window to the wide beach and blue ocean.

"So far, she went snorkeling, spent a little time in a kayak, drove a Jet Ski. Now she wants to go Para-Sailing."

"What the—" Alex stared out the window this time, looking for Mallory and Todd. "You told her she couldn't do it, right?"

"I did. She wasn't very happy about it. Said you and I were as bad as her father," he said.

"Where the hell are you?"

"At the Rigger Resort," Todd said. "It's about four hotels west of the Megalos complex. I bought her a drink in the Tiki bar to distract her, but I don't think it's going to work."

"Okay, I'll be there in a few minutes," Alex said.

"But I'm your driver," he said.

"I'll be there in five," Alex insisted as he left the suite.

Alex easily commandeered a hotel shuttle and walked into the Tiki bar. He spotted Mallory immediately. Dressed in a scant black bikini that emphasized her curves she wore a joyous smile on her face and her long, dark hair was slick against her back. She was riveting. Blinking, he noticed other men were equally riveted. The land sharks were moving in while Todd tried to push them back.

Alex parted the crowd and stood in front of Mallory. As soon as she recognized him, she jumped from her stool and stopped just sort of throwing her arms around him. "Oops. I don't want to get you wet."

"Hey, baby, you can get me wet anytime," a male voice called from a few feet away.

Alex shot the man a quelling glance that sent a hush over the crowd. Then he turned back to Mallory. "You've been busy."

Her eyes sparkled. "I've had so much fun. Loved the Jet Ski. I definitely want to do that again. And snorkel. And snuba. You said you would take me to snuba. I'm almost ready for deep-sea diving." Her brow furrowed and she leaned closer to him. "The only thing is that Todd here is being a spoilsport. I was all set to Para-Sail, but he nixed it. Now it's too late."

He pulled her to the side. "You don't need to do everything in one day," he pointed out. "We can snuba and Para-Sail tomorrow, together."

She searched his face. "I didn't know if you would be busy tomorrow, too."

He shook his head. "Not a chance. And I want to make sure we get the best Para-Sail group. I won't have you risking your gorgeous body with some fly-by-night company."

Her lips curved in a slow smile. "So *you* were the one who nixed the Para-Sail excursion."

"Damn right," he said offering no excuses. "You can wait one more day and do it tandem with me. That way, you'll always associate the experience with me."

"That sounds a little possessive," she said.

"Does that upset you?" he asked.

A moment of silence passed between them where he felt a fist of longing build in his gut, surprising him with its force. He saw the same dark longing reflected in her eyes.

"No," she finally said.

"Good," he said. "Now put on a T-shirt or a robe or something. You're sending the poor locals into a frenzy."

She laughed with delight. "Omigoodness, if I believed half of what you say, then I would be convinced I'm the most desirable woman in the world."

"By the end of this trip, you will be," he told her and slid his arm around her for the benefit of everyone who was watching. He wanted them to know she was with him. "Any chance you could do something boring like shopping or getting one of those spa treatments women like so much."

Biting her lip, she looked into his eyes and he felt an unexpected jolt. "Am I making you nervous? Am I making the man who drives race cars for fun nervous?" she asked in disbelief.

"I wouldn't use the word nervous," he said.

"Then what word would you use?"

"Let's just say you're keeping me on my toes," he said and gave in to the urge to brush his lips over hers. "I'll see you after the dinner meeting and my speech.

Order anything you want from room service then put on a beautiful dress and get ready for a walk on the beach."

"What if I didn't bring a beautiful dress with me?"

"Then go shopping," he said. "I need to leave. Todd will take you anywhere you want to go within reason," he added when he remembered the Para-Sailing.

Within minutes, Mallory finished her fruity beverage and went back to the hotel. She'd packed some cute dresses, but nothing she would consider beautiful, so the pressure was on to find something. She showered and left the resort, and Todd took her to several recommended shops. Nothing grabbed her, so she returned to the resort and looked through the shops there.

Surprisingly enough, she found a hot-pink silk halter-neck dress with sparkles at the bodice and a few scattered throughout. The shopping goddess was on her side. The shop had the dress in her size.

She took it upstairs and immediately changed into it. She curled her hair and added a touch of exotic eye makeup and lip gloss. Hungry, but too excited to eat, she turned on the television and sat on the bed.

Thirty minutes turned into an hour. An hour turned into two. Restless and wondering what had held up Alex, she turned off the television and walked onto the balcony. She closed her eyes as the sea breeze brushed over her. The sound of the surf soothed her.

If her mind weren't whirling a mile a minute, the sound would lull her to sleep.

She couldn't help wondering what she was doing here in Alex's suite. Yes, the suite featured five bedrooms, four bathrooms, full kitchen, formal dining room and a large living area that offered every convenience imaginable, but she was starting to think she'd lost her mind by joining him.

Inhaling a deep breath in search of calm, she caught a hint of his cologne. She opened her eyes and found him standing in front of her.

"You looked so beautiful," he said, lifting his hand to touch a strand of her hair. "So peaceful."

"The sound of the ocean helps," she said, looking at him, noticing that his tie was askew and his shirt pulled loose. "Everything okay?"

"It could be better. I finished my speech and was leaving the ballroom when my ex came out of nowhere."

Mallory stared at him in shock. "Your ex?" she echoed. "Which ex?"

He shot her a dark look. "Chloe Renfro."

"Oh," Mallory said, recalling a willowy blonde. She felt a stab of jealousy, but refused to give in to it. "How did that happen? Does she live here? Have a place here?"

"No to both. She must have found out about my appearance from someone." He pulled his tie the rest of the way loose. "I knew she was going to have a difficult time with the breakup, but I never predicted this."

"You can't totally blame her for having a hard time getting over you. I mean, if a woman grew accustomed to receiving your undivided attention, it could be pretty difficult when your attention goes elsewhere."

"I never gave her my undivided attention," Alex said. "I made it perfectly clear from the beginning that there would be no strings for either of us. Our relationship was not headed for anything permanent."

Ouch. "I wonder how she knew to find you here." An uneasy thought occurred to her. "Unless you brought her here another time." The image tainted the trip for her so swiftly that she tried to push it aside. "But that's none of my business."

He put his hand on her arm. "Mallory, I haven't brought any other woman here but you."

She exhaled, feeling a trickle of relief. "What did you do about her?"

"I arranged for her to get on a flight back to the States," he said with a grim expression on his face.

It dawned on Mallory that this was the flip side of the positive attention and adoration Alex received. "Do you have to deal with this kind of thing often?"

He shook his head. "Despite your impression, I've grown very selective with my dating partners. Just because I'm photographed with a woman doesn't mean I'm intimate with her." He shook his head and shrugged off his jacket. "Enough. I won't allow this to spoil the rest of our evening."

She watched him pull off his socks and step into a pair of canvas shoes. He extended his hand to her. "Ready for that walk on the beach?"

She smiled slowly and accepted his hand. "Sure, let's go."

They took the elevator down to the lobby. At the luxe lounge, Alex bought her a fruity drink and a beer for himself and excused himself from employees who approached him.

Feeling their curious gazes, Mallory was relieved when they stepped outside. "So much better," she said when her feet encountered cool sand.

Alex kicked off his shoes and left them at the foot of the steps leading to the resort. "Beautiful woman, beautiful night. What could be better? Come here," he said and pulled her into his arms. He pressed his mouth against her and tasted her with his lips and tongue, making her feel delicious.

"Mmm," he said in approval. "More."

Her heart tripped over itself. She pulled back and laughed breathlessly. "After our walk."

"I'm surprised you have the energy after all you did today," he muttered as they walked toward the shore.

"I had some downtime while I waited for you."

"Second thoughts about coming," he said.

"How did you know?"

"I could tell," he said.

Surprised, she frowned at him. "How is it that you read me so easily?"

He shrugged. "It's mostly because I want to," he said. "I watch your face and body for signs. I do the same kind of thing when I'm negotiating. You're just a lot more fun to watch," he said, sliding his hand to the top of her opposite hip.

Mallory couldn't deny how wonderful she felt at this moment. With the ocean beside her, the sand at her feet and Alex's arms around her, she couldn't imagine anywhere she would rather be.

"I had a wonderful time today. Thank you for bringing me," she said, looking up at him.

"You were supposed to say you missed me desperately," he said in a mocking tone.

"Just as you missed me," she said innocently.

"Trust me, you had more fun than I did." He shook his head. "Poor Todd couldn't keep the men away from you. It's a wonder I didn't have to fight off a few of them to get to you."

She laughed. "Would you have really done that?"

"You like that idea, do you?" he asked, squeezing her against him.

Heaven help her, she did, at least in theory. How crazy was it that she was preaching liberation on one hand yet loving it when Alex went primitive on her? She couldn't admit it aloud, though. She heard the strains of beach music coming from a resort up ahead. The romantic sound tugged at her.

Alex came to a stop and swung her against him. "Dance?"

Her heart skipped and stuttered. "Yes," she said and began to follow his lead. "You're a good dancer," she said. "When did you learn?"

"When I was young. It was a requirement in my family. My mother was determined that her sons would be civilized and have good manners. I hated every minute of it until I started noticing the opposite sex. Then I figured out that dancing is a damn good way to get close to a woman you want to get to know better. But there's an even better way," he said, sliding his hand down to the back of her waist and drawing her intimately against him.

He felt so good, so strong, and Mallory was so tired of resisting him. She'd always told herself he was the perfect man for a fling. He brought out a wildness in her and made her feel as if it were okay.

She felt something inside her rip so strongly she could almost hear it. Restraint, resistance, she was impatient with living under her code of caution.

"If you and I get closer," she began, her heart beating like a drum in her chest.

"We will," he said, dipping his mouth over hers and away, revving up her temptation.

"I want to keep it confidential," she said. "Secret."

He paused a half-beat. "You want me to be your secret lover?"

"I don't want my parents hurt by any sort of publicity," she said. "And that's the last sensible thing I want to say."

"Are you ready to go wild?" he asked and lifted the inside of her wrist to his mouth. "You taste so good. I can't wait to taste every inch of you."

"Then don't," she whispered. "Don't wait."

Six

But he did wait, and the waiting just made the tension inside her stronger. Mallory had expected Alex to whisk her back to the hotel and immediately devour her. Instead he continued to dance with her on the beach, taking her mouth in long, drugging kisses that made her knees turn to liquid.

The darkness surrounded them like a cocoon of privacy. No one else was anywhere within sight. She wasn't aware of anyone else. She was solely focused on Alex.

He slid one of his hands all the way up her side to the outer edge of her breast and caressed her from the outside of her dress. She felt her nipple harden from the indirect touch. She craved feeling his skin on hers.

An edginess built inside her. "Shouldn't we go back to the suite?" she asked, biting her lip against a moan as he slid one of his fingers just inside her dress to her bare breast.

"We will," he said. "Trust me. I want to take my time with you. Once we get back to the room and I take off your clothes, it will be hard for me to slow down.

"Your skin feels so soft, so edible," he murmured, dipping his mouth to her throat again.

Her pulse spiked.

"I love the way your body responds to me," he whispered. "When I touch you, you take a little breath and hold it. Is that because you want more? Or less?"

She bit her lip at the sharp wanting he caused inside her. "More," she whispered and boldly pulled at the buttons at the top of his shirt. She splayed one of her hands across his smoothly muscled chest. "I want to feel you, too."

He sucked in a sharp breath as if she'd surprised him. Tipping her head backward, he slipped one of his hands through her hair and took her mouth again. This time his kiss was more aggressive, more purposeful. He slid his thigh between hers, and Mallory's breath just stopped.

Feeling his arousal pressed against her, she reacted purely on instinct, undulating against him.

Alex swore under his breath. "Time to go. But if

this were a private beach," he said, and a shocking visual raced through her mind of Alex, naked and taking her right there. The power of it shook her.

She stumbled as he led her toward the resort. He caught her against him. "Okay?"

Mallory had never been this aroused in her life. Never wanted so much to take and be taken by a man. "Yes. No." She swallowed over the emotion building in her throat, a combination of apprehension and anticipation. "I—just—really—want you."

He met her gaze and she saw the same hunger mirrored in his eyes that she felt in every pore of her body. He took her mouth in a quick, but thorough kiss. "You're going to get me," he promised in a gritty, sexy voice and urged her toward the resort.

As soon as they stepped inside, he took a right down a different hallway. "Let's take the back elevators. I'm not in the mood for small talk with one of my employees."

As if even the elevator knew not to impede Alex, it immediately appeared and Alex pulled her inside. As soon as the doors closed, he took her mouth again, urgency emanating from him.

Dizzy from his touch and the heat he generated inside her, Mallory clung to him as the elevator door swept open. A man stepped inside, giving her a second and third look before he got off the elevator three floors later.

Self-consciousness trickled through her and she closed her eyes.

"Did you know him?" he asked.

She shook her head and met his gaze. "Does it show on my face? How I feel?" she asked. "That I'm so turned on I can't—"

He covered her lips with his finger. "You're not alone," he told her, and the elevator finally arrived at their floor.

Alex led her to the suite and before he'd closed the door, he was pulling her into his arms. "There's something about you," he said in a rough voice. "It must be in your skin, in your voice, deeper. I just know I have to have you. All of you."

Tugging her farther into the suite, he pulled her down on the sofa with him and took her mouth in a consuming kiss that made every cell inside her buzz with need and pleasure.

Skimming one of his hands up her side, he found the side zipper of her dress and pulled it down. With his other hand, he untied the knot of silk at the back of her neck. He pulled the soft, sensual material down, baring her breasts.

She felt a whisper of coolness from the sudden exposure, but the heat of his gaze warmed her. He lifted his hands to her breasts, taunting her already sensitized nipples and she looked away, swallowing a moan.

"Oh, no," he said, putting his hand under her chin

and drawing her gaze back to his. "No hiding," he said. "No holding back. I want to see every look, feel every response, hear every sound you make."

Shoving aside her doubts and insecurities, she reached for his shirt and unfastened the rest of the buttons. "Fair is fair," she said, her heart racing like the wind. Urged on by his gaze and her need to be close to him, she pushed his shirt down and pressed her swollen breasts against his chest.

Her moan mingled with his. She felt the muscles of his biceps tense beneath her hand. He swore and took her mouth in a searing kiss.

In the middle of that endless kiss, he pushed her dress aside and slid his hand between her thighs. With unerring instinct, he found her most sensitive, most secret place.

His groan vibrated throughout her. "You're so hot, so wet," he said, his low voice full of approval and need. "I want you everywhere at once," he said and pushed her against an oversize pillow. He skimmed his mouth down her throat to her chest and then he slid his tongue over one of her nipples. A second later, he drew the aching tip into his mouth and she felt a corresponding twist of sensation low in her belly.

As he stroked her between her thighs at the same time he consumed her breasts, Mallory felt her head began to spin. Tension, need and a wanting so vast it shook her to the core. She felt herself climbing to a precipice. He'd taken her there before in the car. But this time, she didn't want to go without him.

"Alex," she managed to say, pulling herself upward. "I want—" She broke off and swallowed. "I need you to—" Meeting his gaze, she lowered her hands to his slacks and tugged his belt loose. "Inside me," she said in a voice that sounded husky to her own ears.

His eyes nearly black with arousal, he stood, stripping off his slacks and underwear. Transfixed by the sight of him, she stared at his muscular body from his strong, wide shoulders over his well-built chest, flat abdomen and his large masculinity jutting from his pelvis.

His size made her wonder if she was ready for him.

Still watching her, he pulled a packet from his pocket and put on the protection. Then he slowly covered her body with his. She felt his erection between her thighs and everything except being with him fled her mind.

He rubbed against her intimately and she arched to take him inside. Sliding his hand between their bodies, he played with her again. Each stroke made her more desperate for him. "Please," she whispered, but she didn't want to beg.

"Hold on," he told her and pushed her thighs apart and thrust inside her.

His invasion stole her breath. "Alex," she breathed and they began to move in an age-old rhythm of possession and surrender. She could feel how much he wanted her, how much he craved her. It was as if he wanted to capture her spirit and soul to light the darkness in his, and Mallory knew nothing would ever be the same for her again.

The next morning, Alex awakened early as he always did. Propping his head on his elbow, he looked down at Mallory, stretched out on her side with the sheet wrapped around her waist. Her brown hair fell in shiny, sensual waves over the top her chest and shoulders. The sight of her voluptuous bare breasts taunted him. During their multiple rounds of lovemaking last night, he'd noticed how her nipples hardened just by him looking at them. Everything about Mallory's body responded to him.

Her responsiveness seemed to go deeper than her skin, although he sensed she wanted to hold some part of herself back. The more Alex was around Mallory, the more he wanted all of her.

He liked the way she pushed back at him. She didn't need his money, and wasn't at all interested in the notoriety her relationship with him could bring her. Her desire to keep their affair secret amused him at the same time that it pinched his pride. If he decided he wanted more from her, though, he would change her mind. Some might consider him arrogant, but for Alex it was just the truth. It was very rare that he didn't get what he wanted. He wanted Mallory and he intended to enjoy every minute of their secret lover weekend. He would make sure she enjoyed every minute, too, but he would give her a little break, noting the violet shadows under her curly eyelashes. He knew he'd worn her out last night.

Sliding out of bed, he went into the den and called room service for breakfast. The newspaper would be delivered in mere minutes, so he grabbed a quick shower and pulled on a pair of shorts. As expected, breakfast, along with three newspapers, arrived shortly. He directed the staff to set the breakfast on the large wraparound balcony.

If Mallory didn't awaken soon, then he would read the papers and reorder for her when she rose. He'd barely finished his first article from the *Wall Street Journal* when she appeared, wrapped in a fluffy robe with sexy, sleepy eyes, as she peeked from the bedroom sliding doors.

"Good morning," he said. "You're just in time for breakfast."

"There's some for me?" she asked, moving toward the table. "The smell of something heavenly woke me up."

"Coffee?"

"Bacon," she corrected, sitting down in the chair opposite him. "The most useless food on the planet."

"But too good to resist," he said, lifting a slice and offering it to her.

She took it and devoured it, closing her eyes as she

ate it as if it were a sensual experience. He wondered how a woman could make eating bacon so arousing, but damn if she didn't.

"I'm starving. I didn't eat dinner last night—"

He frowned. "Why not? I told you to order anything you wanted from room service."

She met his gaze. "I was a little nervous," she confessed.

Something inside him tugged and twisted at her admission. "The prospect of Para-Sailing didn't bother you, but I did?"

"Oh, being with you is much more—" She broke off. "Much more everything than Para-Sailing. They told me Para-Sailing is over in five minutes."

"I hope I lasted longer than that."

She giggled, covering her eyes. "Oh, wow."

Her response was addictive. He tugged her hand and pulled. "Come here. Have some breakfast."

She sat on his lap with no protest. Surveying the plates he'd ordered, she made a little moan of approval. "I want a bite or two of everything," she said and took a bite of the omelet. "Delicious. Have you ever noticed how everything tastes like gourmet food when you're starving?"

He nodded. "Even a stale sandwich from the deli because you don't have time to get anything else."

"Exactly. But since you're a big whoopty-doo VP, I would think your employees would always make sure you get perfectly fresh food."

"Contrary to rumor, I don't force my employees to work the same hours I do. I sometimes work late nights and have been known to grab a package of crackers from the vending machine."

She made a tsking sound of false sympathy. "Poor big whoopty-doo VP."

"You're heartless."

"That's me, heartless Mallory." She smiled then glanced at the food again. "Oh, don't tell me that's a chocolate croissant."

"It is," he said, enjoying every minute of having this woman on his lap.

She sighed. "I may have to eat more than two bites of that."

He snatched the croissant from the plate. "You may have to kiss me to get it."

She met his gaze with soft, but searching eyes. "I would have thought you'd gotten so many kisses last night that you wouldn't want anymore."

"In that case, you would have been very wrong," he said and took her mouth with his.

Mallory was in beach and man heaven. She'd known Alex's attention could be intoxicating, but she'd really had no idea how intoxicating. Doing snuba, a combination of snorkeling and scuba diving, with Alex, Mallory felt as if she were discovering a whole new wonderland. The vibrant colors of the reefs and fishes were spectacular and joining hands with Alex while twenty-five feet underwater upped the thrill exponentially.

As promised, they Para-Sailed tandem. Surprisingly when they hovered above an inlet, it felt more peaceful than frightening. Alex took her mouth in a kiss that sent her heart soaring into the stratosphere. Every once in a while, she wondered how she could possibly return to her claustrophobic existence after experiencing so much freedom.

After their busy morning and early afternoon, they enjoyed a gourmet picnic lunch on a private beach. Mallory guzzled an ice-cold bottle of water.

"You're turning pink," Alex said, pressing his finger against her arm. "Get under the umbrella. Do you need more sunscreen?"

She moved to the double chaise lounge underneath the umbrella. "I've applied it a gajillion times today."

He joined her on the lounge, his skin gleaming bronze from their time in the sun. "Not exaggerating, are you?"

"No," she said, admiring and resenting his tanned skin at the same time. "It isn't fair that you don't burn."

"My ancestry. I guess it's one thing I can thank my father for," he said with a dry laugh and pulled out a bottle of sunscreen. He poured some cream into his palm then rubbed it onto her shoulders.

"Do you miss him?" she asked after a long moment.

"Who?"

"Your father. I can't imagine not being able to talk to my father whenever I want." The idea actually hurt her heart.

"I've gotten used to it," he said with a shrug, rubbing the sunscreen onto her belly.

"I think that's a lie," she said.

He met her gaze and lifted a brow. "And who made you the expert on me?"

Her heart twisted like a vise and it hit her that she wished she could be an expert on Alex. She wished she could know him in every possible way. "Am I right?" she asked.

He laced his fingers through hers. "You keep surprising me," he said. "One minute you're wild, the next you're deep and thoughtful."

"You didn't answer my question," she said, willing him to meet her gaze. A long silence followed, and she resisted the urge to fill it.

"I miss what could have been. Sometimes the death of dream is worse than a real death." He met her gaze and the naked emotion in his green eyes took her breath and stole a piece of her heart. "Satisfied?"

She wondered if she would ever be satisfied. If she could ever know enough of him and not want more. She rose and pressed her lips to his. It seemed the right thing to do.

When she pulled back, he trailed his finger between her breasts. "You know this is a private beach. There's no one else but you and me here." He slid his finger around the edges of the cups of her bathing suit. "You could take this off…."

Her pulse raced at the invitation in his voice. It was more an invite than a dare. "I've never gone topless on a beach before."

"Have you wanted to?" he asked.

"Not before," she said, but she liked the idea of taunting and tempting him. With his experience, he always seemed to have the upper hand.

"And now?" he asked, sliding his finger beneath the edge of the top of her bathing suit, just a fingertip away from her nipple. She felt her nipple grow hard and fought against the urge to arch against him.

"I could get burned even worse since that skin has never seen the sun," she said, her voice husky to her own ears.

"I would be happy to put sunscreen on you," he said. "Every inch."

Mallory closed her eyes, wondering if she wanted to be this wild, wondering if she could. Still keeping her eyes closed, she lifted her hand and untied the strings at the back of her neck. She pushed the cups down and reached behind to unfasten the other strings at her back, then pulled the top of her bathing suit from her body.

She finally opened her eyes.

Alex gazed at her possessively, his nostrils flaring slightly in sudden arousal. She was surprised, but gratified by the speed of his response.

He met her gaze. "You have no idea how you affect me."

An illicit thrill raced through her. "Maybe you should show me."

He slid his hands over her breasts. "My pleasure," he said.

He taunted her with his hands, then replaced his hands with his mouth. He nibbled at the hard, sensitive tips of her breasts, making her want more and more. He took her mouth in a French kiss and rolled on top of her, pushing her thighs apart.

In the afternoon sun, shielded only by the umbrella, he took her with a glorious, consuming intensity. She reveled in the sound of the waves as he thrust inside her. The scents of salt, sand, coconut oil and musk filled her head. She wanted him to take her. She wanted him to fill her completely and in his taking, she wanted him to feel completely full. It was the most carnal yet spiritual experience in her life, and she wondered how she would possibly survive being separated from him.

The next day, they had to return to Las Vegas. Both she and Alex were quiet. He studied designs and reports. Mallory looked through the same magazine for the fifth time, not seeing a single image, not reading a single word. The weekend had been the most glorious of her life, but she was searching for a way to pull herself together. She'd been stretched sexually and emotionally. How was she supposed to go back to her parents' home and be the Mallory she'd been before? How could she?

Thirty minutes before they were scheduled to land, she sensed Alex looking at her. "I want you to move in with me," he said.

Her heart leaped in her chest. She couldn't. Not for her peace of mind, not for her parents' peace of mind. "I can't do that. Right now," she added.

"Why not?" he asked.

"My parents are old-fashioned. They would be horrified and hurt. Besides, you and I need to be sensible. I told you before I didn't want a public affair." She shook her head. "I need to get my own place. If you still want to see me—" She broke off, floundering.

"Want," Alex echoed, taking her hand in his. "You've given new meaning to the word. You can't believe social conventions are bigger than what is going on between you and me."

Her heart twisted and she met his gaze. "This isn't about conventions. I've got to recover from being with you. I don't want to be one of those women who can't get over you. I'm starting to feel more and more sympathy for them," she said.

"This is different," he said, swearing. "It's wrong for you to not be with me."

Every cell in her urged her to say *yes*. Her connection with Alex had been so powerful it had seemed almost otherworldly. Her brain stepped in like a sharp elbow-jab. Alex was a player. This could be over in a second and she would be picking up the pieces of her heart. By herself. "It's too fast," she said, meeting his green gaze, rocked by the emotion she saw there. "I need more time."

Seven

"You're glowing," Lilli De Luca said, two days later, as she joined Mallory for lunch at an outdoor café shielded by umbrellas. "If it's a new spa treatment, please tell me what it is. My sweet little David is wearing me out with his teething."

Mallory smiled, thinking of Alex. "I took a trip to the beach over the weekend. Maybe you should try to do the same soon."

The waiter refilled their glasses of mint iced tea. Mallory remembered how good the iced bottle of water had felt on her throat the afternoon she and Alex had spent on the beach.

Lilli made a face. "Max and I were supposed to

go to the beach this past weekend, but David got sick and I just couldn't leave him."

"I know," Mallory said then tried to take back the words. "I mean, I heard something about David being sick."

Lilli lifted her eyebrows in surprise. "Really? From who?"

Mallory shifted in her wrought-iron chair. "Um, I think Alex Megalos may have mentioned it."

Lilli's eyes widened farther. "Alex? When did you see him?"

"Oh, he's everywhere," Mallory said, waving her hand. "You know, Mr. Social, in the spotlight."

"Hmm," Lilli said, studying Mallory. "I remember how you used to have a crush on him."

"Most single women do," Mallory said, her stomach tightening. "Probably some married women, too. He's charming, good-looking and sexy," she tried to say in a matter-of-fact voice.

Lilli took a bite of her sandwich and swallowed it. "Is there something you're not telling me that you want to tell me?"

Mallory's throat tightened. "I'm not sure. Off the record, just how much of a hound dog would you say Alex Megalos is?"

Lilli furrowed her eyebrows. "Aside from my husband, he is one of the most charming men I've ever met. He actually hit on me when I was pregnant. Very flattering."

"But you were gorgeous when you were pregnant," Mallory said, pushing aside a stupid twinge of jealousy. "And gorgeous when not pregnant, too."

Lilli smiled. "You're such a good friend." She paused. "Here's the thing. Alex is a paradox. He's a terrible flirt. But do you know what he gave David as a gift? A year of tuition at any college and a Tonka truck he can ride. And get this, Alex made me swear that I would support David if he decided to be a sous-chef instead of a tycoon for Megalos-De Luca. How can you not love him for that?"

Mallory thought of Alex's unrelationship with his own father and tears filled her eyes. "How can you?" she echoed.

Lilli studied Mallory for a long moment. "You're still not telling me something."

Mallory blinked her eyes against the tears. "I've kinda gotten involved with Alex," she confided.

Lilli's eyes widened. "How involved?"

Mallory bit her lip. "Pretty involved. Too involved. I'm scared."

"If he hurts you, I'll kill him. I'll make Max kill him, too."

Mallory shook her head. "No murder needed. He asked me to move in with him."

Lilli stared at her, speechless. It took her a full moment to find her voice. "Move in? As in his house?"

"Or condo," Mallory said. "I told him no. My parents would freak. I don't want to make Dad's blood pressure spike through the roof. And my mother is finally coming out of her bedroom since I spent the weekend with Alex. At the beach."

Lilli shook her head. "One surprise after the other. I always thought there was more to Alex than met the eye. He's so good-looking and charming you're tempted not to look any further."

"And once you do, you're hooked," Mallory said.

"Oh," Lilli said and gave a sympathetic smile. "I don't know what to say."

"Just say you'll be my friend whatever happens," Mallory said, unable to avoid an impending sense of doom about her relationship with Alex. She couldn't imagine being able to hold his attention for long.

Lilli covered Mallory's hand. "Always," she said. "I'm always your friend, just as you've been mine since the first time we met. Just remember, both Max and I will kill Alex if he hurts you."

Twenty-four hours later, Alex called her. "You and I need to meet. There's been a development. Come to my office immediately."

Entrenched in research for her term paper, Mallory frowned into her cell phone. "Development?" she echoed. "That's a little vague. I'm in the middle of this paper. Can't you give me more information?"

"Mallory," he said and she could hear the stretched

patience in his voice. "I won't discuss this on the phone. I'll send my driver to—"

She sighed. "No, no. I can drive myself. Give me an hour."

"Thirty minutes," he countered and hung up.

Mallory stared at her cell phone and felt a frisson of fear. Alex had never sounded like this before. There was an eerie calm to his voice. A chill passed over her and she took a deep breath. Saving her file, she shut down her computer, changed her clothes, applied lipstick and mascara and headed for Megalos-De Luca Enterprises.

A valet attendant greeted her and took her car. Mallory walked inside the skyscraper, and security took her name and immediately allowed her to pass. Alex had clearly prepared everyone for her arrival.

With each passing second, she felt her tension increase. What could possibly be so important that he couldn't discuss it with her on the phone? As she took the elevator to the top floor, she tried to conjure the worst scenario. Her heart sank. If he wanted to banish her from his life, this was an odd way to do it.

The steel elevator doors opened and she stepped outside. She spoke with a receptionist who pointed her toward a corner office. She approached a woman outside the corner office. "I'm looking for Alex Megalos's office."

The young woman nodded. "And you are?"

"Oh, I'm sorry. I should have introduced myself. Mallory James."

The woman smiled. "Miss James. It's nice to meet you. I'm Alex's assistant, Emma. Please go on in. He's waiting for you."

"Thank you," Mallory said and took a deep breath as she opened the door to Alex's office.

Alex looked up, then immediately stood. "Come in. Please close the door behind you."

Mallory did as he asked. "I can't tell if I feel like I've got an appointment with the CIA or the principal from my elementary school."

He didn't smile at her remark. That made her more nervous. "Have a seat," he said.

She gingerly sat in the chair across from his desk. "I'm already nervous and you're not making it better."

"Unfortunately it's going to get worse before it gets better," he said.

Her heart sank further. "I can't stand it, Alex. Just tell me."

"You remember that day we spent on the beach on the island," he said.

She nodded. "We ate and talked and…"

"Made love," he said for her.

She nodded again. "Yes."

"We were supposed to be alone. It was supposed to be private."

She frowned in confusion. "There was no one around."

His eyes turned to chips of green ice. "No one we could see. Someone using a long-range lens took photos."

Shock coursed through. She lifted her hand to her mouth. "Oh, my God. You can't mean…"

"The photographs are grainy, but they've shown up on the Internet."

Alarm turned her blood to ice. "The Internet?" she echoed, trying to comprehend what he was saying. "Our pictures are on the Internet. *We* are on the Internet?"

His face grim, he nodded. "Yes. We're putting together a number of action plans to counter the negative impact of—"

"*We?*" she said weakly. "Who is *we?* How many people know about this?"

"So far, just the company's top PR official, your father and me," Alex said. "I'll handle this," he said. "I'll protect you."

"How can you?" she asked, numb and humiliated at the same time. "And my father." She shook her head.

"I will," he promised and his phone buzzed.

He picked up the receiver. "Yes, Emma." His face turned more grim. "Let him in."

Seconds later, Edwin James, Mallory's father, walked through Alex's door with murder in his eyes. "You've destroyed my daughter's reputation," he said to Alex. "What kind of man are you to take advantage of a young lady like Mallory?"

"Daddy," Mallory exclaimed.

"I'm going to take care of this," Alex said in that eerily calm tone.

"There's only one way you can do that," her father said.

"I know."

"The two of you have to get married."

Mallory gasped. "That's ridiculous."

Alex met her gaze. "No. It's not."

She shook her head, feeling as if the whole situation had turned completely surreal. "This is the twenty-first century. It's true my reputation may suffer a little," she said.

"A little," her father said.

Mallory's stomach dipped. "This will just be the scandal of the moment. It will pass. There's no reason to make a permanent decision because of it."

"You want people thinking you're some kind of—" Her father broke off as if he couldn't say the words. "Loose woman. You want people thinking you're a—" He shook his head again as if he couldn't stand the very notion of it. "I won't have it. You were a sweet and innocent woman until you hooked up with Megalos here. He's ruined you."

"He hasn't ruined me," she protested.

"There's only one solution to this problem," her father interjected. "You and Megalos need to get married and soon. Now don't argue, Mallory," he said, shaking his finger at her. "Even Alex agrees with me. I just hope I can keep this from your mother. The disappointment would devastate her."

Guilt sliced through Mallory. In this, her father was right. Her mother was fragile. Although Mallory chafed against the constraints her parents had placed on her, she loved them both deeply and hated that she was causing them pain. She bit her lip. "This is such a huge move to make just for the sake of covering a scandal. Neither Alex nor I were anywhere near ready to make that kind of commitment."

Alex moved from behind his desk, his green gaze wrapping around hers and holding tight. "I can't agree with you. You know I'd already told you I wanted you to move in with me."

Her father swore under his breath.

Mallory's stomach knotted. "Did you have to say that in front of him?" she whispered even though she knew her father could hear her.

"This discussion is a waste of time," her father said, pounding his fist on the desk. "The solution is obvious to everyone." He pursed his lips at Mallory. "It should be obvious to you."

Confused and overwhelmed, she looked at her father. "Daddy, could I please have a moment alone with Alex?"

He clenched his jaw. "Seems to me you've had a few too many moments alone with him."

"Daddy," she said in a chastising voice.

"Please, Mr. James," Alex said, surprising Mallory with his support.

"Okay," her father said. "I'll be outside."

"You don't need to go all the way downstairs," Mallory said.

"I need a cigar," he said.

"You're not supposed to be smoking," she called after him as he stormed out of Alex's office. Her heart swirling with a dozen different emotions, she turned to Alex. "This is crazy."

"Lots of things that happen in this world are crazy. Who would have thought the photographers would have followed us onto that beach?"

"They couldn't have been interested in *me*."

He raised his eyebrows. "Wealthy heiress takes off her shirt for tycoon."

She cringed. "Was that the headline?"

"No, but it could have been." He shook his head. "What I'm saying is these are the cards we've been dealt. We need to do the best we can with this hand." His gaze darkened and he laced his fingers through hers. "In my mind, it could be a winning hand."

Her heart stuttered and she swallowed over a lump in her throat. "How can you feel that way? My father is practically forcing you to marry me."

"No, he's not. I told you before that I'm not a man to be forced into anything by anyone. Especially marriage." He lifted one of his hands to her jaw. "We have something between us. Yeah, the sexual chemistry is outrageous. But there's something else. I like how I feel when I'm with you. I like who I am when I'm with you."

"You're serious," she said, searching his gaze. "But don't you feel trapped? That's what I couldn't bear. The idea of trapping you."

"Before you walked in that door today, I knew we needed to get married."

"But it's so archaic," she said, fear and hope warring inside her.

"It's not archaic," he said. "It's right. Tell me that deep down there isn't something inside you that feels good about this idea. You feel good about being with me all the time, about having me as your husband. Down the line, having babies together," he said, putting his hand on her belly.

Mallory's breath froze somewhere between her lungs and her throat. "I always thought you were trying to avoid marriage. Why would you be willing to make a commitment now?"

"I told you. Because it's the right thing to do. You know it, too."

Mallory closed her eyes. Her head was spinning. Alex wasn't professing undying love. In fact, he hadn't mentioned love at all. She felt a twist of longing inside her. This wasn't what she'd pictured for her marriage.

She forced her eyes open. "What if this is a disaster?"

He gave a rough chuckle and pulled her into his arms. "Mallory, in our own way, you and I are over-achievers. There's no way this will be a disaster."

She buried her head in his shoulder. "I just wish things could be different."

"They will be," he said. "After we're married."

Just like that, the decision was made and wedding plans were put into motion. Exhibiting more enthusiasm than she had in years, her mother plunged into making the arrangements. Her father insisted the wedding take place in ten days.

Alex presented her with a ring that felt strange on her finger. Mallory enlisted Lilli's assistance to help her find a dress.

Standing in front of a three-way mirror after she'd tried on six dresses, Mallory shook her head. "I look like I'm wearing meringue. None of these seem right," she said.

Lilli chuckled, adjusting the gown slightly. "Are you sure it's the dresses?" she asked gently. "Or is it the man?"

"I can't think about that," Mallory said, returning to the dressing room. She hadn't told Lilli about the scandalous photographs of her and Alex. It was too humiliating. "Just trust me, when I tell you that Alex and I have our reasons for getting married."

"But so quickly," Lilli said, following her. "Why can't you take your time?"

"There's a good reason," she said, pushing the gown down and stepping out of it.

Lilli shook it out and returned the garment to the hanger. Then she turned to Mallory. "Are you pregnant?" she asked in a quiet voice.

"No," Mallory instantly replied. "Pregnancy would be easier than—" She broke off and shook her head.

Lilli gave her a blank stare. "I'm dying of curiosity, but if you don't want to tell me, I won't force it."

Mallory sighed and closed her eyes. "It's just so embarrassing. When Alex and I took our trip together, we visited a private beach and…" She opened her eyes and waved her hand.

Lilli's eyes widened. "Oh." She paused. "But I still don't see why you would need to rush into marriage."

"Because someone took pictures of us," Mallory whispered, misery and shame rushing through her again.

"Oh, no," Lilli said, putting her arm around Mallory's shoulder in sympathy.

"They've shown up on the Internet on an obscure site, but it's just a matter of time before someone figures out who the couple in the photos are. My father wants Alex and I married before the story really comes out so it will seem like old news."

Lilli nodded. "And what do you want?"

Mallory shook her head. "I don't know. Alex and

I had begun to connect in a way I'd never thought possible, and I mean more than sexually. But we weren't ready for this."

"He'd asked you to move in with him," Lilli pointed out.

"Yes, but—" Mallory broke off, feeling a sharp twist in her stomach. "He hasn't said he loves me," she admitted.

"Have you told him that you love him?" Lilli asked.

"No," Mallory said and fiddled with the elaborate skirt of the slip. "It seemed too soon."

"I can tell you from personal experience that just because a couple doesn't say I love you before the wedding doesn't mean they will never say it," she said with a soft smile. "It also doesn't mean their marriage can't become a dream come true."

Mallory looked into Lilli's clear blue eyes and found a drop of hope that soothed some of her doubts. "How can we make this work?"

Lilli smiled again. "Just take it one step at a time."

A knock sounded on the dressing room door. "Hello, ladies," the bridal consultant said. "I have some more dresses for you to try."

Mallory met Lilli's gaze and gave a wry smile. "Step one, find a dress I can live with."

Eight

"This was supposed to be simple and small," Mallory said to her father, gaping at the number of people packed into the chapel as she peeked from a tiny window. "How many people are in there?"

Her father patted her hand. "I don't know. Your mother said the guest list kept growing. I haven't seen her this excited about anything in a long, long time," he said.

Mallory met his gaze. "Since Wynn died," she said, feeling a tug of sadness.

Her father nodded. "I know it's been difficult for you to become our only child. We probably didn't handle everything the way we should. And your mother's depression—" He broke off as if he were overcome with emotion.

Mallory was caught off guard by the display. "You two have been wonderful parents."

Her father smiled. "You're so sweet. You sure as hell didn't get that from me." He inhaled deeply. "I just want you to know that I've always been proud of you, and you are a beautiful bride. Megalos is a lucky man."

Her heart twisted with emotions she hadn't expected to feel. She'd been in such a rush to prepare herself for today that she hadn't had much time to think about her parents' feelings. Her eyes swelled with tears. "I love you, Daddy. I hope you'll always be proud of me."

"Always," he said and kissed her cheek. He pulled back and stood taller. "It's time."

She nodded, her stomach fluttering like a hummingbird's wings. Her father gave a soft tap on the door and it immediately opened. At the sight of everyone in that chapel turning to look at her, then standing, her throat tightened with anxiety. She bit the inside of her lip to keep it from quivering.

Then she looked ahead and saw Alex. Gorgeous Alex with so many more layers than she'd dreamed. Wearing a classic black tux, he stood with his feet slightly apart, his hands folded in front of him. With his gaze fixed on hers, she felt as if she was the only other person in the room.

His lips lifted just a bit, giving a hint of his pleasure at seeing her as she walked down the aisle. She smiled and gave her mother a tiny wave just before she arrived at the front of the chapel. Her mother smiled broadly in response.

She finished the last few steps and looked at Alex as he joined her and her father in front of the chaplain. Her heart turned over like a whirling tumbleweed.

"Dearly beloved," she heard the minister say, but her awareness of Alex squeezed everything else from her mind. She was only aware of him, his height, his strength, his incredible magnetism. Was she really going to be his wife?

"Her mother and I," her father said in reply to something the chaplain had asked. Mallory blinked as her father kissed her cheek and joined her hand with Alex's.

His hand felt strong wrapped around hers. Today, more than ever, she needed that strength. She wondered if he suffered from doubts. Surely he did. This had been as much a surprise to him as it had been to her.

Seconds passed and Alex turned her toward him. She stared into his handsome face and wanted to know his heart. She wanted to be in his heart.

His eyes burned into hers. In his green gaze, she saw encouragement, support, strength and…possibilities. Oh, how she wanted those possibilities to come true for both of them.

"Do you, Alex, take Mallory to be your wife? To have and to hold…"

"I do," Alex said, and she felt the click of a lock. She knew he was tying himself to her and her to him. Heaven help them both.

The reception was held in an exquisite private ballroom with marble floors, gold mirrors and crystal chandeliers. Her parents had spared no expense. The menu was sumptuous and the room dripped with white roses on every available surface from the tables to the piano.

She thanked another couple for coming and felt her cheeks ache from smiling. All the tension of the previous ten days was catching up to her and more than anything, she craved a quiet corner. But there was still the first dance and the cake to cut.

Alex dipped his mouth to her ear. "How are you doing?"

She smiled at his timing. It was as if he'd known her energy was starting to flag. "How much longer do we have to stay?" she whispered.

He chuckled. "As far as I'm concerned, we can leave now."

Severely tempted, she shook her head. "We need to do some of the traditional things for the sake of—" She shrugged. "Of whoever cares. We should dance."

"That I don't mind," he said and led her to the dance floor. He spoke with the band for a second and then took her in his arms. The strains of the song that had been playing on the beach began. An old song that had been remade again and again, the tune and words made her smile.

"Up On The Roof," she said, her heart twisting at the romantic selection. "Nice choice."

"I thought so since we'll be spending a lot of evenings on the roof of my penthouse." He spun her around and she laughed. "That's the first real smile I've seen on your face today."

She nodded and closed her eyes so she could seal this moment in her mind. Opening her eyes, she met his gaze, full of hope and wishes. She wondered if he could see them written on her face. She wondered if he felt the same way.

The first dance of their married life together and Mallory whirled from Alex's arms to her father's to partner after partner. The wedding planner finally rescued her, pulling her aside for the cake-cutting.

"It's that time," the woman said in a cheerful voice. "Now if we could just find your groom."

Mallory looked around the room, unable to find Alex. "I don't see—" She double tracked over a corner where a tall blond woman and Alex appeared to be engaged in an intense conversation. The woman lifted her hand to his cheek and Mallory felt as she'd been stabbed. She looked away. "I'm sure he'll be here soon. I would love a sip of water, please," she said.

"Let me get that for you," the woman said. "Can't have our bride getting parched."

Mallory bit her lip, wondering who the woman was. She looked familiar, but she couldn't quite place her. A guest approached her and she plastered on a smile.

Minutes later, the wedding planner returned with Alex, who wore an inscrutable expression. She felt him studying her face, but couldn't bear to look him in the eye.

"I think we need to call it a night," Alex said to the wedding planner. "Mallory is tired."

The wedding planner pressed the bottle of water into her hand. "Just a little longer, I promise. Cut the cake and ten minutes of pleasantries, then out the door."

"Five minutes," Alex said in a firm voice. "My wife is tired."

The wedding planner raised her eyebrows in surprise, but nodded. "This way, then."

Alex led Mallory to the table and she still couldn't look at him. "What's wrong?" he asked in a low voice.

"I could ask you the same," she said and accepted the knife. Alex placed his hand over hers and they cut the first piece. Cameras flashed.

Alex lifted a bite to her lips and Mallory wondered if she would be able to swallow even that small bite. She took it into her mouth and forced it down her dry throat then offered his bite to him.

He surprised her, capturing her hand and kissing

it after he swallowed his bite. The wedding guests roared in approval.

Mallory was filled with confusion. A champagne glass was placed in her hand and she looped her hand through Alex's. Forced to look at him, she saw the possessiveness in his gaze and felt her stomach drop to her knees. What had she let herself in for?

Alex took her glass and his, placed them on the table then pulled her into his arms. She stiffened.

"It's almost over," he promised and covered her mouth with his, surprising her again with his passion. When he pulled away, she was trembling.

Alex lifted his hand to the applauding crowd. "Thank you for coming. Please enjoy the rest of the party. Good night," he said and guests tossed rose petals as he led her out of the room.

Alex had arranged for them to stay in the resort's penthouse suite for the night. He guided her to the private elevator. As soon as the doors whooshed closed, he turned to her. "What's wrong?"

She leaned her head back against the cool steel wall and closed her eyes. She didn't know whether to cry or scream.

"Mallory, why are you upset?"

She sucked in an indignant breath and met his gaze. "Why in the world would I be upset when you are in the corner with a beautiful blond woman at our wedding reception?"

Realization crossed his face and he sighed,

rubbing his hand over his face. "You weren't supposed to see that."

She blinked. "That makes everything better." The elevator doors opened and she stalked toward the doors decorated in ivy and roses.

"Dammit, wait a minute," he said, catching her arm. "I meant I didn't want you upset. That was Chloe. She crashed the reception. I was trying to avoid a big scene by having security remove her from the room."

Mallory met his gaze. "Really?"

He nodded. "Really."

She took an extra breath. "Do you always have this kind of problem when you break up with a woman?"

"Never like this. I'm starting to see the reason for restraining orders," he said, his gaze troubled.

"Should we do something about this? About her?" Mallory asked.

Alex looked at her for a long moment and lifted his hand to her cheek. "You just gave me an amazing gift."

"What?" she asked, confused.

"You said *we*. Should *we* do something? Even though you're miffed," he said, rubbing his finger over her mouth as if it were a lush flower.

Mallory felt some of the fight drain out of her. "Just imagine if the tables were turned," she said. "If you'd seen me in the corner with another man at our wedding reception."

"That's easy," Alex said. "I would have made a scene and given him a bloody nose. You handled it with much more class." He glanced at the door. "Why are we standing outside?"

With no warning, he picked her up and carried her to the door, pushed it open and brought her inside where the room was lit with oodles of candles and dozens of white roses. "What are you—"

"The threshold tradition," he said. "It's supposed to bring good luck. Everyone can use good luck."

He looked down at her and took her mouth with his in a searing, possessive kiss that left her breathless. "What was that for?"

"Because I've been wanting to kiss you all night," he said, sinking onto a white leather sofa and holding her on his lap.

"You've already kissed me several times today."

"Not like I wanted," he said. "Not enough." He rubbed his lip over hers from side to side in delicious, sensual movements. "You feel so good," he said, sliding his tongue over her bottom lip. "Taste so good."

"It's the cake," she said. "I taste like wedding cake."

He gave a dirty chuckle. "Trust me. It's not the cake," he said and took her mouth in another kiss. After a moment, he pulled back and tugged off her shoes. "Bet you're ready to get rid of these."

She nodded and it began to sink in that she had gotten married. She was now his wife. The notion made her chest tighten with a strange mixture of emotion.

"And your dress," he said with a devil's look in his eyes. "Bet you're ready to get rid of that, too."

She couldn't keep a smile of amusement from her face. "Good luck. This dress has fifty buttons."

He shot her a look of disbelief then glanced at her book. "What idiot thought of that?"

"A very famous designer."

"Who is clearly a man-hater," he said and lifted his hand to the buttons. "Good thing I've got staying power."

She lifted her hand to his shoulder and met his gaze. "Do you?" she asked. "Do you really have staying power?"

He paused, clearly hearing her serious tone. "Yes, I do."

Mallory bit her lip, but felt a resolve strengthen inside her. "I don't want to be married to you if you're going to have other women."

His face turned dead serious. "There will be no other women for me, no other men for you," he said in a low, rough voice.

His latter comment caught her off guard. She would never consider being with another man. Now that she'd been with him, now that she'd been his wife, how could she think of anyone but Alex?

"Do you understand?" he asked, lacing his long fingers with hers.

She nodded. "Of course."

"I take my wedding vows seriously, Mallory. I'm committed to you," he said.

She nodded, but her mind was still full of questions. The biggest was would he ever love her?

"I'm your husband," he said, his hands moving over her buttons, releasing them with a speed that surprised her. "Soon enough, there won't be an inch of you that doesn't know that you are my wife."

They spent the night making love until Mallory was too exhausted to continue. She fell asleep in Alex's strong arms and awakened to his kisses. He made love to her again and they shared a delicious meal before it was time to leave.

Alex's job made it impossible to leave his work for a honeymoon. He swept her off her feet and carried her inside his condo. "Welcome home, Mrs. Megalos," he said and allowed her to slide down his body until her feet touched the floor. "The movers will bring anything you want from your parents' place. Just give instructions to the housekeeper and she'll handle everything. I want you to feel comfortable here, so feel free to convert one of the other bedrooms into an office if you like. I'll leave a charge card for you in the morning. Something's up with the board of directors, so I'll need to go in early."

Her heart twisted at the notion of him leaving, which was silly. Having his undivided attention for the last twenty-four hours had knocked her equilibrium completely off-kilter.

He studied her face as if he could read her mind. "You'll be okay, won't you?"

"Of course," she said, refusing to give into her weakness for him. Alex would need a strong woman for his wife, so she needed to buck up and pull herself together. "I have plenty to do to get settled here and make-up work for my class. We can have dinner tomorrow night on the upper terrace."

"Sounds good," he said. "But it may need to be late. I only got half the story from Max at the reception, but it's sounding like we may be in for a major reorganization. I'll send in the housekeeper to unpack for you while I check my messages and give you a chance to relax."

Two hours later she sat propped up in bed, staring at her laptop screen. Feeling a shadow cross over her, she glanced up to see her husband leaning over her wearing a towel looped around his waist and, she suspected nothing else.

His green eyes full of seduction, he shot a quick glance at the laptop. "Anything you need to save?" he asked.

She nodded tearing her gaze from the sight of his amazing body. She wondered if the time would ever come when he didn't take her breath away. She marked the Web site for future research, saved her notes and turned off her laptop.

He immediately took the laptop from her and set it on the dresser. Dropping his towel seconds before he turned off the bedside lamp, he climbed into bed, covering her body with his.

Mallory shivered in anticipation.

"You're not cold, are you?" he asked, sliding his warm hands under her pajama tank top.

"No."

"Good, because you're wearing entirely too many clothes," he said and pulled her top over her head. His hard chest rubbed deliciously against hers, causing a riot in all her most sensitive places. He took her mouth in a hot kiss and pushed her shorts and panties down her legs.

He immediately found her sweet spot with his talented fingers. After a few strokes, he had her panting. "Open up, sweetheart," he told her and as she slid her thighs apart, he thrust inside her, claiming her again, all the way to her core.

Alex left before she woke the next morning. Their days fell into a pattern where Alex left early, arrived home late, worked a couple hours after dinner, made love to Mallory and fell asleep.

An uneasiness inside her began to grow. Was this going to be their future? A distracted dinner followed by late-night sex? It almost seemed as if they talked less now than they had before they'd married.

She wanted to get through to Alex. She wanted him to see her. She wanted him to, heaven help her, love her. Mallory racked her brain for ways to get to him. She tried to meet him for lunch during the day. She invited him to play golf. He was always apologetic, but always too busy.

One evening when Alex was working late again and Mallory was trying her best not to sulk, the condo phone rang and when she answered it, she knew she'd found a way to get Alex's attention.

"Thursday night's not good for me," Alex said absently to Mallory as he made a mental note to himself about the resort in West Virginia. "I'm working late."

"Not on Thursday night. Change your plans," she said in an airy, but confident voice as she sipped her wine during their late dinner.

Surprised that she would disagree with him, he shook his head. "I can't change them. I have a late meeting with marketing then I have a conference call with three contractors in West Virginia."

"Reschedule," she said, surprising him again with her insistence.

"Sweetheart, you don't understand—"

"No," she corrected. "You don't understand. I need you to be available on Thursday night. I need you to go somewhere with me."

"Mallory, be reasonable."

"I am. Do you know how many evenings you've spent with me since we got married?"

"I told you this month was going to be tough. I have an unusually heavy workload partly due to the construction project in West Virginia. Maybe we could schedule something for Sunday night."

She shook her head stubbornly. "No. It has to be Thursday."

"Tell me what it is," he said.

She took a deep breath. "A surprise."

She was such a tenderhearted woman, he thought. Lord he was lucky he hadn't married one of those sharp, brittle women he'd dated during the last several years. "That's sweet," he said. "But I really can't cancel—"

"You have to," she said. "Or I—I'll have to do something desperate."

Alex blinked at her. "What the hell—"

She rose from the table, her meal nearly untouched. "I mean it. I've made plans. I need your presence on Thursday night, and as your wife, I shouldn't have to—" Her voice broke and she bit her lip. "Beg."

Swearing under his breath, Alex stood and reached for her. "You're feeling neglected. Dammit. I can't change my schedule."

She pulled back and lifted her hands. "Don't try to charm me. Don't use seduction. Do you realize I've seen you for an average of sixty waking minutes each day since we got married? I'm just asking for one night," she said, her voice breaking again. Clearly appalled at herself, she spun around and ran from the dining room to the terrace, whisking the door closed behind her.

Alex swore under his breath and rubbed a hand

over his face. The downside of marrying a woman with heart was dealing with her sensitivities. Alex's primary focus was his career. His role at Megalos-De Luca Enterprises was his destiny. Everything else came second. Relationships, his needs, his desires. Everything. Now that he was forging ahead on his individual resort project, more was demanded from him than ever.

As his wife, she would need to grow accustomed to his schedule. His first mistress was his work. This once, however, he would bend, but he would make it clear that in the future, she should never make plans that required his presence without consulting him first.

Thursday night arrived and Alex's chauffeur drove Alex and Mallory to the address she'd given him. Mallory was scared spitless. Her palms were clammy, her heart raced. Her only saving grace was that Alex was distracted by a call he'd received on his cell phone. For once, she was thankful for the interruption.

The more she thought about it, the more she feared this may not have been such a good idea after all. Alex might not appreciate his new wife interfering. By the end of the evening, he could very well be furious with her.

Her stomach twisted into another knot and she tried to rein in her fear. Her instincts had screamed that this was the right thing for her to do. She prayed she was right.

Todd pulled in front of the entrance to the lecture hall and he opened the door for Alex and Mallory to exit the Bentley. Alex wrapped up his call and curiously glanced at the building. "Thanks, Todd," Alex said then turned to Mallory as he escorted her inside. "Are you going to tell me what this is all about now?"

"No," she said, forcing a smile to her face as they approached an auditorium. "You'll know soon enough."

Alex gave a long-suffering sigh. "Do we have assigned seats?"

"Yes," she said, her stomach twisting and turning. "Near the front."

They took their seats and Mallory held her breath.

"You're really not going to tell me," Alex murmured in her ear.

"I'm really not," she said and prayed this would all turn out right.

Finally the lights dimmed and a gray-haired man mounted the platform. "Ladies and gentleman, as director of bio-genetic studies for the University of Nevada, it is my honor and pleasure to introduce this evening's speaker, Dr. Gustavas Megalos…"

Mallory slid a sideways glance at Alex as his brother's name was announced. His eyes rounded in surprise and his gaze was fixed on the podium as a man with dark hair and glasses climbed the platform.

"Gus," he whispered, leaning toward her. "How the hell did you know he was coming to town?"

"He called and said he wanted to see you," she said, trying unsuccessfully to read her husband.

"You couldn't just tell me," he said.

"I didn't know how you would respond. It was too important to risk you saying no."

His jaw tightened. "That's why you said you would do something desperate."

She swallowed over the knot in her throat. "Yes. Are you angry?"

"I'm surprised," he said and focused on his brother.

Mallory suffered in limbo as Alex's brother discussed the importance of genetic studies and the advancements that had been made. She stole glances at Alex throughout the lecture, trying to read him, but his expression was inscrutable.

She hoped she'd made the right decision. That time Alex had opened up to her, she'd glimpsed a longing for his family. She prayed this would be a turning point, and that Alex could reconnect with his family.

Alex's brother finished his speech and the crowd applauded. Alex turned to Mallory. "You want to tell me the rest of the plan now?"

"There's a bar next door. You and your brother can go there and have a beer together," she said, feeling a spark of hope.

"What about you?" Alex asked.

"I'll go home."

Alex shook his head. "I want my brother to meet my wife," he said, standing and extending his hand to her.

Her heart dipped at his words and the emotions she read in his eyes. Maybe, she felt herself begin to hope more and more, maybe Alex could grow to love her after all.

Nine

One week later, Mallory and Alex attended a charity gala held at the Grand Trillion Resort and Casino. After Alex's successful visit with his brother, Mallory's confidence had begun to climb. Although Alex still worked late, he'd begun to call her during the day, and if she wasn't mistaken, she was seeing a new light in his eyes when he looked at her. As for her own feelings, she felt as if she was glowing from the inside out. Her heart was traveling in uncharted waters with him. She'd never felt so strongly about a man, but now she had reason to hope their marriage would work.

Unable to keep a smile from her face, she glanced

around the room and saw her father wave. She and Alex visited him at the bar.

Mallory kissed her father on the cheek. "Hi, Daddy. How's business? Ready to hire me?"

Her father choked on his whiskey, pounding his chest. He scowled at her. "You shouldn't frighten an old man like that when he's got half a glass of whiskey in his throat."

"I'm not that scary," she said.

"No, but you don't need a job," he told her giving her a quick squeeze. "You have a husband to take care of you now."

Getting married hadn't changed Mallory's desire to prove herself professionally, but she could see that it would be futile to argue with her father. "Where's Mom?" she asked, looking around the beautiful room.

"She's over there talking to one of our neighbors. I have to tell you, Mallory. Your wedding did wonders for her. She's getting out more, taking some kind of exercise class. Plating or something."

"Pilates," Mallory said, trading a smile of amusement with Alex.

"She's trying to get me to go with her," he said, clearly appalled.

"You should try it," she said. "It would be good for you."

He shook his head. "I'll stick to golf. Go give her a kiss. She'll be glad to see you."

Spotting her mother in a cluster of women, Mallory walked toward her. Her mother glanced up and smiled, breaking slightly away from the other women. "Hi, sweetheart. I told your father I was looking forward to seeing you tonight."

"Thanks." Mallory kissed her mother on her cheek. "It's good to see you, too. You look wonderful."

"You look wonderful, too," her mother said. "Something about seeing you get married made an impact on me. Life does go on, doesn't it?" she asked, with a hint of her former fragility in her eyes.

Mallory knew what her mother was saying. She still suffered over Wynn, but after all this time, it seemed she finally saw the need to start living again. "Yes, it does. I know I've told you this before, but thank you for all the work you did for my wedding."

Her mother smiled. "That was my pleasure. You're my only daughter, so that was my only chance. I'm doing pretty well. I've even started exercising."

"That's what Daddy told me. That's great," Mallory said.

"Now if I can just talk him into quitting cigars and Scotch," her mother said.

"Then you'll be performing a miracle," Mallory said.

Her mother laughed. Although it was an odd rusty, unfamiliar sound, Mallory felt a rush of tenderness.

"You may be right," her mother said. "I should let you get back to your handsome, new husband."

Mallory looked over her shoulder at Alex and felt her heart skip over itself. Longing, deep and powerful, twisted through her. As every day passed, she found herself wanting his love more and more. "I'm sure I'll see you again later," she said and kissed her mother once more.

She walked toward her father and Alex. With their backs facing her, she decided to surprise them. As she crept closer, she heard her father talking.

"I told you I would reward the man who could get my daughter happily down the aisle. It may have taken some extra pushing, but you succeeded. Her mother and I are very pleased. Mallory just doesn't understand that she needs a protective influence in her life. You provide that for her."

Mallory frowned at her father's words. *Reward? Happily down the aisle? A protective influence?* Had her father actually offered Alex a reward to marry her? Her stomach twisted with nausea. She stared at the two men in disbelief. It couldn't be true, she thought. It couldn't be.

"She's more adventurous than I originally thought," Alex said. "When you first talked about matchmaking, I thought she would need a much milder, more conservative man than me. After spending some time with her, I wasn't sure any of my friends could keep her busy enough to stay out of trouble."

Mallory gasped, unable to keep the shocked sound

from escaping her throat. Alex must have heard her because he immediately turned around. His gaze met hers and she instantly knew she'd caught him at his game. The terrible secret was out. He'd never really wanted her as his wife. He'd obviously just wanted something from her father, although she couldn't imagine what Alex could need because her so-called husband was plenty wealthy.

"Mallory, don't misunderstand," Alex began.

"I don't think I do," she said, torn between humiliation and devastating pain. She felt like such a fool, and she'd hoped he would eventually love her. He had no intention of loving her. She was just a game piece he'd used to win something obviously more important to him.

He moved toward her and she shook her head, backing away.

"You didn't want to marry me because of any feelings for me," she said, her throat nearly closing shut from the pain.

"Baby, don't overreact," her father said.

She shot him a quelling glance. "And you made it all happen. I was so stupid," she said, hating that her voice broke. "So stupid. I actually thought you wanted me," she said to Alex. A horrible pressure at the back of her eyelids formed, making her feel as if she would burst into tears any second. She refused to give into it.

"I feel like such an idiot. And here I was trying my

best to be a good wife when it was all a sham." Her voice broke again. "I want a divorce," she said and fled the room.

The hurt Alex saw in Mallory's eyes stabbed him like a dagger. He turned to Edwin James. "Are you okay, sir?" he asked.

Edwin's face was pale. "I could be better, but I'll be okay. I'm not as sure about my daughter," he said then grimly met Alex's gaze. "I'm not so sure about you."

"If you're okay, then I need to go talk to my wife," Alex told him.

Edwin lifted his eyebrows. "By all means, do."

Alex immediately clicked into crisis mode and left the ballroom. He ruthlessly pushed back his emotions, putting a plan together and executing it at the same time. Dammit, he wished Mallory hadn't heard that conversation. Lengthening his stride, he headed for the front door, suspecting she would try to get the car or grab a cab. He took the stairs instead of the elevator and rounded two corners before he arrived at the resort entrance. Mallory was stepping into a cab.

He quickly jogged toward the cab and grabbed the door as she began to close it.

Mallory stared up at him. "What are you doing? Go away. Leave me alone. I don't want anything to do with you." She let out a squeak when he wouldn't let her close the door. *"What are you doing!"* she shrieked.

"I'm getting in this cab with *my wife*," he said and slid into the back seat, pushing her over and pulling the door closed behind him.

Mallory immediately darted for the other side of the cab and reached for the door handle. Alex reached across her to hold down the lock. "Drive," he said to the cabdriver.

"Where?" the driver asked with a wary expression on his face.

"Let me go!" Mallory yelled.

"Around," Alex said, absorbing the ineffective blows from Mallory's pelting hands.

The driver glanced at him doubtfully from the rearview mirror. "I'm not sure I should—"

"I'm her husband," Alex said, lifting his head when Mallory aimed her hand at his face. "Please note. She's hitting me, not the other way around."

The cabdriver nodded. "Oh, okay," he said and moved the car forward.

"Damn you," Mallory said. "I have nothing to say to you. The only reason you married me was to get something from my father. I have nothing but disgust for you."

"I didn't marry you just because of your father," he said, determined to remain calm.

"But that was part of the reason."

He shook his head. "As you know, there were several factors. The photos from the beach pushed things along," he said.

"If there even were photos from the beach. I never saw them," she retorted.

"I can show you if you'd like to see them. I was trying to protect you from embarrassment," he said.

"Protection," she echoed vehemently. "Who are you protecting? Yourself or me?"

Alex gritted his teeth. "As I said, I can show you—"

"But the photos weren't really the big deal, were they? The dealmaker for our marriage was my father," she told him, her eyes full of hostility.

"You're upset. You're not thinking clearly," he told her. "There's no way I would have married you if there wasn't something between us, something strong," he said.

"But not love," she said bluntly. "And don't tell me I'm not thinking clearly. This is the first clear thought I've had since I met you. So tell me, did it all work out well for you? Was the deal you made with my father really worth being tied to me? After all, you could have easily been through a dozen women since you met me."

He took her wrist in his hand. "Our marriage wasn't about your father. Have you forgotten that I asked you to move in with me when we were in the islands?"

"You'd already negotiated some kind of deal with my father," she said and looked away, shaking her hand. "I should have known. It was just so easy and you were so attentive. It couldn't have been real."

"It was real," he told her. "Everything you and I did was real. It was between you and me."

"You never took a second look at me until you made your deal with my father," she said, her gaze damning him with the disillusionment he saw there.

"The truth is your father told me you needed a husband and he flat out told me he knew I wasn't the right man for you," he told her.

Her eyes widened in surprise. "What?"

"He asked me if I knew anyone who would be a good match for you. In the beginning, when I first tried to get you to meet with me, it was so I could find out your likes and dislikes and introduce you to some men who might work for you."

Her jaw dropped. "You've got to be kidding."

He shook his head. "Trouble was the more I got to know you, the more men I eliminated from the list. I decided I was the right one for you."

She stared at him for a long moment as if she were trying to digest his explanation. She shook her head. "That's ridiculous. I don't believe it."

"Fine. Ask your father," he said.

"As if he would tell the truth," she said. "He would agree with anything you say."

"*Your father* would agree to *anything?*" he said more than asked.

She met his gaze for a long moment then looked away. "This is still ridiculous. And I'm still getting a divorce. I won't stay in this sham of a marriage."

Despite the fact that Alex was known as a master persuader, a master negotiator, he was rock-solid on some issues. Marriage was one of them. "There will be no divorce," he said quietly.

She looked at him as if he were crazy. "Excuse me? You can't force me to stay with you. It's perfectly reasonable that I wouldn't want to stay in a marriage based on lies."

He gave a harsh laugh. "Every couple who gets married is lying to each other. The woman lies about liking sports. The man lies about liking her family. Marriage is often based on a pack of lies. The deception may be made with good intentions, but it's still deception."

She shook her head, looking at him as if she didn't know him at all. "You're so full of cynicism. No wonder you don't believe in love." She glanced away. "How stupid of me to hope that you and I—" She broke off and stared out the window. "I still want a divorce."

"I've already said that's not an option. A Megalos never divorces," he said.

"Interesting time for you to pull out the family card given the fact that you don't even speak to your family anymore," she said.

He withstood the low blow. "That wasn't like you, Mallory."

He watched her take a deep breath. "Perhaps not," she said. "This situation isn't bringing out the best in me. *You* aren't bringing out the best in me. The wisest thing to do is for us to quietly divorce and get on with our lives. It would take very little time to—"

"I told you we're not getting a divorce. I'll fight you every inch of the way."

"Why?" she demanded, turning around, full of fire and fury. "I could name a dozen reasons why we shouldn't stay together."

"We've made a commitment," he said. "We've taken vows. Those are the reasons we'll stay together."

"But those vows have nothing to do with love, past, present or future. You don't even really believe in love. Why be miserable?"

"Misery isn't necessary. Just because you're facing reality instead of relying on romantic wishful thinking doesn't mean we can't be happy. We can work it out and reach a deal to make a happy life for ourselves," he said.

She made a face. "You make it sound like a business negotiation."

"Ask you father. Ask your friend. Ask anyone who's been married. Marriage is one negotiation after another."

"And the reason you married me is because you thought you could win them all because I was so easy," she said, full of resentment. "I need to be away from you. I need some space." She turned to the cabdriver. "Drop me off at the Bellagio, please."

"No. Take us here instead," he said and gave the

address for his house on the outskirts of town. He wanted privacy.

"I'm not staying with you," Mallory said. "I can't. And you can't make me. I can't bear to be with you one more night."

The change from her adoring, loving attitude cut him to the quick, but he didn't give into it. "There are plenty of bedrooms in my home. Choose one. We can discuss this in the morning."

As soon as Alex opened the door to his home, Mallory flew past him hardly noticing the beautiful decor. She was so upset she barely took in the sight of lush, intricately designed carpets, antique wooden furniture and the sparkle of crystal and mirrors.

"Would you like something to drink?" he asked from behind her.

She quivered at the intimate sound of his voice and despised herself for her reaction to him. She refused to look at him. "While I'm tempted to ask for the biggest bottle of wine you have, I'll just take water," she said. "Can you please point me in the direction of your kitchen?"

"It's down the hall to the left, but all the bedrooms have small refrigerators and bottled water," he said.

She nodded. "Thank you. Now, if you could point me in the direction of the master bedroom?"

His eyebrows lifted in surprise. "Upstairs, far left."

She nodded. "I'll be sleeping at the other end of the house. Good night," she said and felt his gaze taking in her every step. Taking a sharp right at the top of the stairs, she walked all the way to the end and opened the door to a guest room decorated in shades of restful green.

She might have appreciated it more if she weren't so upset. After some searching, she found the mini-fridge discreetly hidden in a cabinet. She pulled out a bottle of water and took several swallows as she paced the carpet.

Mallory rubbed her forehead. How had she gotten herself into this situation? Her father had deceived her. Alex had deceived her. A bitter taste filled her mouth. Perhaps she had even deceived herself.

Sure, in the beginning, she had kept her guard up around Alex. She'd continually reminded herself that he was a player and she would never hold his interest. The more time she'd spent with him, though, the more she'd wanted to believe he was sincere. *What a fool.*

A knock sounded on the door. Alex, she thought and scowled. "Go away."

A brief silence followed. "Mr. Megalos asked me to bring you some things for your stay," said a timid female voice.

Cringing at her rudeness, Mallory rushed to the door. "I'll just leave them—"

Mallory opened the door to a woman dressed in a black uniform with a hesitant expression on her face. The woman held a large basket that contained toiletries and a robe.

"I'm so sorry. I thought you were—" Mallory broke off. "Someone else. Thank you. This is lovely."

"You're very welcome," the woman said, smiling cautiously. "I'm Gloria, and may I congratulate you on your recent marriage to Mr. Megalos."

Please don't, Mallory wanted to say, but swallowed the urge. "Thank you."

"May I get anything else for you?" Gloria asked. "A snack?"

Mallory's stomach was still upset. She didn't know when she would want to eat again. "No, thank you. This will be fine. Thank you again, and good night," she said and closed the door. Waiting a few seconds for Gloria to walk away, Mallory locked the door. She didn't want a surprise intruder, particularly one that stood six feet tall and was entirely too handsome and charming.

She couldn't believe the two most important men in her life could have done such a thing to her. Did her father truly believe she was incapable of making good decisions for herself?

Her stomach twisted into another knot.

She felt so betrayed. She would do anything to escape to somewhere far, far away from both Alex and her father. Europe, she fantasized, or Australia.

Not likely. Mallory frowned. Both Alex and her father would have their goons watching her every move.

Sinking onto the bed, she crossed her arms over her chest. Everything inside her ached. It was a wrenching sensation as if she were being ripped apart. Even though she and Alex had only been married for a month, she'd become his wife in her mind, and heaven help her in her heart and soul.

And it had all been a trick.

Remnants of the first overwhelming rush of anger still lingered, but other unwanted emotions trickled through her fury. Bone-deep sadness and gaping loss the size of a black hole sucked her downward.

Her chest and throat tightened like a vise closing around her. She felt so lost. A sob escaped her throat, then another. She'd been determined not to cry in front of Alex, but it was as if a dam broke and unleashed her tears.

Stripping off her clothes, she crawled into bed and cried herself to sleep.

A sliver of dawn crept through the window the next morning, waking Mallory. She lay in bed in a semisleep state, wondering if Alex was already up and drinking his coffee. He rose earlier than anyone she knew, even her father.

Her eyes still closed, she sniffed the air for the

scent of coffee, but the only thing she smelled was the unfamiliar scent of lavender. She frowned to herself.

Any minute he would walk back in the room and look at her. She would pretend to be asleep for a maximum of thirty excruciating seconds, then she would open her eyes and smile, and he would lean over her and kiss her good-morning....

Mallory sighed, waiting for the sound of his footsteps. She heard nothing and forced her eyes open even though they felt weighted down with concrete blocks.

Everything that had happened last night hit her at once. Emotions jabbed at her ruthlessly. Humiliation. Loss. Anger.

She pulled the sheet over her head to hide. Oh, heaven help her, what was she going to do now?

She'd seen the expression on his face. He wouldn't let her go. Alex possessed the personality of a conqueror, and he knew far more about winning than she did. Any chance of her resistance was doomed.

She burrowed deeper under the covers. All she wanted to do was hide. How long, some rational part of her mind asked. How many years would she hide?

The same way her mother had.

Mallory immediately tossed back the sheet and sat up in one swift motion. "Damn it," she said. "Damn him."

Alex may have destroyed one of the deepest wishes in her heart, but she had other goals, other dreams. Mallory refused to stop living.

Ten

"I want a job," Mallory said, her hands folded in her lap, her gaze steadfast. Her glorious wavy hair was pulled back into a ponytail at her nape and she emanated as much warmth as an icicle.

Alex could hardly believe the change from his sweet, adoring and passionate bride to the cool, remote woman sitting on the chair opposite him.

"A job," he echoed, rolling the word around his mouth as he stood.

"That's right. If you insist on us remaining together, then the least you owe me is the opportunity to pursue some of my dreams." She paused a half-beat and her eyes flickered with deep sadness.

"Since some of my dreams will never come true, helping me get a job is the least you can do."

Alex stuffed his hands into his pockets in frustration. "Why do you want to work? You can lead a life of leisure. Or at the least, you can set your own schedule. That's the dream of most American women *and* men."

"This isn't a new goal for me. I mentioned it to you some time ago. If you're deadset against it, you better tell me now. This is a deal breaker," she said in a crisp voice.

Alex was stunned at her inflexibility. He didn't want his wife working. He didn't want his wife to feel it was necessary to work. "You're making this difficult."

"In the grand scheme of things, I'm not asking for all that much."

Resting his hands on his hips, he looked down at her, wondering where the sweet woman who'd been his wife had gone. "I can provide for you. You don't need to work."

"Yes, I do. I *need* to feel as if I'm accomplishing something. I don't want to feel like I'm under someone's thumb." She took a quick breath.

"A job," he said again. Alex hadn't spent much time thinking about his future wife, but he'd always expected his wife to retire from her job once they married. After all, he could provide everything a woman could wish for.

He looked into Mallory's eyes and saw the combination of hurt and determination. The hurt made him feel restless. Resting his hands on his hips, he considered options.

"I'll have to think about it. It's not as if any job would do since you're my wife," he said.

"I'll give you two weeks," she said, coolly meeting his gaze.

He lifted an eyebrow. "Or what?" he asked, surprised again that she would have the nerve to give him a deadline. Daddy's little girl was pushing back.

"Or I walk," she said, rising from her seat. "You may not agree to a divorce, but I don't have to agree to live with you, either."

Even though Alex knew he would eventually win any arguments she presented about living apart, he couldn't help feeling a shocking illicit thrill at the challenge in her eyes, her voice, her body. She oozed a dare to him.

"Fine," he said. "I'll find a position for you. You'll be reviewed by someone other than me. If you don't cut it, then it's back to charity work and being my wife."

She glowered at him. "I can cut anything you throw at me. And as far as being your wife, this has become a business arrangement. It was from the beginning. I just didn't know it. If we're going to have a loveless marriage, it's going to be a sexless marriage."

Alex blinked. She couldn't be serious, not with the chemistry they shared. He laughed. "Good joke."

"I am not joking," she said, looking so furious he

wondered if steam would come pouring out of her ears any minute. "Why should I continue to humiliate myself—"

"I didn't know you found sex with me humiliating," he cut in. "I could have sworn those were sounds of pleasure you were making."

She inhaled sharply. "This marriage is a sham. Everything between us is a sham."

"That's not true and you know it. You're exaggerating because you're still upset," he said and shook his head when she opened her mouth. "This argument is unnecessary. You can stay in another bedroom if that's what you want, but it won't last. Now, is that all?"

She silently met his gaze for a long moment, her hands knotted in fury, her cheeks pink from barely restrained temper. She looked like she wanted to slap him. "Yes," she hissed.

"Then I need to get to work. You can either ride with me or I'll send a driver for you."

"I'm not riding with you," she said. "In fact, I think I'll stay here for the next two weeks."

Alex shook his head. "No. I said you may choose another bedroom, not another house. Besides, we have appearances scheduled for this weekend."

"You can't really expect me to appear with you in public and act as if everything between us is all lovey-dovey."

"I can and I do," he said. "I'll leave you with

something to think about. We didn't profess our love to each other before we were married, and you had no aversion to sharing my bed then. I'll see you tonight at dinner." He leaned toward her to kiss her goodbye, but she turned her head.

Even though Alex had won the argument, the victory was hollow. He hadn't realized how much the affection in Mallory's gaze had felt like a ray of sunshine.

Malloy rode to the condo in a sedan driven by Todd. Scowling at the sunny day, she pumped her foot as she crossed one leg over the other. What she wouldn't give to wring Alex's neck and wipe that insufferable confidence off his face.

She'd never felt more trapped in her life. She felt as if the very life was being choked out of her. How could he possibly expect her to pretend their marriage wasn't just a big show? How could she possibly act as if she adored him when she was already fantasizing about fixing a dinner that would cause him a week's worth of indigestion?

After a while, she would wear him down. He would tire of having a wife in name only. He may not love her, but he wanted her to warm his bed. She scowled again at the thought. She'd been so easy, so eager to please. Now Alex would see a different side of her. A side that would make him give her the freedom she deserved.

Mallory allowed herself to stew over the situation

until she arrived at the condo. Then she chose her new bedroom, the one farthest away from Alex's. No need to tempt him. She wouldn't need to worry about being tempted by him. Now that she knew the truth about him, she couldn't possibly feel even a spark of lust, let alone love. She moved all her clothes and belongings to the room and studied how she could make her new bedroom a place of comfort and solace.

She decided to go shopping for candles, pillows and anything else that caught her attention. At the mall, the local animal league was holding a fund and adoption drive. Mallory stroked the soft fur of the dogs and cats. She'd always wanted a pet, but her mother had been allergic.

But she no longer lived in the same house as her mother. An idea occurred to her as she petted a kitten. If she was looking for comfort, a pet would be perfect. She wondered how Alex would feel about having a pet. It would be inconsiderate to get one without asking his opinion.

On the other hand, it had been incredibly inconsiderate for him to marry her for business reasons, too. Mallory smiled to herself as she looked at the animals. Alex would probably hate having a pet. All the more reason for her to get one, although Mallory would never adopt an animal out of spite. Adopting a pet would be one little dream of hers that she could still make come true. If she and Alex remained married, there would be no children. The realization saddened her. She would need to give her affection to some other living being.

Mallory spent the rest of the afternoon shopping for her new bedroom and the two cats she adopted from the animal shelter. New collars, cat food, an electronic litter box, cat carriers.

As she pulled up to the entrance of the condo, the valet opened the door for her and glanced in her back seat. "Would you like some help taking your bags upstairs?"

"Yes, please. That would be wonderful," Mallory said, grabbing the two cat carriers while her new furry friends made plaintive cries. "I don't think they like the carriers, but I don't trust them loose yet."

The nice valet helped her carry everything up to the penthouse.

As she opened the door, she caught the scent of dinner cooking. Surprised because she hadn't requested anything, she wondered if Alex had called from work with instructions. The prospect of seeing him again almost destroyed her good mood, but when she looked at her new kitties again, she had to smile.

Jean, the housekeeper, walked into the foyer and blinked at the sight of the cat carriers. "Cats?" she said in disbelief.

"Yes, aren't they darling?" Mallory asked. "I'll put them in my room for now, but later—"

"Your room," Jean echoed, grabbing several bags

the valet had deposited at the front door and trying to keep up with Mallory.

"Yes," Mallory said, walking through the den and down the long hallway to the end. "I guess Alex didn't have a chance to tell you, but this will be my room. I may redecorate, but I'll figure that out later." She bent down to let out the long-haired black cat with glowing green eyes. "His name is Gorgeous," she said as she stroked his silky, soft fur.

The other cat mewed in envy and Mallory laughed. "I know. It's your turn, Indie," she said, releasing the short-haired calico and rubbing her under her chin. "Aren't they sweet?"

The housekeeper shot a wary eye at Gorgeous, who'd sprang onto an upholstered chair. She cleared her throat. "Mrs. Megalos, I'm not sure Mr. Megalos is a cat lover."

"That's okay. I'll take care of them," Mallory said.

Jean cleared her throat again then nodded. "Mr. Megalos asked me to tell you as soon as you arrived that the two of you are having dinner on the upper terrace. He asked the chef to prepare your favorite dish."

I'm sure he did, Mallory thought as she narrowed her eyes. If Alex thought Crab Imperial on the terrace was going to be enough to win her back to his bed, then he was sadly mistaken. "Thanks. How soon will it be ready?" Mallory asked.

"He requested that you join him as soon as you arrive," Jean said.

Mallory nodded. "Please tell him I'll be upstairs as soon as I set up the litter box and wash up."

"You want me to mention the litter box?" Jean asked in a strained voice, clearly reluctant to be the bearer of that news.

"Good thinking," Mallory said. "Ask him to come in here so I can surprise him."

The housekeeper looked at her as if she'd lost her mind, but nodded. "As you wish."

As Indie circled around her, Mallory pulled out the litter box and poured the litter into it.

"What the hell—"

Mallory glanced up to find Alex staring at Indie. He met her gaze and even though the real reason she'd gotten the cats was for her own edification, she got a tiny thrill at the look of shock on his face. "A cat?"

"Two," she said with a smile that was completely sincere. She pointed at Gorgeous sitting in the chair. "The volunteers at the animal rescue league told me cats are happier in pairs. I was going to get kittens, but I decided on adults because not as many people want them. Meet Gorgeous and Indie," she said and picked up the calico. "I love cats. Don't you?"

He opened his mouth then rubbed his hand over it. "Tell me again why you got two," he said.

"So they won't be lonely while I'm at work," she said.

Alex clenched his jaw and gave a short nod.

"Dinner's ready. I asked the chef to prepare your favorite."

"Yes, thank you. Jean told me. I'll wash up and join you," she said, feeling the strain between them pull like an overstretched rubber band. She hated the sensation.

Leaving her new furry friends in her new room, she freshened up and climbed the stairs to the upper level of the terrace. A light breeze softened the blazing heat. Alex stood, looking over the balcony, his mind seemingly a million miles away. The wind ruffled his wavy hair and his white shirt. He appeared so isolated. She wondered if he would ever admit to feeling lonely. She wondered if he would ever admit to needing someone. Needing her?

Slamming the door on such useless thoughts, she lifted her chin. She could and would get through this. "The Crab Imperial smells delicious," she said, taking a seat at the table.

Alex glanced up and walked to the table. It struck her that he moved with the grace of a primitive, wild animal. A tiger, she decided. He moved his chair next to hers and sat down, his leg immediately brushing hers.

Mallory's heart skipped and she moved her leg away from his. She wished she wasn't so aware of him. She shouldn't be, she thought, taking a sip of white wine. Not after what he'd done.

"You've been busy today," he said, picking up his fork and taking a bite.

"I had a lot to do," she said and took a bite of the Crab Imperial. It tasted like sawdust.

"You didn't need to move into another room so quickly," he said. "You could have slept on your decision."

"No, I couldn't," she said, suspecting that if she'd slept on her decision she would have never moved out. She would have simply remained under Alex's spell forever, feeling and acting like a weak fool.

She took another bite and it tasted the same, sawdust. Blast it. "What did you find out about jobs for me today?"

He took a long sip of wine and speared a piece of crab with his fork. "Technically nothing."

Mallory's blood pressure immediately rose. "I really meant it when I said I wanted a job. I can interview for one on my own."

"That won't be necessary. I've decided you'll work for me," he said.

She blinked. "How?"

"I've been working double time because of the resort I'm developing in West Virginia. Your father has supplied the investors."

"In trade for you being my husband," she said, a bitter taste filling her mouth.

"He would have done it, anyway. It's a good investment."

"Why was it necessary? You have enough money on your own," she blurted out.

"One of the rules of wealth management is that you use other people's money to accomplish your goals. You don't risk your own."

She was surprised at his acumen, but shouldn't have been. "Where do I fit in with this?"

"I want you to interface with my contacts in West Virginia. There will be very limited travel," he said. "I don't want my wife spending most of her time away from me. I'm balancing several demands at Megalos-De Luca Enterprises and the personal resort start-up, so I won't be able to get your job in place for another week or so."

"As long as it's within two weeks," she said, feeling as if she had to hold the line. Alex had made her forget everything but him. She couldn't let that happen again.

"I'll make it worth the wait," he said in such a sexy way that it sent a shiver down her all the way to her toes.

Upset by her reaction to him, Mallory rushed down a couple of bites of the dish and gulped some wine. "That was delicious. I'm full. If you don't mind excusing me—"

"Already?" he said with a raised eyebrow that could have made her back down in other circumstances. But not now.

"The cats," she said. "I need to get them acclimated to their new home."

He gave a slow nod that made her feel as if she

may have won round one, but the game was far from over. "We have a cocktail party with the other VPs, CEO and board members of Megalos-De Luca Enterprises the day after tomorrow."

She blinked in surprise. "That's not much notice."

"No, it isn't," he said. "The board is introducing a reengineering specialist."

"You don't sound happy," she said.

"I'm not. Neither is Max De Luca."

She shivered at the cold expression on his face. "I can't imagine anyone in their right mind who would want to go up against the two of you."

He lifted his mouth in a smile that bared his teeth like a wolf. "I always thought you were a clever woman."

She stood. "Just not clever enough to see through the ruse you and my father cooked up."

Alex shot from his chair and snagged her wrist. "There was always something between us, Mallory. You can't deny that."

She knew she'd always had feelings for him. That was all. She shook her head. "I have no idea what your true feelings, if any, are for me."

"I can show you," he offered and lowered his head.

She turned her head away and his mouth seared her cheek. Her heart was hammering a mile a minute. "I want more than a man who's interested in me for the money my father can find for him. I want more than sex."

Eleven

The tension at the Megalos-De Luca cocktail party was so thick it reminded Mallory of trying to breathe in a dust storm. The room vibrated with such suspicion she couldn't wait to leave.

Spotting Lilli De Luca, she felt a smidgeon of relief and waved. Lilli smiled in return and moved toward Mallory. "Hi," she said, giving Mallory a quick hug. "This is horrible, isn't it?" she said in a low voice.

Mallory gave a short laugh, nodding in agreement. "I couldn't agree more. It feels like we're waiting for the gallows."

Lilli's pretty features wrinkled in concern. "I know. Max has been very upset about this. He won't talk about it, but he's not sleeping well at all. What about Alex?"

Mallory felt a twist of self-consciousness. She didn't know how Alex was sleeping because she wasn't sharing his bed. "He's bothered, too."

Lilli nodded. "The two of them are talking more and more. It's interesting how something like this can turn two men who were competitors into more of a team. You find out a lot about a man by how he acts when the pressure's on."

The discussion made Mallory even more uncomfortable. She would examine why later. "How's David?"

Lilli lit up. She lifted her hand and showed a miniscule of space between her thumb and forefinger. "He's this close to crawling. Max is egging him on even though I keep telling Max we'll both be doing a lot more chasing once David is mobile."

Mallory felt a stab of loss as she thought about the babies she wouldn't have with Alex.

"I'm sure you're still enjoying your honeymoon period," Lilli said with a knowing smile. "What's new at the Megalos house?"

"Cats," Mallory said. "I adopted two cats."

Lilli gaped. "Oh, my gosh. How did Alex react to that?"

"Surprisingly well," Mallory said and shook her head. "And they seem to love him. They wind around his ankles every night when he comes home." She still couldn't believe it, but she supposed she shouldn't have been surprised. Alex could turn every woman to putty. She just hadn't known his powers extended to felines.

Lilli glanced at the other side of the room. "It looks like there's going to be an announcement. We should join our husbands."

Mallory walked to Alex's side. He held a glass of Scotch in his hand and appeared attentive, but relaxed. She knew better, though. He hadn't touched his drink and every once in a while his jaw clenched.

She shouldn't care, and she told herself it was just human nature not to want to see another human being suffer, but Mallory knew that the first wave of her white-hot anger and indignation against Alex had finally cooled. "Are you okay?" she asked in a low voice.

He met her gaze and she saw a flash of turbulence before he covered it. "Yes. You're drinking water. Did you want something else?"

She shook her head, thinking she would just like to leave the oppressive atmosphere. "Who is he?" she asked, nodding toward the man getting ready to speak.

"James Oldham, one of the board of directors," he said.

"He has shifty eyes," she whispered.

Alex chuckled. "You continue to delight me."

His statement was so natural it caught her off guard. Mallory often dismissed Alex's compliments because she assumed a hidden agenda. This time there was none and she couldn't suppress a burst of pleasure.

"Ladies and gentlemen, thank you for joining us on such short notice," James Oldham said. "As you know, Megalos-De Luca Enterprises has long provided travelers all over the world with the ultimate resort luxury experience. We continue to do that. We also continue to refine the bottom line so that we keep our stockholders happy. To best facilitate that continued refinement, we are bringing in the best of the best in reengineering consulting firms to help us improve our financial edge in this complicated world market. Please welcome Damien Medici," he said and the door to the room opened, revealing a tall, dark man with black hair, olive skin and dark, watchful eyes. His lips lifted in the barest of smiles. He turned his head and she glimpsed a jagged scar along his jaw.

Mallory watched Alex give a nod and a soundless clap of his hands while the rest of the room applauded. Max leaned toward Alex and said something. Mallory felt the tension in the room grow exponentially and took a sip of her water.

"No relation to Santa Claus, is he?" she said to Alex.

His lips twisted in humor and he slid his hand behind her back. "Not exactly. He goes by a couple nicknames. The Terminator. Switch for switchblade. Here he comes," he said.

Mallory turned to find Damien Medici studying

the four of them intently, with particular interest in Alex and Max. He extended his hand. "The two namesakes of the company. I've heard much about you. Max, Alex," he said, shaking each of their hands. "We have more in common than you probably think. I look forward to working with you."

Damien turned to Lilli. "Mrs. De Luca?" he enquired and smiled. "Max did well." He then turned to Mallory and extended his hand. "As did Alex, Mrs. Megalos."

Mallory reluctantly accepted his hand. "Mr. Medici," she said.

"I'll be meeting with each of you individually soon," Damien said to Max and Alex.

"Welcome to Megalos-De Luca Enterprises," Alex said in his regular charming voice, but Mallory didn't miss the emphasis on the company name. Alex and Max would protect the company. Damien might not know it, but he would be facing the fight of his life if he wrangled with the two of them.

Damien nodded and walked away. Alex and Max exchanged a look then Alex glanced down, pulling his BlackBerry from his pocket. He frowned. "We should go," he said to Mallory and escorted her from the gathering.

Alex was completely silent during the drive to the condo. That should have been fine, but Mallory couldn't stop herself from being concerned. She knew he was bothered about Damien Medici, but she wondered if there was something else bringing that dark look to his face. Could it be something about the development in West Virginia?

He absently wished her good-night, and Mallory went to bed, but didn't sleep well. Rising early despite her lack of sleep, she showered and got dressed. Entering the kitchen, she was surprised to see Alex seated at the table talking on the phone.

As soon as he caught sight of her, he cut off the conversation. "Please have a seat," he said, standing and pulling out a chair for her.

Mallory felt a ripple of uneasiness. Although she glimpsed slight shadows beneath his eyes, Alex seemed almost too controlled, too calm. She took the seat he offered. "Okay."

He took a deep breath. "I'll give you the divorce you want."

Shock hit her like a cannonball. Surely she hadn't heard him correctly. "Excuse me?"

"I said I'll give you a divorce," he said in that too calm voice.

Shock hit her again, followed by confusion. "I don't understand."

He shoved his hands into his pockets, one sign that he wasn't as calm as he seemed. "I don't expect you to understand. That's why I'm giving you the divorce. Chloe," he began.

"Your ex-girlfriend?" Mallory could hardly forget the woman since the willowy blonde had shown up during her trip to the islands and the wedding reception.

"We were briefly involved, which was a terrible mistake on my part," he said in a cold, crisp voice. "I can't allow you to suffer as a result of my mistake."

Mallory shook her head, still confused. "I don't understand. Would you please sit down? This is a strange enough conversation without my having to crane to look up at you."

Alex reluctantly sat. "Chloe is threatening to go to the press with a story that she's pregnant with my child. She's claiming she got pregnant while you and I were seeing each other."

Mallory's heart stopped. "Oh, my God," she whispered. "She's pregnant with your child?"

He shook his head. "No, she isn't."

"How can you be sure?"

"I always wore protection and we were only together twice," he said.

"But condoms don't provide perfect protection," Mallory said more to herself than to Alex, her mind spinning with the news. She felt a deep twist of resentment and jealousy at the thought of Chloe bearing Alex's child.

"The woman is a pathological liar," Alex said. "I wouldn't be surprised if she's not pregnant at all."

Mallory stared at him. "Really?"

"Really," he said and finally swore. "She showed up uninvited at our wedding reception, for God's sake."

"Were you still seeing her when you and I—"

"Absolutely not," he said and took her hand in his. "I swear it. I broke up with her before you and I got involved. Once there was you, there was no one else."

Mallory felt a shiver run down her body at the naked honesty in Alex's eyes. Her emotions running all over the place, she looked at him helplessly. "If she's lying, then why do you want to divorce me?"

"I can't put you through this kind of scandal. I refuse to do it. You don't deserve it. The only way I can protect you is to divorce you." He drew in a slow breath. "I'll take care of it quickly and quietly. I have to leave town on business for the next few days. While I'm gone you can choose where you'd like to move. I think it's best that you leave Vegas, at least for a while, so you won't have to answer questions." He paused. "I'm sorry. Divorcing you is that last thing I want to do, but it's the only choice. Chloe is promising a long, drawn-out fight, and I know you would never escape the whispers. Chloe was my mistake, not yours. You deserve the fresh start that I can't give you."

Fifteen minutes later, she watched him walk out of the condo. Mallory felt as if she'd been sucked into a killer tornado and spit out in pieces. She wandered the condo, shell-shocked.

She should be happy, shouldn't she? This was what she'd wanted, no, demanded of Alex. Now she could be free to pursue her own life, her own dreams. Freedom was what she'd been craving for years.

Why did she feel like crying? Why did she feel as if someone important to her had died? Biting her lip, Mallory walked to her new bedroom and felt tears stinging her eyes. She blinked furiously to make them stop, but they streamed down her face.

Sinking onto the bed, she tried to come to terms with what Alex had told her and his solution. Her cats hopped onto the bed and rubbed against her. She grabbed Gorgeous and held him against her. He mewed in sympathy.

She glanced at the books for her online class sitting on her dresser. She'd had a hard time concentrating lately. How much harder would it be now?

She tried to formulate a plan. While she packed her belongings, she would figure out where to go. California, she thought, and immediately rejected the idea. Somewhere different. Somewhere that no one knew her. The East Coast. Florida. A remote, sunny island. A downpour of images of the time she and Alex had shared in Cabo stormed through her. The memories were so sweet she ached from them.

She pulled a suitcase from the closet and began to fill it with clothes. Heaven help her, she was confused. She'd spent most of her life doing what everyone else had told her to do. During the last month, she'd been tricked into marrying the man of her dreams. Now she was getting a divorce. She hadn't wanted to get married. She didn't want a divorce.

The thought took her by surprise. She opened

another drawer and dumped the clothes into the suitcase then stopped. A question echoed in her mind, throughout her body. What did she *really* want?

Four days later, Alex returned from his business trip. Riding the elevator to the penthouse, he dreaded walking into his home. He'd been tempted to stay at the resort downtown. Even though Mallory had been furious with him during the last week they'd been together, he'd still looked forward to her presence.

He despised the fact that his life had become tabloid fodder. He despised the fact that he'd been forced to cut Mallory out of his life for her protection. He felt gutted, empty. He'd always been so sure a woman couldn't get to his soul. Until Mallory.

He'd even started liking her cats.

The elevator stopped at the top floor and the doors opened. Swearing under his breath, he braced himself for utter quiet. He opened the door to the condo and gritted his teeth. He had never known he could be this miserable.

Closing the door behind him, he dropped his suitcase in the foyer and walked into the den. The calico sprinted out to greet him with the black male at her heels. He stared at the cats in confusion.

"What the—"

The cats wove around his ankles, mewing. Untangling himself, Alex raced to Mallory's room. Empty except for the furniture that had been there before she moved. His heart fell to his stomach.

Why the hell were the cats here? Had she left them with him for some sick reason? He backtracked to the kitchen, searching for Jean, but there was no sign of the housekeeper. He noticed, however, that the sliding door to the deck was slightly ajar. He stood very still. Was that music playing?

Confusion and anticipation coursed through him. He stepped outside and heard the music coming from the upper deck. He couldn't imagine why she would still be here. He'd made it perfectly clear to Mallory that he would give her a divorce. He hadn't softened the scandal he was facing.

Climbing the stairs to the upper terrace, he didn't know what to expect. It certainly wasn't finding Mallory reclined on a chaise lounge wearing a silky gown.

She glanced up to meet his gaze and smiled. A knot of longing formed in his throat. He wondered if he was dreaming.

"Welcome home," she said and sat up in the chair. "I poured a glass of Scotch for you. It's on the bar if you want it."

He did. Lifting the small glass from the bar, he took a long sip, feeling the burn all the way down. He met her gaze again. "I thought you would be gone."

"I almost was," she said, rising to her feet. "I packed up everything. But the whole time I couldn't stop asking myself what I really wanted." She moved toward him.

His heart pounded hard and deep. "And what was your answer?"

"I want to be the woman of your dreams," she said. "I want to be the woman you choose above all the other women. I want to be the woman you love even though you never thought you would fall in love."

He narrowed his eyes, steeling himself against the temptation to take her in his arms. "Love won't fix the mess with Chloe."

Her eyes flashed with sadness then she lifted her chin in determination. "Do you love me?"

Stunned by her boldness, he stared at her for a full moment before responding. "It doesn't matter. I won't put you through this scandal."

She pressed her lips together. "Afraid I can't take it, right?"

"I didn't say that," he said.

"You may as well. Are you going to underestimate me like everyone else has?"

Surprised again, Alex felt as if she were taking him on a ride with hairpin turns and gut-wrenching drops. "I don't underestimate you. I know you're an amazing woman. Adventurous, kind, sexy."

She made a moue of her lips. "Sounds like you might like me a little bit."

"A little bit," he echoed and swore. He took

another swallow of his drink. He didn't know how it had happened, but he was tied up in knots over her.

"I wouldn't have thought you were the quitting kind," she said. "Not if it was something you really wanted."

"I'm not," he said.

"Then you must not want me very much," she said.

His breath left his body. "Dammit," he said reaching for her. "I want you too much. I can't stand to see you hurt by all this. I finally find a woman who makes me feel like a human being, who makes me feel alive inside and I have to give her up. Dammit, it's killing me, Mallory. Don't make it any harder."

Mallory blinked, dropping her jaw and working it for a few seconds. She shook her head. "I'm going to make it very hard. I love you and I'm tired of being told what I should want and what I should do. You and I got married and I can stomp my foot and scream and rail at you because of the deal you made with my father, but the truth is I wouldn't have married you if I didn't want to." She took a deep breath. "And I don't think anyone, including my father, could have forced you to marry me. So, Mr. Megalos, consider yourself stuck with me."

Alex stared at her in amazement, not quite able to believe her. "Are you sure? This is going to get messy."

"Life is messy," she said. "I want to spend mine with you."

In that moment she made all Alex's dreams come

true at once. He pulled her against him. "I love you more than I can tell you. You really are the woman of my dreams."

He took her mouth in a soul-searing kiss that went on and on. He felt dampness against his cheeks and realized she was crying. Pulling back, he searched her face. "Mallory?"

"I was so afraid," she said. "So afraid that maybe I was wrong, that maybe you didn't love me."

"Oh, sweetheart," he said, pulling her against him. "I guess I'll just have to spend the rest of my life telling you and showing you how very much I love you."

She took a trembling breath. "Starting now?"

He swung her into his arms and headed down the steps. "Starting now."

Epilogue

Six weeks later...

Poring over lists, charts and plans for Alex's resort in West Virginia, Mallory sneaked a peek through the glass oven door and felt a twinge of relief. Good, she hadn't burned anything this time. Cooking wasn't her forte, and even though it wasn't technically necessary for her to cook, she wanted to be able to fix something special for Alex. He'd been working so hard, engaged in a constant corporate battle with Damien Medici. The master of reorganization had been a major pain in the rear and she just wished he would go far, far away. The planet Jupiter sounded like a good place for him.

With both her kitties snoozing at her feet, she glanced back at her work. She took her job for Alex very seriously. In fact, Alex joked that she took it too seriously sometimes when she was glued to her cell phone getting answers to questions and smoothing out rough spots. She could tell, however, that he was proud of her. It was amazing how much their relationship had changed once they'd admitted their love to each other. The difference was night and day.

Hearing the front door open, she watched the cats race out of the room. Seconds later they began to mew in welcome.

"Good afternoon, you spoiled, beautiful felines," Alex said in an affectionate voice at odds with his words. "What have you been up to today? Shredding curtains, ripping upholstery? Mallory?" he called.

Her heart still hiccupped at the sound of his voice. "In the kitchen," she said, rising from the table and peeking into the oven again. So far, so good.

Alex strode into the room and pulled her into his arms. If she didn't know better, she would say he was even more gorgeous than the first day she'd seen him. "How was your day?" he asked. "Tell me you're finished with your work," he said before she could answer, and lowered his mouth to hers.

Mallory bubbled with laughter, then sank into his kiss and his embrace. He kissed her as if she were the only woman on earth, and she was starting to believe that maybe she was for him.

She pulled back and took a couple of quick breaths. "I had one more thing I wanted to do before—"

"No," he said, shaking his head. "You're done. I have plans for you."

She wondered what was behind the mysterious glint in his green eyes. "Really?"

"I do, and there'll be no stalling, no excuses due to homework or anything else," he said firmly and paused a half-beat. "What is that amazing smell?"

Mallory smiled. "Apple pie. I made it myself. And we have ice cream."

His gaze softened. "You didn't have to do that. You could ask the cook—"

"I know. I wanted to." She glanced over his shoulder. "Time to take it out," she said, and pulled the pie from the oven and set it on a hot pad. "You've been working so hard lately in so many ways," she said, her mind drifting to the problems with Chloe. "I thought you deserved a little treat."

He came up behind her and put his arms around her waist. "We may have to take the pie with us. I've arranged for a celebration."

She turned in his arms and searched his face. "Why? Did Damien move to the other side of the world?"

Alex's face hardened. "No, but he's taking some time away from Megalos-De Luca to handle a crisis somewhere else." He gave a deep sigh. "My good news is that Chloe submitted to a pregnancy test and she's not pregnant."

Relief washed over Mallory. She knew how much Alex had suffered over this. "She can't threaten to sue you anymore."

"Exactly. So I've decided to celebrate by getting your passport stamped."

Mallory dropped her mouth in amazement. "How? When?"

"Tonight," he said. "We'll take my personal jet. We can sleep or do other things on the way," he said in a suggestive voice. "We'll take the pie with us, too."

Mallory's mind flew in a half-dozen different directions. "But I really do have a paper due and I've got to stay on top of those people in West Virginia or they won't get things done the way they should—"

Alex placed his index finger over her mouth. "This is part one of our honeymoon. We're gong to Paris."

"Paris," she echoed. "I've never been."

His lips curved in sexy *gotcha* smile. "I know. I see it as my personal duty to fill up all the pages in your passport the same way I fill up…"

Her face flaming at his intimate suggestion, she covered his mouth with her hand.

He kissed her fingers. "Not blushing, are you?" he teased.

"Stop it. You're making it hard for me to think straight."

He lowered his mouth to a breath away from hers. "One of my other jobs," he said.

She groaned. "Part one. Why did you say this is part one of our honeymoon?"

"Because numbers are infinite," he said, his face turning solemn. "They go on forever. The same way our love will."

"Pinch me," she said. "I can't believe I'm this lucky. Pinch me."

Alex shook his head. "Wait until I get you on the plane. I'll do a lot more pleasurable things than pinch you."

Mallory sighed as he kissed her. She knew he would deliver on his promise. Loving Alex and being loved by him would be the greatest adventure of her life.

* * * * *

RICH MAN'S
FAKE FIANCÉE

by
Catherine Mann

Dear Reader,

Welcome to the first book in my new LANDIS BROTHERS series!

I especially enjoyed the opportunity to set these stories in South Carolina where I grew up. Furthermore, while my sisters and I were at the College of Charleston, we all met our future husbands, cadets at The Citadel. Charleston will always be the city of romance to me. I hope you find the area as enchanting as I still do!

I very much enjoy hearing from readers. If you would like to contact me, I can be reached at PO Box 6065, Navarre, FL 32566, USA or www.catherinemann.com.

Happy reading!

Catherine Mann

CATHERINE MANN

RITA® Award winner Catherine Mann resides on a sunny Florida beach with her military flyboy husband and their four children. Although after nine moves in twenty years, she hasn't given away her winter gear! With more than a million books in print in fifteen countries, she has also celebrated five RITA® finals, three Maggie Award of Excellence finals and a Booksellers' Best win. A former theatre school director and university teacher, she graduated with a master's degree in theatre from UNC-Greensboro and a bachelor's degree in fine arts from the College of Charleston. Catherine enjoys hearing from readers and chatting on her message board – thanks to the wonders of the wireless internet that allows her to cyber-network with her laptop by the water!

To learn more about her work, visit her website at www.catherinemann.com.

To my sisters, Julie Morrison and Beth Reaves,
and to their South Carolina husbands,
Todd Morrison and Jerry Reaves.
Much love to you all!

And a great big thanks to my editor
Melissa Jeglinski for giving me the
opportunity to tell the Landis Brothers' stories!

One

Only one thing sucked worse than wearing boring white cotton underwear on the night she finally landed in bed with her secret fantasy man.

Having him walk out on her before daylight.

Ashley Carson tensed under her down comforter. Through the veil of her eyelashes, she watched her new lover quietly zip his custom-fit pants. She'd taken a bold step—unusual for her—by falling into bed with Matthew Landis the night before. Her still-tingly sated body cheered the risk. Her good sense, however, told her she'd made a whopper mistake with none other than South Carolina's most high-profile senatorial candidate.

Moonlight streaked through the dormer window, glinting off his dark hair trimmed short but still mussed from her fingers. Broad shoulders showcased his beacon white shirt, crisp even though she'd stripped it from him just hours ago when their planning session for his fund-raiser dinner at her restaurant/home had taken an unexpected turn down the hall to her bedroom.

Matthew may have been dream material, but safely so since she'd always thought there wasn't a chance they could actually end up together. *She* preferred a sedentary, quiet life running her business, with simple pleasures she never took for granted after her foster child upbringing. *He* worked in the spotlight as a powerful member of the House of Representatives just as adept at negotiating high-profile legislation as swinging a hammer at a Habitat for Humanity site.

People gravitated to his natural charisma and sense of purpose.

Matthew reached for his suit jacket draped over the back of a corner chair. Would he say goodbye or simply walk away? She wanted to think he would speak to her, but couldn't bear to find out otherwise so she sat up, floral sheet clutched to her chest.

"That floorboard by the door creaks, Matthew. You might want to sidestep it or I'll hear you sneaking out."

He stopped, wide shoulders stiffening before he turned slowly. He hadn't shaved, his five-o'clock shadow having thickened into something much darker—just below the guilty glint in his jewel-green eyes that had helped win him a seat in the U.S. House of Representatives. Five months from now, come November, he could well be the handsome sexy-eyed *Senator* Landis if he won the seat to be vacated by his mother.

With one quick blink, Matthew masked the hint of emotion. "Excuse me? I haven't snuck anywhere since I was twelve, trying to steal my cousin's magazines from under his mattress." He stuffed his tie in his pocket. "I was getting dressed."

"Oh, my mistake." She slid from the bed, keeping the sheet tucked around her naked body. The room smelled of potpourri and musk, but she wouldn't let either distract her. "Since yesterday, you've developed a light step and a penchant for walking around in your socks."

Ashley nodded toward his Gucci loafers dangling from two fingers.

"You were sleeping soundly," he stated simply.

A lot of great sex tends to wear a woman out. Apparently she hadn't accomplished the same for him, not that she intended to voice her vulnerability to him. "How polite of you."

He dropped the shoes to the floor and toed them

on one after the other. Seeing his expensive loafers on her worn hardwood floors with a cotton rag rug, she couldn't miss the hints that this polished, soon-to-be senator wasn't at home in her world. Too bad those reminders didn't stop her from wanting to drag him back onto her bed.

"Ashley, last night was amazing—"

"Stop right there. I don't need platitudes or explanations. We're both single adults, not dating each other or anyone else." She snagged a terry-cloth robe off a brass hook by the bathroom door and ducked inside to swap the sheet for the robe. "We're not even really friends for that matter. More like business acquaintances who happened to indulge in a momentary attraction."

Okay, momentary for him maybe. But she'd been salivating over him during the few times they'd met to plan social functions at her Beachcombers Restaurant and Bar.

Ashley stepped back into the bedroom, tugging the robe tie tight around her waist.

"Right, we're on the same page then." He braced a hand on the doorframe, his gold cuff links glinting.

"You should get going if you plan to make it home in time to change."

He hesitated for three long thumps of her heart before pivoting away on his heel. Ashley followed him down the hall of her Southern antebellum home-turned-restaurant she ran with her two foster sisters. She'd recently taken up residence in the back room off her office, watching over the accounting books as well as the building since her recently married sisters had moved out.

Sure enough, more than one floorboard creaked under his confident strides as they made their way past the gift shop and into the lobby. She unlocked the towering front door, avoiding his eyes. "I'll send copies of the signed contract for the fund-raising dinner to your campaign manager."

The night before, Matthew had stayed late after the business dinner to pass along some last-minute paperwork. She never could have guessed how combustible a simple brush of their bodies against each other could become. Her fantasies about this man had always revolved around far more exotic scenarios.

But they were just that. Fantasies. As much as he tried to hide his emotions, she couldn't miss how fast he'd made tracks out of her room. She'd been rejected often enough as a kid by her parents and even classmates. These days, pride starched her spine far better than any back brace she'd been forced to wear to combat scoliosis.

Matthew flattened a palm to the mahogany door. "I will call you later."

Sure. Right. "No calls." She didn't even want the

possibility of waiting by the phone, or worse yet, succumbing to the humiliating urge to dial him up, only to get stuck in voicejail as she navigated his answering service. "Let's end this encounter on the same note it started. Business."

She extended her hand. He eyed her warily. She pasted her poise in place through pride alone. Matthew enfolded her hand in his, not shaking after all, rather holding as he leaned forward to press a kiss…

On her cheek.

Damn.

He slipped out into the muggy summer night. "It's still dark. You should go back to sleep."

Sleep? He had to be freaking kidding.

Thank goodness she had plenty to keep her busy now that Matthew had left, because she was fairly certain she wouldn't be sleeping again. She watched his brisk pace down the steps and into the shadowy parking lot, which held only his Lexus sedan and her tiny Kia Rio. What was she doing, staring after him? She shoved the door closed with a heavy click.

All her poise melted. She still had her pride but her ability to stand was sorely in question. Ashley sagged against the counter by the antique cash register in the foyer.

She couldn't even blame him. She'd been a willing participant all night long. They'd been in the kitchen where she'd planned to give him a taste of the dessert pastries her sister added to the menu for his fund-raiser. Standing near each other in the close confines of the open refrigerator, they had brushed against each other, once, twice.

His hand had slowly raised to thumb away cream filling at the corner of her mouth…

She'd forgotten all about her white cotton underwear until he'd peeled it from her body on the way back to her bedroom. Then she hadn't been able to think of much else for hours to come.

Her bruised emotions needed some serious indulging. She gazed into the gift shop, her eyes locking on a rack of vintage-style lingerie. She padded on bare feet straight toward the pale pink satin nightgown dangling on the end. Her fingers gravitated to the wide bands of peekaboo lace crisscrossing over the bodice, rimming the hem, outlining the V slit in the front of the 1920s-looking garment.

How she'd ached for whispery soft underthings during her childhood, but had always been forced to opt for the more practical cotton, a sturdier fabric not so easily snagged by her back brace. She didn't need the brace any longer. Just a slight lift to her left shoulder remained, only noticeable if someone knew to check. But while she'd ditched the brace once it finished the job, she still felt each striation on her heart.

Ashley snatched the hanger from the rack and

dashed past the shelved volumes of poetry, around a bubble bath display to the public powder room. Too bad she hadn't worn this yesterday. Her night with Matthew might not have ended any differently, but at least she would have had the satisfaction of stamping a helluva sexier imprint on his memory.

A quick shrug landed her robe on the floor around her feet.

Ashley avoided the mirror, a habit long ingrained. She focused instead on the nightgown's beauty. One bridal shower after another, she'd gifted her two foster sisters with the same style.

Satin slid along her skin like a cool shower over a body still flushed from the joys of heated sex with Matthew. She sunk onto the tapestry chaise, a French Restoration piece she'd bargained for at an estate auction. She lit the candle next to her to complete the sensory saturation. The flame flickered shadows across the faded wallpaper, wafting relaxing hints of lavender.

One deep breath at a time, she willed her anger to roll free as she drifted into the pillowy cloud of sensation. She tugged a decorative afghan over her. Maybe she could snag a nano nap after all.

Timeless relaxing moments later, Ashley inhaled again, deeper. And coughed. She sat up bolt right, sniffing not lavender, but…

Smoke.

* * *

Staring out at the summer sunrise just peeking up from the ocean, Matthew Landis worked like hell to get his head together before he powered back up those steps to retrieve the briefcase he'd left behind at Beachcombers.

He slid his car into Park for the second time that day, back where he'd started—with Ashley Carson. He prided himself on never making a misstep thanks to diligent planning. His impulsive tumble with her definitely hadn't been planned.

As a public servant he'd vowed to look out for the best interests of the people, protect and help others, especially the vulnerable. Yet last night he'd taken advantage of one of the most vulnerable women he knew.

He'd always been careful in choosing bed partners, because while he never intended to marry, he damn well couldn't live his life as a monk. He'd already had his one shot at forever in college, only to lose her to heart failure from a rare birth defect. He'd never even gotten the chance to introduce Dana to his family. No one knew about their engagement to this day. The notion of sharing that information with anyone had always felt like he would be giving up a part of their short time together.

After that, he'd focused on finishing his MBA at Duke University and entering the family business of politics. His inheritance afforded him the option of serving others without concerns about his bank balance. His life was full.

So what the hell was he doing here?

Ashley Carson was sexy, no question, her prettiness increased all the more by the way she didn't seem to realize her own appeal. Still, he worked around beautiful women all the time and held himself in check. Something he would continue to do when he retrieved his briefcase—and no, damn it, leaving it there wasn't a subconscious slip on his part. Matthew opened the sedan door—

And heard the smoke alarm *beep, beep, beeping* from inside the restaurant.

An even louder alert sounded in his head as a whiff of smoke brushed his nose. He scoured the lot. Her small blue sedan sat in the same spot it had when he'd left.

"Ashley?" he shouted, hoping she'd already come outside.

No answer.

His muscles contracted and he sprinted toward the porch while dialing 9-1-1 on his cell to call the fire department. He gripped the front doorknob, the metal hot in his hand. In spite of its scorching heat, he twisted the knob. Thank God she'd left it unlocked after he'd gone. The leash snapped on Matthew's restraint and he shoved into the lobby.

Heat swamped him, but he saw no flames in the old mansion's foyer.

Through the shadowy glow, the fire seemed contained to the gift shop and his feet beat a path in that direction. Flames licked upward from the racks of clothing in the small store. Paint bubbled, popped and peeled on aged wood.

"Ashley?" Matthew shouted. "Ashley!"

Bottles of perfume exploded. Glass spewed through the archway onto the wooden floor. Colognes ignited, feeding the blaze inside the gift shop.

He pressed deeper inside. Boards creaked and shifted, plaster falling nearby, all leading him to wonder about the structural integrity of the hundred-and-seventy-year-old house. How much time did he have to find her?

As long as it took.

His leather loafers crunched broken glass. "Ashley, answer me, damn it."

Smoke rolled through the hallway. He ducked lower, his arm in front of his face as he called out for her again and again.

Then he heard her.

"Help!" A thud sounded against the wall. "Anybody, I'm in here."

Relief made him dizzier than the acrid smoke.

"Hold on, Ashley, I'm coming," he yelled.

The pounding stopped. "Matthew?"

Her husky drawl of his name blindsided him. A gust of heat at his back snapped him back to the moment. "Keep talking."

"I'm over here, in the powder room."

Her hoarse tones drove Matthew the last few feet. The door rattled, then stopped. A handle lay on the ground. "Get as far away from the door as you can. I'm coming in."

"Okay," Ashley said, her raspy voice softer. "I'm out of the way."

Straightening, he slid his body into the suffocating cloud. He didn't have much time left. If the blaze snaked down the hall, it would tunnel out of control.

Matthew shoved with his shoulder, again, harder, but the door didn't budge, the old wood apparently sturdier than the handle. He took three steps back for a running start.

And rammed a final time. The force shuddered through him as finally the panel gave way and crashed inward.

He scanned the dim cubicle and found Ashley— thank God—sitting, wedged in a corner by the sink, wrapped in a wet blanket. Smart woman.

Matthew wove around the fallen door toward her. He sidestepped a broken chair, the whole room in shambles. She'd obviously fought to free herself. This subdued woman apparently packed the wallop of a pocket-size warrior.

"Thanks for coming back," she gasped out, thrusting out a hand with a dripping wet hand towel. "Wrap this around your face."

Very smart woman. He looped the cloth around his face, scarf style, to filter the air.

Ashley rose to her feet, coughed, gasped. Damn. She needed air, but she wouldn't be able to walk over the shards of glass and sparking embers with her bare feet.

He hunkered down, dipping his shoulder into her midsection and swooping her up. "Hang on."

"Just get us out of here." She hacked through another rasping cough.

Matthew charged through the shop, now more of a kiln. Greedy flames crawled along a counter. Packs of stationery blackened, disintegrated.

Move faster. Don't stop. Don't think.

A bookshelf wobbled. Matthew rocked on his heels. Instinctively, he curved himself over Ashley. The towering shelves crashed forward, exploding into a pyre, stinging his face. Blocking his exit.

His fist convulsed around the blanket. A burning wood chip sizzled through his leather shoe.

"The other entrance, through the kitchen," Ashley hollered through wrenching coughs and her fireproof cocoon. "To the left."

"Got it." Backtracking, he rounded the corner

into the narrow hall. The smoke thinned enough for light to seep through the glass door.

Ashley jostled against him, a slight weight. Relief slammed him with at least twice the force. Too damn much relief for someone he barely knew.

Suddenly the air outside felt as thick and heavy as the smoldering atmosphere back inside.

Ashley gasped fresh air by the Dumpster behind her store. Hysteria hummed inside her.

At least the humid air out here was fresher than the alternative inside her ruined restaurant. Soon to be her entirely ruined home if firefighters didn't show up ASAP and knock back the flames spitting through two kitchen windows.

The distant siren brought some relief, which only freed her mind to fill with other concerns. How could the blaze have started? Had one of the candles been to blame? How much damage waited back inside?

Matthew's shoulder dug into her stomach. Each loping step punched precious gasps from her and brought a painful reminder of her undignified position. "You can put me down now."

"No need to thank me," he answered, his drawl raspier. "Save your breath."

How could he be both a hero and an insensitive jerk in the space of a few hours?

Her teeth chattered. Delayed reaction, no doubt.

The fine stitching along the bottom of his Brooks Brothers suit coat bobbed in front of her eyes. The graveled parking lot passed below. Now that the imminent danger of burning to death had ended, she could distract herself with an almost equally daunting problem.

Earlier she'd bemoaned the fact Matthew hadn't seen her in the pink satin nightgown—and now she wished he could see her in anything but that scrap of lingerie underneath her soggy blanket.

"Matthew," Ashley squeaked. "I can walk. Let me go, please."

"Not a chance." He shifted her more securely in place. The move nudged the blanket aside, baring her shoulder. His feet pounded the narrow strip of pavement at a fast jog. "You're going straight to the hospital to be checked over."

"You don't need to carry me. I'm fine." She gagged on a dry cough, gripping the edges of the slipping blanket. "Really."

"And stubborn."

"Not at all. I just hate for you to wear yourself out." Except after last night she knew just how much stamina his honed body possessed.

She grappled with the edges of the wet afghan, succeeding only in loosening the folds further and nearly flipping herself sideways off Matthew's shoulder.

"Quit wiggling, Ashley." He cupped her bottom.
Oh, my.

His touch tingled clear to the roots of her long red hair swishing as she hung upside down.

Two firefighters rounded the corner, dragging a hose as they sprinted past, reminding her of bigger concerns than the impact of Matthew's touch and her lack of clothing. Her restaurant was burning down, her business started with her two foster sisters in the only real home she'd ever known. The place had been willed to them by dear "Aunt" Libby who'd taken them in.

Tears clogged her nose until another coughing jag ripped through her. Matthew broke into a run. She gripped the hem of his jacket.

A second rig jerked to a halt in front. With unmistakable synergy, the additional firefighters shot into action. Oh God. What if the fire spread? A wasted minute could carry the blaze to the other historic, wooden structures lining the beachfront property. Her foster sister Starr even lived next door with her new husband.

The fire chief shouted clipped orders. A small crowd of neighbors swelled forward, backlit by the ocean sunrise.

"Ashley?"

She heard her name through the mishmash of noises. Turning her head, Ashley peeked through her curtain of hair to find her foster sister Starr pushing forward.

Ashley wanted to warn Starr to get back, but dizziness swirled. From hanging upside down, too much gasping, or too much Matthew, she couldn't tell. Lights from fire trucks and an EMS vehicle strobed over the crowd, making Ashley queasy. She needed to lie down.

She wanted out of Matthew's arms before their warmth destroyed more than any fire.

He halted by the gurney, cradling Ashley's head as he leaned forward. She should look away. And she would, soon. But right now with her head fuzzy from smoke inhalation, she couldn't help reliving the moment when he'd laid her on her bed. His deep emerald eyes had held her then as firmly as they did now. His lean face ended in a stubborn jaw almost too prominent, but saved from harshness by a dent dimpling the end.

In her world filled with things appealing to the eye, he still took the prize.

"Please, let me go," she whispered, her voice hoarse from hacking, smoke and emotion.

Matthew finished lowering her to the stretcher. "The EMS folks will take care of you now."

His hands slid from beneath her, a long, slow caress scorching her skin through the blanket. He stepped back, the vibrant June sunrise shimmering behind his shoulders.

Already edgy, she looked away, needing distance. Her burning business provided ample distraction. Smoke swelled through her shattered front window, belching clouds toward the shoreline. Soot tinged her wooden sign, staining the painstakingly stenciled *Beachcombers.*

What was left inside their beautiful home inherited from their foster mother? She and her two sisters had invested all their heart and funds to start Beachcombers. She raised herself on her elbows for a better view, sadness and loss weighting her already labored breathing.

"Ashley." Her sister—Starr—elbowed through to her side. She wrapped her in a hug, an awkward hug Ashley couldn't quite settle into and suddenly she realized why.

Starr was tugging the wet blanket back up. Damn. The satin nighty. Maybe no one else had seen.

Who was she kidding? She only hoped Matthew had been looking the other way.

Her eyes shot straight to him and... His hot gaze said it all. The jerk who'd walked out on her had suddenly experienced a change of heart because of her lingerie, not because of her.

Damn. She wanted her white cotton back.

Two

"Ashley?" Matthew blinked, half certain smoke inhalation must have messed with his head.

He blinked again to get a better view in the morning sun. Ashley was now covered back up in the blanket. Except one creamy shoulder peeked free with a pink satin strap that told him he'd seen exactly what he thought when the soggy covering slipped. Ashley Carson had a secret side.

Something he didn't want anyone else seeing. He angled his body between Ashley and the small gathering behind them.

A burly EMS worker waved him aside. "Back

up, please, Congressman. The technician over there will check on you while I see to this lady." The EMS worker secured an oxygen mask over Ashley's face, his beefy, scarred hands surprisingly gentle. "Breathe. That's right, ma'am. Again. Just relax."

Vaguely Matthew registered someone taking his vitals, hands cleaning his temple and applying a bandage. He willed his breathing to regulate, as if that could help Ashley. She needed to be in the hospital. He should be thinking of that, not last night.

A light touch on his sooty sleeve cut through his focus. Ashley's foster sister stood beside him— Starr Reis. He remembered her name from other political events hosted at Beachcombers. Long dark hair tumbled over her shoulders, her eyes crinkled with worry.

"Congressman? What happened in there?"

"I wish I knew." How had the place caught on fire so quickly? He hadn't been gone that long.

"If only I hadn't overslept this morning, maybe I would have heard the smoke alarm." Starr shifted from one bare foot to another, her paint-splattered shirt and baggy sleep pants all but swallowing the petite woman. "I just called David. He's on his way home from an assignment in Europe."

"I'm glad you could reach him." He recalled her Air Force husband worked assignments around the world. A photographic memory for faces and names came in handy on the campaign trail.

This had to be hell for the woman, seeing her sister in danger and watching her business burn. At least the flames hadn't spread next door to Starr's home.

"Thank you for going in there." Starr blinked back tears and shoved a hank of wild curls from her face. "We'll never be able to repay you."

Matthew tugged at his tie, too aware of Ashley a few inches away, close enough she could overhear. He doubted Starr would keep thanking him if she knew the full story about what had happened last night and how it had ended.

He settled for a neutral, "I'm just glad to have been in the right place at the right time."

"What amazing good luck you were around." Starr smoothed a hand over her sister's head. "Why were you here? Beachcombers doesn't open for another hour."

His eyes snapped to Ashley's. He didn't expect she would say anything here, now. But would she be sharing sister girl talk later? He sure as hell didn't intend to exchange locker-room confidences with anyone about this. Keeping his life private was tough enough with the press hounding him and everyone around him for a top-dollar tidbit of gossip.

Starr frowned. "Matthew?"

"I came by for—"

"He came to—" Ashley brushed aside Starr's hand and lifted the oxygen mask. "He needed to pick up contracts for the fund-raiser. Please, don't worry about me. What's going on with Beachcombers? Is that another police siren?"

She tugged the blanket tighter and tried to stand. No surprise. While he hadn't known Ashley for more than a few months, she clearly preferred people didn't make a fuss over her. A problem for her at this particular moment, because he wasn't budging until he heard the all-clear from her EMS tech.

Matthew turned to the burly guy who tucked a length of gauze back into a first-aid kit. "Shouldn't she be in a hospital?"

"Congressman Landis?" a voice called from behind him, drew closer, louder. "Just one statement for the record before you go."

Holy hell. He glanced over his shoulder and took in the well-dressed reporter holding a microphone, her cameraman scurrying behind her with a boom mike and video recorder. He recognized this woman as an up-and-coming scrapper of a journalist who was convinced he would be her ticket to a big story this election season.

How could he have forgotten to look out for the press, even here, at a restaurant buried in an exclusive stretch of beachside historic homes? He'd been a politician's son for most of his life. A South

Carolina congressman in his own right. Now a candidate for the U.S. Senate.

He might not always be able to keep his private life quiet, but he would make sure Ashley's stayed protected. He'd hurt her enough already.

Matthew pivoted and before he could finish saying, "No comment," he heard a camera click. So much for his resolve to close the book on his time with Ashley.

Showering in the hospital bathroom, Ashley finished lathering her soot-reeking hair and ducked her head under the spray. The *tap, tap, tap* of the water on green tile reminded her of the sound of cameras snapping photographs earlier. At least the EMS technicians had hustled her into the ambulance and slammed the doors before any members of the media could push past Matthew's barricading body.

Still, no matter how long she stood under the soothing spray, she couldn't wash away the frustration burning along her nerves. Matthew Landis had only blown through Charleston a few times and already he'd turned her life inside out, like a garment tugged off too quickly.

Had he really stared at her for a second too long when the blanket slipped? Part of her gloried in his wide-eyed expression, especially after his hasty retreat earlier that morning. Then tormenting images came to mind of him risking his life to save her when she'd been trapped in the powder room. Ashley grabbed the washcloth and scrubbed away the lingering sensation of smoke and Matthew's touch.

Once she'd dried off and wrapped her hair in a towel, she felt somewhat steadier. She slipped into the nightgown and robe her sister had brought by her hospital room, giving only a passing thought to the ruined pink peignoir. Yes, she was well on her way to putting the whole debacle behind her. She had more important things to concentrate on anyway—like the fiery mess. Ashley yanked open the bathroom door.

And stopped short.

Matthew Landis sat on the hospital room's one chair, stretching his legs in front of him. He wore a fresh gray suit with a silver tie tack that she could swear bore the South Carolina state tree—a palmetto. How he managed such relaxed composure—especially given today's circumstances—she would never know.

He appeared completely confident and unfazed by their near-death experience. The small square bandage on his temple offered the only sign he'd blasted into a burning building and saved her life.

Her throat closed up again as she thought of all that could have happened to him in that fire. She needed to establish distance from him. Fast.

He held a long-stemmed red rose in one hand. She refused to consider he'd brought it for her. He'd undoubtedly plucked it from one of the arrangements already filling the rolling tray and windowsill. He twirled the stem between his thumb and forefinger. Why had he stuck around Charleston rather than returning to his family's Hilton Head compound?

Ashley cinched the belt on her hospital robe tighter. Her other hand clutched the travel pack of shampoo, mouthwash and toothpaste. "I didn't, uh, expect...."

He didn't move other than a slow blink and two twirls of the flower. "I knocked."

She unwrapped the towel, her hair unfurling down her back. "Obviously I didn't hear you."

Silence mingled with the scent of all those floral arrangements. Matthew stood. Ashley backed up a step. She hooked the towel over the doorknob and looked everywhere but at his piercing green eyes that had so captivated constituents for years.

Everyone in this part of the country had watched the four strapping Landis brothers grow up in the news, first while their father occupied the senate. Then after their dad's tragic death, their mother had taken over his senatorial seat.

Matthew had followed in his family's footsteps by running for the U.S. House of Representatives after completing his MBA, and now that his mom was moving on to become the secretary of state, Matthew was campaigning for her vacated senate seat.

The name Landis equaled old money, privilege, power and all the confidence that came with the influential package. She wanted to resent him for being born into all of those things so far outside her reach. Except his family had always lived lives beyond reproach. They were known to be genuinely good people. Even their political adversaries had been hard-pressed to find a reason to criticize the Landises for much of anything other than their stubborn streak.

He cleared his throat. "Are you okay?"

She spun to face him. "I'm fine."

"Ashley." He shook his head.

"What?"

He stuffed his hands in his pockets. "I'm a politician. Word nuances don't escape me. 'Fine' means you're only telling me what I want to hear."

Why did he have to look so crisp and appealing while she felt disheveled and unsettled? The scene felt too parallel to the one they'd played out just this morning. "Well, I am fine all the same."

"It's good to hear that. What's the doctor's verdict?"

"Dr. Kwan says I can leave in the morning." She skirted around Matthew toward the bedside table to put away her toiletries. "He diagnosed a mild to moderate case of smoke inhalation. My throat's still a little raw but my lungs are fine. I have a lot to be grateful for."

"I'm glad you're going to be all right." Still he watched her with that steady gaze of his that read too much while revealing only what he chose.

"I've sucked down more cups of ice chips than I care to count. I'm lucky, though, and I know it. Thank you for risking your life to save me." She tightened the cap on her toothpaste, then rolled the end to inflate the thumbprint in the middle. The question she'd been aching to ask pushed up her throat just as surely as the toothpaste made its way toward the top of the tube. "Why did you come back this morning?"

"I forgot my briefcase." He set the flower aside on the rolling tray.

Her thumb pushed deeper into the tube of Crest. She looked down quickly so he wouldn't be able to catch her disappointment. "I hope you didn't have anything irreplaceable in there because I'm pretty sure that even if it didn't burn up, the papers are suffering from a serious case of waterlog."

She tried to laugh but it got stuck somewhere between her heart and her throat. For once, she was grateful for the cough that followed. Except she couldn't stop.

Matthew edged into sight, a cup of water in his hand. She took it from him, careful not to brush fingers, gripped the straw and gulped until her throat cleared.

Ashley sunk to the edge of the bed, gasping. "Thank you."

"I should have gotten you out faster." His brow furrowed, puckering the bandage.

"Don't be ridiculous. I'm alive because of you." Her bare feet swinging an inch from the floor, she crumpled the crisp sheets between her fingers to keep from checking the bandage on his temple. "Uh, how bad was the damage to Beachcombers? Starr gave me some information, but I'm afraid she might have soft-soaped things for fear of upsetting me."

He pulled the chair in front of her and sat. "The structure is intact, the fire damage appears contained to downstairs, but everything is going to be water-logged from the fire hoses. That's all I could tell from the outside."

"Inspectors will probably have more information for us soon."

"If they show any signs of giving you trouble, just let me know and I'll get the family lawyers on it right away."

"Starr said pretty much the same when she came by earlier. She just kept repeating how glad she is that I'm alive."

Their other foster sister, Claire, had echoed the sentiment when she'd called from her cruise with her husband and daughter. Insurance would take care of the cost. But Ashley still couldn't help feeling responsible. The fire had happened on her watch and she'd been so preoccupied with Matthew she may well have screwed up in some way. How could she help but blame herself?

Matthew shifted from the chair to sit beside her on the bed and pulled her close before she could think to protest. His fingers tunneling under her damp hair, he patted between her shoulder blades. Slowly, she relaxed against his chest, drawn by the now-familiar scent of his aftershave, the steady thud of his heart beneath his starched shirt. After a hellish day such as the one she'd been through, who could fault her for stealing a moment's comfort?

"It'll be okay," he chanted, his husky Southern drawl stroking her tattered nerves as surely as his hands skimmed over her back. "You've got plenty of people to help."

His jacket rasped against her cheek and she couldn't resist tracing the palmetto tree tie tack. Being in his arms felt every bit as wonderful as she remembered. And here they were again.

Could she have misread his early departure this morning? "Thank you for stopping by to check on me."

"Of course. And I was careful not to be seen."

Her heart stuttered and it had nothing to do with the whiff of his aftershave. "What?"

He smoothed her hair from her face, his strong

hands gentle along her cheeks. "I was able to dodge the media on my way inside the hospital."

She thought back to the barrage of questions shouted their way as she'd been loaded into the ambulance. Uneasily, she inched out of his arms. "I imagine there will be plenty of coverage of your heroic save."

Matthew scrubbed a hand along his jaw. "That's not exactly the angle the media's working."

Apprehension prickled along her spine nearly managing to nudge aside the awareness of his touch still humming through her veins. "Is there a problem?"

"Don't worry." His smile almost reassured her. Almost. "I'll take care of everything with the press and the photos that are popping up on the Internet. Once my campaign manager works his magic with a new spin, nobody will think for even a second that we're a couple."

Three

Not a couple? Wow, he sure could use some lessons on how to let a girl down easy.

Ashley shoved her palms against his chest. His big arrogant chest. So much for assuming he'd been attracted to her after all. It would be a cold day in hell before she fell into those mesmerizing eyes again. "Glad to hear you've got everything under control."

Matthew eased to his feet, confidence and that damned air of sincerity mucking up the air around him. "My campaign manager, Brent Davis, is top—"

Ashley raised a hand to stop him. "Great. I'm not surprised. You can handle anything."

He searched her with his gaze. "Is there something wrong? I thought you would be pleased to know about the damage control."

Damage control? Her experience with him fell under the header of freaking *damage* control? Her anger burned hotter than any fire.

But the last thing she needed was for him to get a perceptive peek into her emotions. She scrambled for a plausible excuse in case he picked up on her feelings. "I'm dreading going over to the store tomorrow, but at the same time can't wait to set things in order. It's a relief to know I don't have anything to worry about with the press." Damn it all, she was babbling now, but anything was better than an awkward silence during which she might do something rash—like punch him. "So that's that then."

He didn't leave, just stood, his brows knitting together. Her heart tapped an unsteady beat in spite of herself.

Okay, so he was *hot* and confident and sincere looking. And he didn't want her. She shouldn't be this pissed off. It was just an impulsive one-night stand. People did that sort of thing.

She just never had. But she wasn't totally inexperienced. Why then did a single lapse against his chest plummet her into a world of sensation that a bolt of silk couldn't hope to rival?

She wanted, needed, him gone now. "Thanks again for visiting, but I have to dry my hair."

Oh great. Really original brush-off line.

He massaged his temple beside the bandage. "Promise me you'll be careful. Don't rush into Beachcombers until you get official notice that it's safe."

"I pinky swear. Now you really can go." Why wouldn't he leave the hospital? Better yet, return to Hilton Head altogether.

"About this morning… Ah, hell." He stuffed his hands in his pockets. "You're still okay with everything. Right?"

Full-scale alert. The man was rolling out the pity party. How mortifying.

If he said anything more, she might well slug him after all, which would rumple his perfectly tailored suit and show far more than she wanted him to see concerning his effect over her. "I have bigger concerns in my life right now than thinking about bed partners."

"Fair enough."

"I have to deal with the shop, my sisters, insurance claims." She was a competent businesswoman and he should respect her for that. No pity.

"I've got it." He held up his hands, a one-sided smile crooking up. "You're ready for me to leave."

Sheesh. How had he managed to turn the tables so fast until she felt guilty? Blast his politician skills that made her feel suddenly witchy.

She softened her stance and allowed herself to smile benignly back. "Last night was…nice. But it's back to real life now."

He arched one aristocratic brow. "Nice? You think the time we spent naked together was *nice?*"

Uh-oh. She'd thrown down a proverbial gauntlet to a man who made a profession out of competition. A chill tightened her scalp.

She shuffled to the window, offering him her back until she could stare away the need to explore the heat in his eyes again. Her poise threatened to snap. Matthew's return had already left her raw, and today she had little control to spare.

"Matthew, I need for you to go *now.*" She toyed with the satin bow in a potted fern, the ribbon's texture reminding her of the gown she'd foolishly donned earlier.

"Of course." His voice rumbled, smoother than the ribbon in her hand or the fabric along her body.

Two echoing footsteps brought him closer. His breath heated through her hair. "I'm sorry about the media mess and for not keeping my distance when I should have. But there's not a chance in hell I would call last night something so bland as 'nice.'"

If he touched her again, she'd snap, or worse yet, kiss him.

Ashley spun to face him, the window ledge biting into her back. His gaze intense, glowing, he stared down at her. The bow crumbled in her clenched hand.

Forget courtesy. "My sister is on her way with a blow-dryer. She forgot to bring one when she brought by my other things."

He nodded simply. "Call me if you have any unexpected troubles with the press or the insurance company."

The door hissed closed behind him. Snatching up the rose he'd held, Ashley congratulated herself on not sprinting after him. Especially since her lips felt swollen and hungry. She'd always been attracted to him. What woman wouldn't be?

Her body wanted him. Her mind knew better— when she bothered to listen. She'd vowed she wouldn't be one of those females who lost twenty IQ points when a charming guy smiled.

She sketched the flower against her cheek, twirling the stem between two fingers. How would she manage to resist him now that she'd experienced just how amazing his touch felt on her naked skin?

Straightening her spine, she stabbed the long stemmed bud back into a vase. The same way she'd done everything else since her parents tossed her out before kindergarten.

With a steely backbone honed by years of restraint.

* * *

It took all his restraint not to blow a gasket when he saw the morning paper.

Matthew gripped the worst of the batch in his fist as he rode the service elevator up to Ashley's hospital room. He'd known the press would dig around. Hell, they had been doing so for most of his life. Overall, he took those times as opportunities to voice his opinions. Calmly and articulately.

Right now, he felt anything but calm.

He unrolled the tabloid rag and looked again at the damning photos splashed across the front page. Somehow, a reporter had managed to get shots of his night with Ashley. Intimate photos that left nothing to the imagination. The most benign of the batch? A picture of him with Ashley at her front door, when she'd been wearing her robe. When he'd leaned to kiss her goodbye.

The photographer had gerrymandered his way to just the right angle to make that peck on the cheek look like a serious liplock.

Then there was the worst of the crop. A telephoto-lens shot through one of the downstairs bay windows when he and Ashley had been in the hall, on their way to her room, ditching clothes faster than you could say "government cheese."

Had she seen or heard about the pictures yet? He would find out soon enough.

The elevator jolted to a stop. Door swished apart to reveal a nurse waiting for him with a speculative gleam in her matronly eyes. He managed not to wince and gestured for her to lead the way.

The nurse's shoes squeaked on the tile floors as he strode behind her, the sounds of televisions and a rattling food cart filling the silence as people stopped talking to stare when he walked past.

He understood well enough the ebb and flow of gossip in this business. For the most part, he could shrug it off. But he wasn't so sure someone as private and reserved as Ashley could do the same.

Matthew nodded his thanks to the nurse and knocked on Ashley's door. "It's me."

The already cracked open door swooshed wider. Ashley sat in the chair by the window, wearing jeans and two layered shirts, all of which cupped her curves the way his hands itched to do.

He shoved the door closed behind him.

Ashley nodded to the paper in his fist. "The political scoop of the year."

Well, that answered one question. She'd already seen the paper. Or watched TV. Or listened to the radio.

Hell. "I am so damn sorry."

"I assume your campaign manager hasn't rolled out of bed yet," she said quietly, as stiff as the industrial chair.

"He's been awake since the phone rang at 4:00 a.m. warning him this was coming."

"And you didn't think it would be prudent to give me a heads-up?" While her voice stayed controlled, her red hair—gathered in a long ponytail—all but crackled with pent-up energy as it swept over her shoulder, along her pink and green layered shirts.

"I would have called, but the hospital's switchboard is on overload."

She squeezed her eyes shut, a long sigh gusting past her lips. Finally, she unclenched her death grip on the chair's arms and looked at him again. "Why does the press care who you're sleeping with?"

She couldn't be that naive. He raised an eyebrow.

"Okay, okay." She shoved to her feet and started pacing restlessly around the small room. "Of course they care. They are interested in anything a politician does, especially a wealthy one. Still why should it matter in regards to the polls? You're young, unattached. I'm single and of legal age. We had sex. Big deal."

As she passed, a drying strand of hair fluttered, snagging on his cuff link and draping over his hand. Each movement of her head as she continued talking shifted the lock of hair without sliding it away.

Why couldn't he twitch the strand free? "You may or may not have read about how my last breakup ended badly. My ex-girlfriend didn't take it well when I ended things and she let that be known in the press. Of course the media never bothered to mention she was cheating while I was in D.C."

Her answer dimly registered in his mind as he stared while the overhead light played with the hints of gold twining through the red lock. He kept his arm motionless. The strand slashed across his hand the way her hair had played along his chest when she'd leaned over him, her beautiful body on display for him.

Naked.

He cleared his throat and his thoughts. He needed to prepare her for what she would face once she left this room. "The media are going to hound you for details. You can't comprehend how intense the scrutiny will be until you've lived with it. Do you have any idea how many reporters are out there waiting for a chance to talk to you right now?"

"When my sister gets here, we'll slip out the back entrance." She eyed the door with a grimace. "I'm sure the hospital staff will be happy to help."

He scratched behind his ear. "It's not that simple. And your sister's not coming."

She pointed to his hand. "Stop scratching."

What the hell? "Pardon?"

"Scratching. It's your poker tell. You only do that when you're trying to think of a way around a question. What are you hiding—" She paused, scowled. "Wait. You told my sister not to come, didn't you?"

Matthew dropped his arm to his side. Damn it, he'd never realized he had a "tell" sign. Why hadn't he or his campaign manager picked up on that before? At least Ashley had alerted him so he could make a conscious effort to avoid it in the future.

Meanwhile, he had to deal with a fired-up female. "Her husband and I thought it would be safer for her to stay out of the mob outside."

"You and David decided? You two have been as busy as your campaign manager." She scooped up her overnight tote bag. "I'll take a cab."

Matthew eased the canvas sack from her hand before she could hitch the thing over her shoulder. "Don't be ridiculous. My car is parked right by the back exit."

Her eyes battled with him for at least a three count before she finally sighed. "Fine. The sooner we go the sooner this will be past us."

A short ride down the elevator later, he opened the service entrance—and found four photographers poised and ready. He shielded Ashley as best he could and hustled her into his car. More pictures of the two of them wouldn't help matters, but better he be there to move this along than having her face them alone.

He plowed past a particularly snap-happy press

hound and slid into the driver's side of his Lexus, closing the door carefully, but firmly after him.

Ashley sagged in her seat. "God, you're right. I didn't realize it would be this bad."

"Bad?" He gunned the gas pedal. "I hate to tell you, but we got off easy, and they're not going to give up anytime soon. They will pry into every aspect of your private life."

Her face paled, but she sat up straighter. "I guess I'll just have to invest in some dark glasses and really cool hats."

He admired her spunk, even more so because he knew how much harder this was for her than it would be for others. "The press isn't going to leave you alone. They've been trying to marry me off for years."

"I'm tough," she said with only a small quiver in her voice. "I can wait it out."

Except she shouldn't have to. This was his fault and he should be the one bearing the fallout. Not her.

Then the answer came to him in a sweep of inspiration as smooth as the luxury car's glide along the four-lane road. Hadn't he already noted how much easier managing the media would be for her with him by her side? He knew the perfect way to keep her close *and* tamp down the negative gossip.

Decision made, he didn't question further, merely forged ahead. "There's a simpler way to make this die down faster."

"And that would be?" She swiped her palms over her jeans again and again, her frayed nerves all the more obvious with each passing palmetto and pine tree.

Stopping for a traffic light, he hitched his arm along the seat behind her head and pinned her with his most persuasive gaze. "We'll get engaged."

"Engaged?" Her eyes went wide and she jerked away from the brush of his arm as if scorched. "You've got to be kidding. Don't you think getting married to pacify the press is a little extreme?"

Marriage. The word stabbed through him like a well-sharpened blade. He absolutely agreed with her point about staying clear of the altar.

The light turned green and he welcomed the chance to shift his eyes back to the road. "It won't go that far. Once the buzz dies down and they focus on the issues again, you and I will quietly break up. We can simply turn the tables and state that the pressure from so much media attention put a strain on our relationship."

Yeah, the idea of lying chafed more than a little since he considered his ethics to be of the utmost importance. But right now, only one thing dominated his thoughts.

Keeping Ashley's reputation from suffering for his mistake.

He would have to live with the fallout from that,

not her. This was the best way to protect her. "We'll set up a press conference of our own to make the official announcement."

She crossed her arms over her chest, her brown eyes glinting nearly black with a determination that warned him he may have underestimated the strength of the woman beside him.

"Congressman Landis, you are absolutely out of your flipping mind. There's not a chance in hell you're putting an engagement ring on my finger."

Four

Uh-oh. She'd thrown down the proverbial gauntlet again.

Ashley gripped the sides of the butter-soft leather seat. She couldn't miss the competitive gleam in Matthew's eyes as he drove the luxurious sedan.

"Matthew," she rushed to backtrack. "I appreciate that you're concerned for my reputation, but one night of sex does not make me your responsibility. And it doesn't make *you* my responsibility, either."

He reached across to loosen her grip and link hands as they sped down the road. She looked away and tried to focus on the towering three-story homes, their deep porches sheltering rocking chairs and ferns. Anything to keep from registering how Matthew's thumb brushed back and forth across the sensitive inside of her wrist.

His callused thumb rasped against her tender skin, bringing to mind thoughts of all those photos of him in the paper featuring the numerous times he'd worked on Habitat homes. He came by the roughened skin and muscles the honest way. Her traitorous heart picked up pace from just his touch, a pulse he could no doubt feel.

Yep, there he went smiling again.

She snatched her hand away and tucked it under her leg. "Stop that. The last thing we need is to provide more photo ops for gossip fodder."

"Be my fiancée." He stated, rather than asking.

"No."

"I'll make it worth your while." He winked.

She covered her ears. "I am Ashley Carson and I do *not* approve this message."

Laughing, he gripped one of her wrists and lowered her arm. "Cute."

"And hopefully understood."

"Ashley, you're a practical woman, an accountant for God's sake. Surely you can see how this is the wisest course of action."

Practical? He wanted her for "practical" reasons? How romantic.

"Thanks, but I'll take my chances with the press." She tried to tug free her recaptured hand.

No such luck.

He held on and teased her with more of those understated but potent touches all the way to her sister's house—which just happened to have a red-and-blue Landis For Senate sign on the front lawn. Ashley shifted her attention to Beachcombers instead. And gasped from the shock and pain.

The sight in front of her doused passion and anger faster than if she'd jumped into the crashing surf in front of them. Beachcombers waited for her like a sad, bedraggled friend. Soot streaked the white clapboard beside broken windows, now boarded over. The grassy lawn was striped with huge muddy ruts from fire trucks and the deluge of water.

If she kept staring, she would cry. Yet, looking away felt like abandoning a loved one. She had bigger problems than her reputation—or some crazy mixed-up need to jump back into bed with a man certain to complicate her life.

She needed to regroup after the devastation, to meet with her sisters and revise her whole future. And no matter what plan they came up with, Matthew Landis would not be figuring into the strategy.

This time, when she pulled her hand back, she would make sure he understood that no meant no.

* * *

Waiting for Starr to come downstairs, Ashley peered through the living room window, watching as Matthew drove away.

A marriage proposal. Her first, and what a sham.

Now that she'd gotten over the shock of his *faux* fiancée proposition, she had to appreciate that he wanted to preserve her reputation. An old-fashioned notion, certainly, but then his monied family was known for their by-the-rules manners. How ironic that Starr belonged in this kind of world for real now that she'd married into an established Charleston family.

The Landis's Hilton Head compound might be more modern than this place—she'd pored over a photo spread in *Southern Living*—but his home proclaimed all the wealth and privilege of this Southern antebellum house that had been in Starr's husband's family for generations.

Her artsy sister had put her own eclectic stamp on the historic landmark, mixing dark wood antiques with fresh new and bright prints. All the dour drapes had been stripped away and replaced with pristine white shutters that let in light while still affording privacy when needed.

Like now.

Ashley wandered across the room past the Steinway grand piano to the music cabinet beside it. Photos in sterling-silver frames packed the top. One of Starr and David on their wedding day. Another of David's mother perched royally in a wingback chair holding her cat.

And yet another of Starr, Claire and Ashley standing in front of the Beachcombers sign when they'd officially opened the business three years ago. Most restaurants failed in the first year, but they had defied the odds despite having no restaurant experience. Their clientele swelled as Charleston's blue-blooded brought their well-attended bridal breakfasts and showers to Beachcombers, drawn by hosting their events in such a scenically placed historic home.

Once Starr lured them in with her decorative eye for creating the perfect ambiance, their sister Claire's catering skills sealed the deal and Ashley tallied the totals. Their foster mother may have used up her entire family fortune taking in children, but she'd left a lasting legacy of love.

Ashley cradled a picture of Aunt Libby.

Their foster mother had lost her fiancé in the Korean War and pledged never to marry another man. Instead, she'd stayed in her childhood house and used all her inheritance to bring in girls who needed a home. Many had come and gone, adopted or returned to their parents. Just Claire, Starr and Ashley had stayed.

God, how she missed Aunt Libby. She could sure

use some of her cut-to-the-chase wisdom right about now. Aunt Libby had never cared what other people thought about her, and heaven knew there had been some hateful things said when Libby brought some of her more troubled teens to this high-end neighborhood

The light tread of footsteps on the stairs pulled her from her thoughts. Ashley turned to find her fireball of a sister sprinting toward her.

"Welcome! I'm so sorry I wasn't here to greet you."

"Not a problem." Ashley stepped into the familiar hug. This woman was as dear to her as any biological sibling ever could be. "Your housekeeper said you've been battling the stomach flu. Are you okay?"

"Nothing to worry about. I'm fine." Starr stepped back and hooked an arm through Ashley's. "Let's go up to my room. I've been sorting through my clothes to find some you can borrow until you get your closet restocked. I'm shorter than you are, but there are a few things that should work."

Starr pulled her sister up the stairs and into her bedroom…and holy cow, she'd meant it when she said she went through all her clothes. The different piles barely left any room to walk, turning the space into a veritable floordrobe.

"Really, you're being too generous. I don't want to put you out."

Starr smiled and slid her hand over her stomach. "Don't worry. I won't be able to fit in my clothes soon anyway. I don't have the stomach flu."

The hint flowered in her mind, stirring happiness and, please forgive her, a little jealousy. "You're pregnant?"

Starr nodded. "Two-and-a-half months. David and I haven't told anyone yet. I would have said something sooner, but it was totally a shock. We weren't planning to start a family yet, but I'm so happy."

"Of course you are. Congratulations." Ashley folded her in a hug. "I'm thrilled for you."

And she was. Truly. Both of her sisters were moving on with their lives, building families. She just wanted the same for herself. Someday. With a man who wasn't proposing a "practical" engagement.

Her sister held tight for a second before pulling back. "Okay, so?"

"So what?"

Starr picked up a newspaper on her bed stand and flopped it open. "Holy crap, kiddo, I can hardly believe my eyes. *You* slept with Matthew Landis?"

"Thanks for the vote of confidence." She knew she wasn't Matthew's type, but it hurt hearing her sister's incredulity. For that matter, why in the world would Matthew think the press would even believe an engagement announcement?

"I'm simply surprised because it's so sudden. I didn't realize you two had known each other that long." She folded the paper to cover the incriminating pictures. "Although given these, I guess you've been keeping a lot from me lately. I can't believe you didn't say anything when I brought the clothes to the hospital." There was no missing the hurt in her tone.

"I'm sorry and you're right—about the not knowing each other part. You already heard or read most of what there is to tell. We've seen each other during the course of planning functions and smaller gatherings for his campaign. That night, was just… well…"

"Spontaneously human?"

"Neither one of us was doing much thinking."

"Well, I'm glad you're all right."

"But?"

"It's such a tight race." Her sister picked at a pile of sparkly painted T-shirts that looked designer made yet had been created by artsy Starr. "I'd hate for his opponent to get any kind of leg up at a time when even a few votes can make a difference. There are some important issues at stake—like Martin Stewart's history in the state legislature and how he has hacked away funds that feed into the foster-care system."

Certainly discussion of the race had been bandied about among Beachcombers clientele with everyone weighing in. Ashley and her sisters had gotten behind Matthew early on given their strong stance on foster care. "That issue hits close to home, no question. But I'm sure the voters will see Martin Stewart for the phony snake he is by the time the campaign runs its course. The guy does the Potomac Two-Step changing his stance on issues so often he's a prime candidate for *Dancing With the Stars.*"

Starr's packing slowed to a near halt. "I wish I could be so certain."

"I truly believe that. Remember when you worked after school in his office? It only took you a couple of months to quit that job. You said he was hell to work for. If you sensed that at seventeen surely older more mature voters will figure it out, too."

Starr resumed stacking piles in the box, quietly. Too quietly. Her sister never ran out of things to say.

Ashley tried to catch her sister's eye. "What's wrong?"

Starr pivoted on her heel, her eyes awash with pain—and anger. "I didn't quit that job. I was fired."

"Oh my God, why?"

"Because I wouldn't sleep with him."

Whoa. The impact of Starr's revelation set Ashley back a step. Then another until she sagged into a chair. "You were only seventeen. He must have been in his thirties then."

"Yeah, exactly." Starr stalked around the room,

dodging piles of clothes. "He fired me, and to top it off, just before that I had asked him to write a recommendation for me to get into that art school in Atlanta. Well, afterward, he made a call that ruined any chance I had at the scholarship."

"Starr, that's horrible." Ashley tried to hide her hurt that her sister hadn't shared something so life critical with her before now, but her firebrand of a sister seemed suddenly fragile. Plus she didn't want to upset a pregnant woman, so Ashley settled for, "I'm surprised Aunt Libby didn't string him up by his toenails."

She smoothed her hand along a bright red angora sweater with jet beads along the neckline, wondering how her vibrant sister had put up with that kind of treatment.

"I didn't tell her. I was embarrassed and—" Starr shrugged a shoulder "—afraid no one would believe me since my parents had been such scam artists. Then as time passed, it seemed best to just put it all behind me. I may seem more outgoing than you, but in those days it was mostly bravado."

Ashley hugged her again, holding on until her sister stopped shaking. "I'm so, so sorry you had to go through that."

Starr inched away and swiped her wrist across her eyes, bracelets jangling a discordant tune. "I could go to the press now, but since I'm your sister…"

"They would assume you're lying to help me out." Which would only make things worse.

"I'm afraid so. Maybe now you understand better why I've been so active in campaigning for Matthew Landis."

What a mess. If Matthew lost the election because of one night of consensual sex between two adults, that would be horribly unjust, but she knew well enough that life wasn't always fair. She had to do something to clean up the mess she'd made. She had to do something for Starr.

The obvious answer sat there in front of her in the way her sister had supported her and been the family she never had. She would do anything for the sisters who'd been so self-sufficient they didn't need much of anything from the youngest of their clan. "Don't worry about it. The press will have plenty to talk about before long."

"What do you mean?"

Ashley sucked in a bracing breath. "You aren't the only one with big news today. Matthew and I are engaged."

She would tell Matthew her decision to go forward with the engagement. Soon, since she'd called and asked him to stop by and pick her up for a late supper after she looked through the charred mess.

Her life would be changing at the speed of light

once she accepted his proposal. Even though she would be staying at Starr's during the Beachcomber renovations, Ashley knew the announcement would bring down a hailstorm of media attention. She only needed a few minutes alone inside her old world first—however wrecked it might be.

The air was heavy with humid dew. Ashley climbed the rear entrance steps toward the only real home she'd ever known while crickets chirped. At least the press couldn't get too close to her in the gated backyard. She panned her flashlight around the lawn and didn't see anyone lurking in the bushes.

Rubbing a hand over the creamy colored clapboard, she thought of the hours she'd spent developing the business with her sisters. A deep breath later, she pushed on the door. It stuck until an extra jolt of her shoulder nudged it loose.

The acrid pall nearly choked her. Who would have thought the smell could linger so long? Soot mingled in the air, hanging on the humidity like whispery spiderwebs.

No doubt, even walking through her shop would be messy, so Ashley tied her hair through itself into a loose slipknot. A quiver of dread fluttered to life. She squashed it before it could rob her of the drive she needed to face the damage.

A soaked rug squished beneath her shoes as she padded down the hallway. Pausing at her office, she tapped the door open, sighing to find all intact. A film of black residue smudged the surfaces of desks and shelves, but just as Matthew had promised, no fire damage.

She would come back to it later. First, she needed to confront the worst. Each step bubbled gray water from beneath her shoes, the squelching sound weakly echoing memories of Matthew's leather loafers pounding down the hall as he'd carried her.

Around the corner waited the main showroom. The horrid sense of helplessness returned, crawling between her shoulder blades like a persistent bug she couldn't swat away. Above all, Ashley hated feeling powerless.

She shook off the wasted emotion. Time to take control and face the nightmare so she could wake up and get her life back. Ashley plowed around the corner and into a broad male chest. She jumped back with a scream, slipping on the squishy rug.

But it wasn't the paparazzi.

Matthew filled the doorway. Apparently she would be talking to him sooner than she'd expected.

"Hold on a minute, darlin'." Matthew gripped her shoulders, his voice rumbling into the silence. "It's just me."

"Matthew, of course it's you." Shuddering with

relief, she instinctively sagged against him—then stiffened defensively.

He pulled her firmly against him anyway until she could only hear the steady thrum of his heart pulsing beneath her ear. His musky scent encircled her, insulating her from the fiery aftermath.

Her skin burned with a prickly sensation, almost painful. A rush of heat deep in the pit of her stomach made her long to melt against him, press her breasts to his chest until the ache subsided, or exploded into something magnificent.

Ashley flatted her palms on his chest and shoved. "You scared the hell out of me."

"Sorry." Matthew squished back a step, hands raised in surrender, his flashlight casting a dome of light. "I saw you crossing the yard and I came in through the front."

"It's okay. Now that I can breathe." It wasn't fair that she felt like death warmed over and he looked so damned good. Even in khakis and a polo shirt, he rippled with power.

Still, she felt tired and cranky, and his appeal left her edgy and vulnerable. She didn't like it—and she still had to tell him they were engaged after all. "What are you doing here so early?"

"You said you were coming to check out the damage." He absently scratched behind his ear, then stopped. "I thought you could use some help."

Miffed with herself for losing her temper, Ashley reined in her wayward emotions. She'd never used anger to get her way before. She couldn't see any reason to start now. Must be nerves from what she had to tell him.

She'd wanted a good night's sleep to brace herself, but so much for wishes. "I apologize and you're right, I did need to speak with you. We can talk while I do my walk-through of the place."

For the first time since she'd slammed into Matthew, his poster-boy-perfect mask slid. Concern wrinkled his brow. "Are you sure you're ready for this? Hire a clean-up crew and spare yourself some heartache."

"I'm not going to clean the place yet. Actually, I can't until the insurance company completes its assessment. I just wanted to look. It shouldn't take long."

He stepped aside. She gasped.

The whole room loomed like a black hole, void of color. Boards over the window even kept out much of the streetlights from lending any relief to the drab grays. Maybe she should have waited until morning after all and seen the place in the light of day. Surely the dark made everything seem worse than it was.

But probably not.

She'd hosted so many beautiful pre-wedding events here in the past, imagining celebrating her own engagement someday. What a crummy, crummy way to get her wish.

Matthew wondered how Ashley could stand so stoically still in the face of such a damn mess.

The second she'd told him she planned to come here, he'd known he would have to be there with her. For safety's sake and for support.

Her chin quivered. Totally understandable. He'd expected just such a reaction. He hadn't anticipated how her sadness would sucker punch him.

Matthew crossed his arms, trapping his hands so he wouldn't reach for her. She eased past him, the sweep of her peasant top brushing against his arm. What did she have on underneath? His throbbing body begged him to discover the answer.

Odd how he'd never considered that practical Ashley might wear her merchandise. Her merchandise. How could he have been so focused on thoughts of getting Ashley naked that he momentarily forgot about the mess around them?

Clothing racks lay on their sides, having been tipped by the force of spraying water. Curled wisps of melted fabrics stuck to the floor and hangers. That same material could have melted to her skin.

Matthew heard a bell chime behind him, followed by Ashley's chuckle. Her laugh rippled over his taut nerves, just as enticing as any slip. Damn. He was in trouble. "What did you find?"

Ashley reached inside the antique gilded cash register and pulled out a soggy stack of bills. "A few blasts with the blow-dryer and I'll be solvent."

Only Ashley could stand in the middle of a charred-out room, holding what probably amounted to a couple of hundred bucks and still manage a laugh.

He stepped deeper into the room. "So supper's on you tonight."

"Sure. I could probably afford to spring for burgers, if you don't mind splitting the Coke?"

"How about I give you some money, just to tide you over?"

Her pride blazed brighter than their two flashlights combined. "I'll be fine once the insurance check arrives. I don't mind working off my deductible with sweat equity."

"It's a standing offer."

"Thanks, but no."

Matthew bit short a rebuttal. He could see she wouldn't be budged. He would just find other ways around her counterproductive need for independence. "All right then."

He followed her back down the hall, her gathered long hair swaying with each step baring a patch of her neck, and just that fast he started forgetting about the charred mess around them.

Until they reached her open bedroom door.

What if she'd been asleep in her bed when the fire started and he hadn't returned? Being inside the dressing room could very well have saved her life.

His chest tightened, his breathing ragged. He braced a forearm against the fire-split molding. His arms trembled with the tension of bunched muscles as he fought the image of Ashley dead.

She made a slow spin around to face him again. "Well, you were right, Matthew. There's not much I can do here for now. I feel better, though. Knowing the worst somehow makes it easier to go forward."

"Right." He only half registered her words, still caught in the hellish scenario of her stuck in this place while it burned. Thank God she wasn't his fiancée, someone like Dana who could wreck his world in a stopped heartbeat.

"I accept."

Ashley's words snapped him back to the present.

"Accept the money?" He was surprised, but damn glad. "Of course. How much do you need?" His eyes swept over her, unable to read her body language but sensing the tension coiling through her.

"Not that. I accept your, uh—" she chewed her lip "—your proposal. If you still think it will help your campaign, I'll be your fiancée."

Five

He was engaged. Hell.

Matthew creaked back in the chair at his bustling campaign headquarters in Hilton Head. Even four hours after Ashley's official acceptance, he still couldn't believe she had actually agreed. He'd gotten his way, but still the whole notion had him itching with the same sensation that had urged him to get out of her place as quickly as he could after their night together.

He stared at the computer screen full of briefing notes in front of him, but it registered as vaguely as the ringing of telephones and hum of the copy machine outside his office.

Thumbing the edge of a shiny red and blue stack of "Landis for Senate" bumper stickers, Matthew wondered why the thought of even a fake engagement floored him so much. After all, he'd gotten exactly what he wanted from her. It wasn't real like with Dana.

He just hadn't expected Ashley to be so damn reluctant in her agreement. Okay, so yeah maybe his ego smarted a little. *He* was the one who wanted to keep his bachelor life.

Wouldn't his brothers enjoy yucking it up over this mess?

A light tap sounded on his open door. He glanced up to find his campaign manager—Brent Davis—filling the opening. "Are you getting enough sleep?"

"You're kidding, right?" Matthew waved Brent to take the chair in front of the mahogany desk.

Older than Matthew by twenty years, the wiry manager had been an energetic force behind Matthew's mother's campaign and had acted as a consultant when Matthew ran for the House of Representatives. Brent had been the natural choice to head the campaign when Matthew made his decision to seek his mother's vacated senatorial seat.

For the first time, Matthew wondered if he'd decided to push too hard, too fast, politically. He could have hung out in the House for another ten years or so and still been on track to run for the senate by the time he was forty. But he'd been so hell-bent on not letting go of the seat that started with his father before shifting to his mom. He'd worried that someone else might get a lock on the spot that couldn't be broken.

Had his ambition pushed him to sacrifice anything—including an innocent person like Ashley?

Damn it all, he was doing this to help preserve her reputation. He'd made his decision and he wouldn't hurt her worse by changing his mind and offering her a trip to the Bahamas to hide out until the frenzy died out. While yes, he could have handled the scandal, it would have been a hell of a lot more taxing on everyone in his campaign who had worked so hard to get him here.

Time to step up to the plate and be a man. He leaned forward on his arms, shirtsleeves rolled up, and looked Brent Davis square in the eye. "Ashley Carson and I are engaged."

His campaign manager froze—no expression, no movement, not so much as a blink to betray his thoughts. Matthew knew from experience the guy only did that when he'd been tossed a curve ball that whacked him upside the skull. The last time Matthew had seen that look on Brent's face, he'd gotten the news flash that Ginger Landis had decided to elope with her longtime friend General Hank Renshaw during a goodwill tour across Europe.

Finally, Brent templed his pointer fingers and tapped them against his nose. "You're joking."

"I'm serious." Matthew straightened, unflinching.

One blink from Brent. Just one, but a fast flick of irritation. "You're engaged to the mouse of a girl in the compromising photos."

Anger blazed hot and fast. "Watch how you talk about Ashley."

Brent's eyes went wide. "Whoa, okay, take it down a notch there, big fella. I hear you loud and clear. You're totally in lust with this female."

"Davis…" Matthew growled his final warning.

Besides, the last thing he needed right now was to dwell on that night with Ashley, a train of thoughts guaranteed to steal what cool he had left at the moment. "She's my fiancée, my choice, deal with it. That's your job."

"Why didn't you tell me you were dating her when those damning photos hit the news?" Brent flattened his palms on the desk. "You left me to spin one helluva nightmare with incomplete informati— Wait." He leaned back with narrowed laser eyes. "This is one of those fake deals, isn't it? The two of you are making this up to get the heat off."

"I never said that," he hedged, unwilling to expose Ashley to any more embarrassment.

"You need to be honest with me if I'm going to help you make it through the November elections on top." Brent tapped the stack of bumper stickers with his pointer finger repeatedly for emphasis. "In fact, you should have told me before you proposed to her in the first place."

On the one hand, Matthew could see his point. On the other, it seemed damned ridiculous—not to mention unromantic—to clear his bridal choice with his campaign manager first.

If he were really getting married. Which he wasn't. But that was beside the point.

He wouldn't sacrifice Ashley to the media hyenas just to win an election. In spite of all his competitive urges that totally agreed with Brent, Matthew couldn't bring himself to say anything that might bring Ashley further embarrassment.

Something deep inside him insisted if he was the kind of man to abandon her, then he didn't deserve to win. "Ashley and I were work acquaintances who were surprised to find there was something more. Call it a whirlwind romance in your press release."

Brent nodded his head slowly, a smile spreading across his angular face for the first time since he'd entered the office. "If we put that out there to the media, then everyone will understand when the two of you decide to break off the impetuous engagement."

"I never said that, either."

"Damn it, Matthew—" his smile went wry "—I

taught you how to use those avoidant answer techniques with the press back when your mother was running for office. Don't think you can get away with using those same techniques on me."

Why couldn't he bring himself to close the office door and tell Brent the truth? It all came back to protecting Ashley, her reputation and her pride as best he could until he set things right again in her life.

Matthew angled forward with a long creak of the wheels on the antique leather chair he'd inherited from his father. "I said Ashley and I are engaged and that's exactly what I mean. We're going to pick out a ring tomorrow."

A ring?

Hell yeah.

Of course they would need a ring. If Ashley balked, he would suggest they could sell it afterward and donate the proceeds to her favorite charity. Ashley with all her generous ways would get into a notion like that. He wasn't actually purchasing any token of commitment, rather protecting Ashley while contributing to a worthy cause.

Brent eyed him narrowly. "Why not give this Ashley Carson woman your mother's ring from her marriage to your father?"

Good question.

"Ashley wants her own," he neatly dodged. "As a foster child, she lived her life receiving hand-medowns from others, rarely getting the chance to choose what suited *her* best. She deserves to have a ring of her choice and start traditions of her own."

Yeah, that sounded plausible enough, especially given he'd only had half a second to come up with an answer. As a matter of fact, it actually resonated as true inside him, the decision he would reach if he and Ashley were doing this couple thing for real.

Matthew aligned the stack of bumper stickers. "I imagine the news will leak from someone in the jewelry store, but we'll still want to make our own official announcement. When do you think is best to call a press conference? Tomorrow night or the next morning?"

"You actually love this woman?" His manager didn't even bother hiding the jaded tone in his voice.

Love? The word brought to mind the endless times he'd heard his mother crying on the other side of the door after Benjamin Landis's death. Ginger had been damn near incapacitated. If it hadn't been for her kids and the surprise offer to take over her husband's senate seat, Matthew still wasn't sure how long it would have taken his mother to enter the world of the living again.

He would have chalked it up to emotions growing over a long-term relationship, but he'd felt much the same crippling pain when his fiancée died in college. No way was he going back for round two of that pathway to hell. The possibility of letting anyone have that kind of control over him again scared the crap out of him.

He'd been right to try and end things after their accidental night together. Circumstances, however, had forced them to bide their time before going their separate and diverse ways.

He thought about Ashley, and yeah, she stirred a protectiveness inside him along with that hefty dose of arousal. Just thinking about her naked body tangled in the sheets with her auburn hair splayed over the pillow…

Damn. He wouldn't be standing up from behind the protective cover of his mahogany desk anytime soon. "I am captivated by her."

Brent stared him down and Matthew held his gaze without wavering. Finally, his old family friend nodded. "Either you're a brilliant liar or in more trouble than you realize, my friend."

The camera flash blinded her.

Ashley blinked to clear the sparks of light as the intense reflection bounced off the marquise-cut diamond on her finger as she stood in front of the podium outside Matthew's campaign headquarters in Hilton Head.

She hadn't wanted him to spend so much on the ring, but he'd swayed her by telling her the proceeds from hocking the rock afterward would go to the charity of her choice. That he knew her and her wishes so well after such a short time swayed her more than anything.

His campaign manager, Mr. Davis, stepped between them and the microphone. "Thank you, ladies and gentlemen of the press. That officially concludes our conference for this afternoon."

Ashley forced a smile on her face as cameras continued to click while Matthew escorted her toward a chauffeur-driven Suburban. The weight of the stone on her hand provided a constant reminder that while she might not be committed to this man, she was committed to her decision to help him with his campaign to beat his scumbag opponent.

She extended her fingers and stared at the brilliant diamond in the shiny gold setting, thought of their night together, followed by his cageyness the next morning.

She feared she'd made a mistake.

Not in deciding on the engagement. She still believed in making sure that rat bastard running against him didn't get to exploit anyone else.

But this ring? She turned her hand to catch fragments of sunlight in the facets of the stone. The ring was perfect, exactly what she would want in a real engagement and now she could never have it because the marquise cut would always remind her of Matthew Landis and the way he'd hurt her.

She couldn't help but think of how he'd hotfooted toward her door. When this relationship didn't benefit him anymore, he would likely hotfoot his way out of her life just that fast. She didn't want to view him in such an unfavorable light, but what else could she think? That's what he'd shown her, and he *was* a politician, after all.

Although she'd seen signs he wasn't the typical politician, she reminded herself he was used to spinning things to his own advantage. She needed to remember that in order to survive this debacle.

Ashley slid into the backseat of the Suburban, the driver closing the door after her while she settled into the decadently soft leather. A built-in television played a twenty-four hour news channel.

Matthew tossed his briefcase to the floor before buckling his seat belt. "Thank God, that's past. We should have some time to talk before we reach my place."

Her ears perked up and she lost focus on the ring. "Your place?"

"Yes, you should familiarize yourself with the property." He angled to face her, his knee brushing against hers and stirring more than nerves in her stomach. "It would seem strange if you're unfamiliar with where I live."

"Of course. That makes sense." She forced her face to stay blasé even though inside she couldn't ignore the frustrated twinge that his reasons for taking her home were merely practical. "Why didn't your campaign manager come along then? Where is he now?"

"Don't know." Matthew shrugged as a golf course with a lush lawn and palm trees whizzed past.

"I thought he wanted to tell me more about the upcoming agenda." She tugged her lightweight sweater closed over her floral sundress she'd borrowed from Starr. The outfit was pretty, but Starr wasn't as busty so the darn thing didn't fit quite right and the press of Matthew's knee against hers was starting to make the dress even more uncomfortably tight as her breasts ached for his touch.

She should have been shopping for clothes rather than a ring in order to pull off this charade.

"Brent and I decided I could give you the information just as easily. He has enough to keep him busy." Matthew clicked open his briefcase and pulled out a printed agenda roster. "I'm slated to speak at a Rotary breakfast in the morning and a stump gathering in the afternoon. On Saturday evening, there's a harbor cruise fund-raising dinner."

He paused reading to glance over at her, seemingly unaware of the havoc he wreaked on her senses with just the touch of his kneecap, for Pete's sake. If only the photographers hadn't caught those compromising photos, she could have gone on with her life, pissed off at him, certainly, but free of this painful attraction.

"Ashley?" He ducked his head into her line of sight. "Are you with me? Do you have a problem with any of this? You don't have to attend everything. It's not like you're a politician's wife."

"Of course I want to come. It's fascinating to hear all of the political ins and outs up close. And it's not as if I have a job at the moment. Everything's at a standstill with Beachcombers until the insurance company finishes its report and cuts us a check."

She forced her eyes to stay dry when more than anything she wanted to shout her frustration over her out-of-control life. She liked simple and uncomplicated.

Matthew Landis was anything and everything except simple and uncomplicated.

His handsome face went somber with concern. "I could always float you a loan—"

"Shut up about the money already." God, he really didn't have a clue about her values and pride in spite of the ring. Still, she eased her words with a smile even as constant reminders of his affluent world whipped by outside in the shape of waterside mansions and high-end cars. "But thank you for the offer. It's very generous of you."

"Don't overrate me. The amount you need wouldn't even put a dent in my portfolio."

She wrinkled her nose and planted her legs firmly on her side of the car—away from his. The leather seats teased at the back of her calves with a reminder of lush accessories she could never afford. "Why did you have to take such a nice offer and downplay it that way?"

"I'm not bragging, only speaking the truth."

That might be so, but it still didn't mean she planned to let him open his wallet to her. Taking money from a man she was sleeping with seemed…icky.

She'd already come too close to crossing a moral conscience line with this fake engagement. She couldn't take one step further. "I see plenty of wealthy people traipsing through Beachcombers who will stiff the waitress on a tip without thinking twice. I know affluence and generosity do not always go hand in hand."

"Since I already have enough debates on my schedule, I won't bother disputing your kind assessment of my character."

She chewed her lip to keep from arguing further and simply listened to the roar and honks of street traffic. The last thing she wanted was to wax on about the wonderful attributes of Matthew Landis. That would do little to bolster her self-control.

He tapped her brow with a warm callused finger. "Penny for them."

She forced a lighthearted smile on her face.

"Come on, surely with your portfolio you can do better than that."

"Touché." He chuckled low, the rumble of his laugh sliding as smoothly over her senses as his arm along the back of the seat to cup her shoulders.

His touch burned along her already heightened nerves, tightening an unwelcome need deep in her belly. She'd always been attracted to him, but the sensual draw was so much more intense now that she knew exactly how high he could nudge her pleasure with even one stroke of his body inside hers.

She inched forward on the seat, her light linen sundress suddenly itchy against her knees. "You don't need to keep up the shows of affection. No one is around to snap a promo shot."

Slowly, torturously so, he slid his arm away, his green eyes glinting with a hint of bad-boy charm that showed he knew exactly how much his touch affected her. "I didn't mean to overstep."

"Apology accepted."

Sheesh, she hated sounding so uptight, but she could barely hold her own with this guy when he *wasn't* touching her. She'd enjoyed having his hands all over her, but she'd hated the way he made her feel the next morning.

"So, what's the going rate for your thoughts?"

"Actually, they're free at the moment." She struggled for some new direction to take their discussion that had nothing to do with touching, needing, wanting. "I'm just not sure if my question is polite."

"I've developed a thick skin over the years."

She wished she could say the same. "All right, then." She tipped her face confidently—and so the vents could shoosh some cooling air against her warming skin. "I can't hush up the accountant in me that's wondering how your family accumulated such a hefty portfolio."

"Dumb luck, as a matter of fact." He scratched his hand along his jaw, which just happened to draw his pointer finger over his top lip in a temptingly seductive manner. "My great-grandfather bought into a big local land deal that paid off well when it just as easily could have tanked."

She remembered clearly how that mouth of his felt exploring every inch of her body, lingering once he discovered a particularly sensitive region. She cleared her throat if not her passion-fogged thoughts. Too easily she could be lured under his sensual spell again and she needed to hold strong. "Uh, where were these land plots?"

"Myrtle Beach." He dropped his hand back to his knee, giving her overloaded senses a momentary reprieve.

"Ah, that explains a lot." Interesting how he downplayed his family's fortune. Wealth that large didn't accumulate on its own or grow by taking care of itself.

"But it doesn't explain everything. Plenty of people blow a fortune before it ever reaches their kids."

"We've invested wisely over the years," he conceded, fingering his cuff links, an antique-looking set that she suspected must have family sentimentality. As she looked closer, she recognized his father's initials. "We've lived well, without question, but always kept an eye on growing the principal."

"Very smart move." Her accounting brain envisioned numerous creative ways to diversify a large holding. Some lucky number cruncher must be having a field day playing with all that capital. "Families expand, so if you don't increase the size of the pie, the pieces will get smaller with each generation."

"Exactly." His thumb polished a rounded cuff link. "We're lucky that we've been able to pursue whatever career dream we wanted without worrying about putting a roof over our heads."

His grass-roots practicality touched her as firmly and stirringly as those callused fingers ever had and that scared her. This man could hurt her, badly, if she wasn't careful.

"It's admirable that you all think that way rather than simply living a life of leisure." The Suburban slowed to a crawl behind cars backed up from a wreck ahead. She forced her drying-up mouth to keep the conversation flowing. "You could simply see the world or something, and nobody would think less of you."

"I could go stark raving nuts, you mean. I like playing golf as much as the next guy—" he gestured at the rolling course packed with players "—but I'm not good enough to make a living at it, therefore it can't be my life's pursuit. For me, politics keeps me in touch with the rest of the world and how they're living. That's a real grounding kind of thing. My brother Kyle says the same about serving in the Air Force."

So this conversation thing wasn't working out as well as she'd expected since he actually got nicer with each sentence. If the traffic jam didn't clear soon she would be in serious trouble. "What about your other brother Sebastian?"

"He's the business lawyer who keeps us all bankrolled for the next generation."

"And Jonah?"

His smile tightened. "The jury's still out on him."

"He's the youngest, right?" She seemed to recall from the publicity photos of Ginger Landis Renshaw with her boys. "I seem to remember reading he only just graduated from college."

"So did you, but you're not jaunting around the world." He thumbed the crease between his eyebrows. "I'm just not sure how my parents brought up a playboy son."

She followed his words and the mounting proof that there might be something more to him than a fat wallet, a handsome face and slick politician's persona. Definitely dangerous with a warm magnetism that radiated from him and reached to her even when they didn't touch.

"You're a good listener, Ashley."

"You're an interesting speaker." And that was the truth, damn it. Why couldn't he have been a pedantic slug? "I look forward to hearing what you have to say at all those functions. I honestly believe you're the better man for this job and I want to do whatever I can to help make that happen."

"Thank you. You sound like you actually mean that."

She shared a quiet smile with him, unable to miss the enclosed intimacy of just the two of them in the back of the Suburban with a privacy window closed. She started to sway toward him, then jerked her body rigid.

"What's the matter then?" He smoothed a finger along her furrowed forehead much the way he'd smoothed the crease between his own eyebrows.

"I don't have a problem with attending the events with you." She forced her best prim tone in place to put things back on a more practical keel. "My concern is actually more logistical. I don't know how I'm going to get to Charleston and back in time to make everything."

"Who says you have to go back and forth to Charleston?"

Her jaw dropped as her pulse skyrocketed. A fake engagement was one thing. But moving in together? Matthew must have been dipping into the vehicle's liquor cabinet.

Six

Ashley considered availing herself of the Suburban's drink selection after all, time of the afternoon be damned. She could be stuck in here with Matthew for hours if the cops didn't clear the wreck soon.

She tugged at the hem of her dress, because yes, she'd felt his heated gaze stray to her calves more than once during the ride to his house. "You can't be suggesting I should move in with you. The press will chew us up."

"We're engaged." He cupped her elbow.

She shrugged her arm free. She'd been lured by

his sexual draw once before and look where that had landed her? Half dressed on the front page of countless newspapers. "Don't be obtuse and stop touching me."

His eyes narrowed and Ashley mentally kicked herself. Another gauntlet moment.

He slowly removed his hand. "So you're still every bit as attracted to me as I am to you."

Ouch. He played tough.

Well, she would have to meet the challenge. "That line of discussion will not go far in persuading me to stay with you."

One side of his mouth kicked up in a smile. "Point well made." He stretched his arm along the back of the seat, this time without so much as brushing any part of her. "I live in a family compound as do two of my brothers. We all have our own quarters. Mom and the general live in both D.C. and South Carolina. The general's at the Pentagon right now, but Mom's around, so you even have a chaperone."

"By living quarters, what do you mean?" She eyed him warily. He'd made it clear he was still attracted to her and that it wasn't an act. Yet having an affair, with a ring on her finger and the intent to break things off felt wrong. How ironic that she'd been willing to consider sleeping with him when there'd been no jewelry or fake commitments involved. "Is everybody in the same house with a suite, but all still bump into each other walking around in the hall?"

"I thought you objected to me not being around in the morning."

She narrowed her gaze and considered elbowing him in the kidney but that would show he had too much sway over her emotions. "Old issue. No longer relevant."

"Fair enough. Jonah and Sebastian both have suites of rooms in the main house since Jonah graduated and Sebastian's separated from his wife. Kyle has a condo near the Air Force Base in Charleston. And I live in the renovated groundskeeper's carriage house behind the main place. Does that work for you?"

His plan sounded solid and her sister's husband had just arrived home from assignment. While Starr and David would say they didn't mind having her around and they had plenty of space, she had to imagine they would want some privacy. They hadn't been married long and they had the pregnancy news to celebrate. She would be most decidedly a third wheel and it was downright silly to drive back and forth from Charleston to Hilton Head multiple times a day.

Matthew's idea was sensible and bottom line, she was painfully practical.

"Okay and thank you. As long as your brothers

don't run around in their boxer shorts, I guess this should work out all right."

"No worries." Matthew's grin stretched from appealing to downright wicked, sending a shiver of premonition up her spine as the Suburban finally jolted forward. "If I find any of them wearing nothing but their skivvies around you, I'll kick their asses."

Wow, Matthew sure new how to deliver a zinger line to close up shop on conversation. His silence left her with nothing to do but stare out the window.

She'd grown up in Charleston, but this exclusive area of coastal beauty had been meticulously manicured in a way that seemed to preserve yet tame the natural magnificence.

Of course, given the size of the mansions and golf courses they'd passed, the people who lived here could obviously afford to sculpt this place into anything they wished.

The driver steered the SUV along a winding paved drive through palm trees and sea grass until the view parted to reveal a sprawling white three-story house with Victorian peaks overlooking the ocean. A lengthy set of stairs stretched upward to the second story wraparound porch that housed the main entrance. Latticework shielded most of the first floor, which appeared to be a large entertainment area.

Just as in Charleston, many homes so close to the water were built up as a safeguard against tidal floods from hurricanes.

The attached garage had so many doors she stopped counting. His SUV rolled to a stop beside the house, providing a view of the brilliant azaleas behind them and the ocean in front of them. An organic-shaped pool was situated between the house and shore, the waters of the hot tub at the base churning a glistening swirl in the afternoon sun.

"My place is over there." He pointed to the cluster of live oaks and palmettos, a two-story carriage house just visible through the branches.

White with slate-blue shutters, this carriage house was larger than most family homes. She understood he came from money. She had even grown up among wealthy types in Aunt Libby's old Charleston neighborhood. But seeing Matthew's lifestyle laid out so grandly only emphasized their different roots.

She walked up the lengthy stretch of white steps toward the large double doors on the second floor. She gripped the railing and looked out over the water view. "This view. It totally rocks."

He slid an arm around her again. This time she couldn't bring herself to pull away and ruin the moment. She let herself believe she leaned into his embrace simply because they might be seen by someone, the staff, his family.

Had he even told his family the truth? She assumed so but hadn't thought to ask. It was one thing to keep his silence with his campaign manager because as much as you thought you could trust someone, she'd learned it never hurt to be extra careful.

The sound of an opening door plucked her from her reverie. She jerked in Matthew's spicy-scented embrace and turned to find an older woman coming through the main entrance. Even if she hadn't recognized the senator from her press coverage, Ashley would have figured out her identity all the same. Her deep green eyes declared her to be Matthew's mother, even if her fair head contrasted with his dark brown hair.

Ginger Landis Renshaw strode toward them, her shoulder length gray-blond hair perfectly styled. Ashley recalled from news reports the woman was around fifty, but she carried the years well. Wearing a pale pink lightweight sweater set with pearls—and blue jeans—Ginger Landis wasn't at all what Ashley had expected. Thank goodness, because the woman in front of her appeared a little less intimidating.

She had seen the woman often enough on the news—always poised and intelligent, sometimes steely, determined. Today, a softer side showed as she looked at her son then over to Ashley.

"Mother, this is Ashley. Ashley, my mother."

Ginger extended her hands and clasped Ashley's. "Welcome to our home. I'm sorry to hear about what happened to your business, but I'm so glad you're all right and that Matthew brought you here to stay with us."

"Thank you for having me on such short notice, Senator."

"Ginger, please, do call me Ginger."

"Of course," she replied, not yet able to envision herself using the first name of this woman who dined with heads of state.

Matthew's mother studied her, inventory-style, and suddenly Ashley realized the reason for the woman's presence here instead of in D.C. with her husband. Matthew's mother must have been called to give her a Cinderella makeover.

Ashley released Ginger's clasp and crossed her arms over her ill-fitting dress. "It's a pleasure and honor to meet you."

Ginger tipped her head to the side. "Is something wrong, dear?"

Visions blossomed to mind of being stuffed into some stiff sequined gown with her hair plastered in an overdone crafted creation that would make her head ache. She might even be able to pull the look off without appearing to be a joke. She might even look presentable enough to turn a head or two.

But she would feel wretchedly fake and uncomfortable the whole time. "No, of course not. I'm grateful for your generosity in letting me stay here."

"But…?" Ginger prodded.

Ashley let the words tumble free before she could restrain them and end up stuffed in a fashion runway mess. "I just can't help but wonder if Matthew's campaign manager expects you to give me some kind of makeover."

"Why would I want to change you? My son obviously finds you perfect as you are."

"That's very kind of you to say. Thank you." Ashley expected relief only to find something different altogether. She resented the twinge of disappointment sticking inside her chest like an annoying thorn. She truly didn't want some fake redo. She liked herself just fine, but still…

Then another implication of his mother's words soaked in. She didn't appear to know the engagement was fake. That Matthew would keep himself so closed off from even his family gave her pause. Except wasn't she doing the same with her own sisters?

Matthew kissed his mother's cheek. "Always the diplomat." He backed a step. "I'll just go help the driver with our luggage."

Ashley couldn't miss how it didn't seem to dawn on him to allow the chauffeur to haul their suitcases by himself. Yet another touch that made Matthew all the more appealing.

Forcing herself to stop watching him lope down the steps with a muscled grace, she turned her attention to following Ginger back into the house. No mere magazine layout could have done the place justice.

A wall of windows let sunshine stream through and bathe the room in light all the way up to the cathedral ceilings. Hardwood floors were scattered with light Persian rugs around two Queen Anne sofas upholstered in a pale blue fabric with white piping. Wingback chairs in a creamy yellow angled off the side. The whole décor was undoubtedly formal, but in an airy comfortable way.

Ginger spun on her low heel. "I'll show you to your room shortly. The view of the ocean is breathtaking."

Having grown up at Aunt Libby's on the water, she appreciated the sense of home she would get from the sound of the waves lulling her to sleep. Come to think of it, this woman had an Aunt-Libby-like air of kindness to her.

"Your home is gorgeous." Ashley turned to the picturesque windows overlooking the pool and ocean. "Thank you again for letting me stay. I can't wait to unpack my suitcase."

"Oh, my dear, don't worry about doing that. You won't need to use your sister's clothes."

Ashley pivoted away from the windows to the

room filled with the beauty and scent of fresh-cut flowers in crystal vases. "Excuse me, but I thought you said we weren't going to do the makeover deal."

"I never said we weren't going shopping."

"You didn't?" This woman was as good at word-plays and nuances as Matthew. Ashley would have to watch her step around both of them. "What do you mean then?"

"Your entire wardrobe was ruined. It's obvious you need new clothes, even more so because of the predicament with my son and all the appearances you'll need to make together."

"I can't let him pay for my clothes."

Matthew's mother planted her fists on her hips in a stance that brooked no argument. "Since he's the reason you have to attend the functions, it's only fair he pay."

Ashley stayed silent because she knew she wouldn't win a war of words with this master stateswoman.

Ginger smiled. "Prideful. I like you more and more by the minute." She waved a manicured hand. "I wasn't born into all of this. I didn't even know about it when I met my first husband, an Air Force jet-jock who swept me off my feet so much we eloped in two weeks."

A sweet-sad smile flickered across her face as the

soft sounds of someone turning on a vacuum in the next room filled the silence.

Ashley touched her arm. "How long has he been gone?"

"Nearly eleven years. I never thought I would fall in love that way again. And in a sense, I was right. Love built slower for me the second time around, but no less strong."

Ginger's eyes took on a faraway look and Ashley realized the woman was staring at an old family photo across the room for at least half a minute before she returned her attention back to the present. "So, Ashley, about the shopping spree. I adore the general and my boys, but there are times I need a girls' day out."

Wow, this lady had a way of working a person around to her side of the argument. "How about this? He can pay for the clothes I use at official functions, but I pay for anything else I wear."

"That sounds entirely fair and wonderfully honorable."

"Matthew's campaign manager says the media will eat me alive."

Ginger cupped her cheek, her charm bracelet jingling. "No one expects you to change who you are. We're only here to help you be comfortable as *yourself*. We'll be doing that with new clothes of your choosing and some helpful tips for dealing with the press."

Ah man, she really didn't want to like this woman so much. Forming any kind of bond with Matthew's family would only make things all the tougher when she walked away.

At least she could take some comfort in the sincerity lacing Ginger's words. Matthew's mother would help her choose appropriate clothes that stayed true to her own tastes.

There wouldn't be a Cinderella makeover after all. Which was a relief. Except that as much as she knew she and Matthew weren't right for each other long-term, a part of her wouldn't have minded knocking him flat on his awesome butt.

He was only just finishing up his first speech of the day and already he was sweating—big-time.

Except he couldn't blame the crowd or the press or even the cranking summer heat. His pumping blood pressure had more to do with the demure woman sitting serenely to his right in his peripheral vision, her attention unwaveringly focused on him.

The way Ashley's sheathe dress kept hitching up over her knees was about to send him into cardiac arrest at thirty years old. His mother had absconded with Ashley yesterday afternoon, not returning until well after supper. Call him crazy, but he'd been expecting pastel suits and pearls like his mother wore.

Instead, his mother had picked an emerald-green form-fitting dress with a scooped neck and a pendant that drew his gaze south. A daring choice given all he'd heard about everyone appearing subdued during a campaign. Yet Ashley, with her long auburn hair pulled back with a simple gold clasp, looked classically elegant. The no-heel strappy sandals accented with gold stones matching the necklace flashed a tribute to her glowing youthfulness. She would easily appeal to a cross section of voters.

She easily appealed to *him* at a time when he'd sworn he would keep his distance.

He resisted the urge to swipe his wrist over his brow, a dead giveaway to anyone with a camera that he was rattled. He glanced quickly at his notes to scoop up his ender. Thank God he must have said something coherent because everyone clapped and smiled.

The Rotary president stepped up to the microphone to invite questions from the media.

An older woman stood, her press pass around her neck tangled in the buttons of her tan sweater. "Miss Carson, tell us how Congressman Landis proposed? Was it before or after the revealing photos of the two of you hit the papers?"

Yeah, that had lots to do with the issues.

His campaign manager on his left shot to his feet. "Come on, Mary." Brent smiled at the seasoned reporter. "You know Ashley's still new to all of this. How about you don't put the screws to her just yet?"

Ashley placed a soft hand on Matthew's arm, gently nudging him from the podium. "It's all right. I would like to answer."

Matthew heard his campaign manager suck in air faster than a dehydrated person gulped down water. Matthew worried more than a little himself, but he wouldn't embarrass Ashley by silencing her. He would simply stand by in case she threw him a panicked "save me" look.

"As you can tell, Matthew has concerns for me and the stresses of campaign scrutiny. That's why he tried to keep me out of the limelight. So I solved the problem by proposing to him."

Chuckles rumbled through the crowd while reporters went wild taking notes. He had to admit, she'd handled the question well while sticking to the truth.

She cast a shy glance through her eyelashes. "You'll have to pardon me if I insist the rest of the details are *very* personal and private." The laughter swelled again. Ashley waited patiently for the hubbub to subside. "And I know when to end on a positive note. Thank you for having us here today."

Matthew palmed the small of her back and ushered her toward the exit behind the podium. The door swooshed behind them, muffling clicking cameras. He leaned and captured her lips with his—hey, wait, where had that idea come from?—but too late, he'd already done it. He was totally entranced with the way she'd glowed behind that podium. So much so, all his good intentions for protecting her with distance had flown right the hell out the window.

Now that he had her against him again, the taste of her fresh on his tongue, he had to savor the moment for an extra stroke longer before easing the kiss to an end. He settled her against his chest instead while he regained control.

"You did a fantastic job handling that reporter, Ashley."

"I answered truthfully." Her fingers gripped his lapels, her words breathy in the narrow corridor leading to a brightly lit Exit sign out of the small community college auditorium.

"You answered artfully." He forced himself to step back, but couldn't bring himself to release her arms, convenient since she still held his jacket. "There's a skill to that."

"It was worth it to hear your campaign manager go on life support."

"I was hoping you wouldn't notice."

"He has no reason to trust me. I don't have a track record." Her eyebrows pinched together. "Matthew, I've been waiting for the right time to ask you something, but there are always people around, so I may as well spill it now. Why haven't you told your family the truth?"

"Why haven't you?"

"Answering a question with a question isn't going to work this time."

He gave her the truth as best he understood it. "So much of my life is an open book. I prefer to keep things private when I can." As he'd done about his relationship with Dana. Ashley had a way of pushing his buttons and making him open up before he realized it, a decidedly uncomfortable feeling. "Besides, my family would only worry if they knew, which I suspect is the same reason you haven't told your sisters."

"You're very perceptive." She relaxed against his chest, soft, sweet smelling and too sexy given the way she'd been turning him inside out all morning long.

"I'm sorry you're in this position at all." And damn but he knew to be more careful in his word choices. Now the word positions had him thinking of all the different ways he would like to have Ashley under him, over him, around him. "If I could go back and do things differently, I—"

He stopped. He couldn't complete the sentence because he realized without question that he wouldn't give up that night with Ashley, even realizing how things would turn out. God, but that made him a selfish bastard.

Her eyes locked with his, her lips parting slightly. She arched up on her toes just as he felt his head magnetically drawn back down toward her. His mouth grazed hers, once, twice, only long enough for a gentle nip that sent his insides aching for more. What harm could there be in exploring the sexual side of things? A brief affair… More of the taste of Ashley…

The door swung open, cutting short the moment if not his desire. His campaign manager barged toward them, not bothering to slam the door, damn him, undoubtedly more than happy for the reporters to snap a shot now.

Brent clapped his hands together. "Okay, love-birds, time to get this show on the road."

Matthew watched Ashley as she followed Brent out the door. He didn't want a committed relationship and he most definitely was not giving his heart away again. However, something told him as he watched Ashley, new confidence swinging in her step, he might not be able to walk away as easily as he'd imagined.

Seven

Enjoying the play of moonlight across the ocean, Ashley gripped the railing of the harbor cruise paddle boat as it docked and thought of the thousand questions she'd answered since yesterday morning. Hands she'd shaken. Babies she'd cradled.

The last part had been the easiest because those little constituents didn't vote. She hadn't realized until the morning paper that she'd been lured into the most cliché campaign moment possible. Thinking about her every move and word was downright exhausting, especially when she and Matthew actually knew so little about each other. She really should make out a questionnaire asking about funky facts from his past.

Tonight had been pleasant with the romantic setting and fairly tasty meal—Beachcombers could have provided better, of course—but the evening had been nice. Except for the fact she'd barely seen Matthew. She rubbed her arms, trying to will away the irritation she had no right to experience. She focused instead on the beauty around her.

Lights were strung along the paddle boat cruiser. Dinner tables were littered along one deck. The upper deck rang with swing-band dance music. A waiter strolled by with a silver platter resting on one palm, perfectly balancing the tray of champagne flutes.

Matthew stepped from the shadows, sipping his seltzer water. His eyes scanned down with obvious approval glinting and she winged a prayer of thanks to Ginger Landis Renshaw, her fairy godmother who'd been wise enough not to try to transform her into Cinderella. Instead, she'd simply helped Ashley fine tune her own tastes in ways she never could have envisioned on her own.

She certainly wouldn't have thought to select a dress that left her shoulders bare. She'd always tried to cover the uneven tilt with layers—the more the better. But then Ginger had pulled out the simple cream dress stitched in gold with a plunging V-neck in the front and back. She'd dreamed of this sort of satiny fabric sliding over her skin. Ginger had added a lightweight, gold shawl.

Matthew tipped back his water glass and drained the whole thing as if his throat were parched.

Ashley savored the moment and searched for small talk to keep him standing with her. "You're not drinking any of that top-notch champagne?"

"Seems like a recipe for disaster, mixing alcohol and reporters." He glanced at Ashley's drink.

She rattled her ice, saddened again that they knew so little about each other. "Seltzer water for me, too, but with a lime."

"My apologies for jumping to conclusions. Let me get you a refill to make up for ignoring you all evening."

"Thank you." Most of all for noticing that she'd been left to her own devices. That eased the sting.

She leaned back against the rail, studying the couples dancing up on the deck. The ocean wind carried snippets of conversations her way from partiers as well as people milling about and disembarking down the gangplank. She paid little attention until her ear snagged on a familiar voice, the campaign manager's brisk baritone.

"She did better than I expected."

"That's not saying much," another man responded, a voice she vaguely recognized from a telephone briefing she'd received earlier. "Your expectations weren't very high."

"Well, what can I say?" Brent answered. "She wasn't what I would have chosen for him on the campaign trail or as a senator's wife. She brings nothing to the table politically except that shy little smile. However, what's done is done. He will have to make the best of things. At least she won't outshine him."

Ouch. That one hurt more than a little. But then eavesdroppers rarely heard good about themselves.

"I thought Ginger did a decent job with the makeover," the other man continued, "not too flashy, not too schoolmarmish. The outfit is classy but Ashley doesn't look like someone playing dress-up with her mother's clothes."

"Yeah, about that age thing. What the hell was Matthew thinking? She's only what, twenty-four? The pressure is going to demolish her."

Ashley had heard enough. She refused to stand around like an insecure wimp, regardless of how much their words hurt, reminding her yet again how she was the wrong kind of woman for Matthew. At least she could make sure they never knew how deeply the barbs dug.

She stepped out of the shadows. "Twenty-*three,* thank you very much. I am twenty-three. You of all people should have your facts in order better than that. But thanks for the extra year of maturity vote of confidence to go along with my honors diploma in accounting from the College of Charleston."

"Ah hell." Brent had the good grace to wince while music echoed on the sea breeze. "We didn't see you there. I'm sorry for speaking out of turn in a public setting."

"Apology accepted." There was no use in making an enemy of the man. She just didn't want his pity because it played on her already pervasive sense that she couldn't be the kind of woman Matthew needed. "Although I would warn you of a very good piece of advice I received at a briefing recently. Never, *never* speak a sound bite you wouldn't want repeated."

"Point well taken," the campaign manager agreed, hesitating only long enough to check for privacy. "But hear me on this. I've been around this business a long time and you're not cut out for this. Most importantly, Martin Stewart is a wily opponent not to be taken lightly and you're not helping Matthew."

Before Ashley could answer, Matthew rounded the corner with her drink in hand. "Here you are, Ashley. I thought I'd lost you to another reporter." He passed the glass to her. "Your sparkling water, complete with a twist of lime."

"Thank you." The tart taste fit right in with her souring mood.

Matthew's eyes narrowed. "Is everything all right here?"

Ashley stirred her drink with the thin straw, unwilling to risk causing any scene or rift between Matthew and his campaign manager.

She stabbed her straw through the ice. "Everything's fine. Why shouldn't it be? Your manager is just discussing ways I can be more helpful on the campaign trail."

Matthew slid an arm around her waist. "She doesn't have to do anything other than be herself."

Ashley appreciated him saying that, but she knew full well she hadn't offered anything substantive to his campaign beyond stopping rumors he was indiscriminately sleeping around.

Brent leaned back on the rail on both elbows. "I worry about the two of you."

"Just do your job." Matthew's voice took on that renowned Landis icy tone. "If you have anything more to say on this subject, we can take it up at headquarters later."

"You're the boss." Brent shoved away from the rail and walked away with his companion.

Matthew narrowed his eyes at the retreating man, then turned back to Ashley. "Did he say something to upset you?"

"Nothing. Really. Everything's fine."

Matthew brushed a thumb over her cheekbone,

glancing around much like Brent when he'd checked to be sure no one could overhear. "You look tired. You've got dark circles under your eyes."

His words, too close to Brent's concerns, pissed her off when her emotions were already raw. She wasn't a weakling, damn it. "What a smooth talker you are."

"Beautiful—but tired. I realize campaigning can be a grind." He stepped away, taking her drink from her and placing it on a deck table alongside his. "We're leaving now."

"You can't go." She looked around at the people still dancing on the upper deck. "This is your party."

"I most certainly can punch out whenever I want. We've docked. Others are disembarking. I learned a while back if I stay 'til lights out at every function I'm on hand when the party turns wild and that never goes well for a politician come picture time."

When he put it that way…. She tucked her hand in the crook of his elbow. "Well, by all means then, let's blow this pop stand before Mrs. Hamilton-Reis hangs her bra in place of the flag."

Chuckling, he shuddered. "Thanks for placing that image in my mind."

"Always happy to please."

His eyes narrowed. "You do please me, you know. Very much, Ashley Carson." He dipped his head and brushed his mouth along her ear. "I'm so very sorry

I messed things up for the chance to please *you* again."

His words sent a thrill of excitement and power up her spine. Sure, Brent Davis's years of political wisdom attested to reasons she wasn't the wisest choice to stand by Matthew's side, at least for tonight, she could have one more memory to tuck away.

And she intended to make the most of it.

Strolling along the private shoreline outside his home with Ashley, Matthew wondered if he'd pushed too hard too fast by saying something suggestive to Ashley on the boat. He wanted an affair with her, but he already sensed they wouldn't have much time. She would cut and run from his lifestyle soon enough, without a doubt.

But all the touching and kissing for the camera was playing hell with his libido. He'd suggested this barefoot walk alone along the shore to cool them both down before they turned in for the night. A long night. Likely alone, because as much as he wanted her, she would have to set the pace this time.

Ashley kicked her way through the rolling surf, her gold shawl billowing behind her in the breeze. Creamy white fabric with its tantalizing glimmers of gold stitching molded to her chest the way he wanted to fit his palms against her curves.

Gathering the hem of her gown up to her knees, she shot ahead a couple of paces before spinning on her bare feet to face him, her loose hair streaking around her face. "What did you dress up as for Halloween as a kid?"

Her question blindsided him more than anything he'd heard from the most seasoned reporter. Of course that could also have something to do with his lust-fogged brain at the moment. "Excuse me? I'm accustomed to obscure questions from the press, but that one came way out of left field."

"Then I guess it's an excellent question." Her gentle laugh carried on the salty breeze as light as any meringue, simple, but damn fine. "It just struck me over the past couple of days that we really don't know that much about each other. Those holes in our knowledge could be a real pitfall in an interview. So? What about your childhood holidays?"

He thought back to all those pictures in his mother's countless family photo albums. "A cop. I trick-or-treated as a cop."

"And?"

Matthew shook his head, his shoes dangling from his fingers. Water slapped at the dock where the family speedboat bucked with each wave. "Always a policeman for Halloween. Drove my mom nuts. She really got into making us new costumes each year and I kept asking for the same one, just in a bigger size."

"If you wanted to be a police officer, what made you want to go into politics?"

"Who said I wanted to be a cop as an adult? Just because I dressed up like one as a kid doesn't mean…" He scratched his head. "Okay, never mind. Fair question. Politics is the family business. It's only natural I would follow this path."

"Your father was in the Air Force before becoming a senator." She scraped her hair back from her face. "And your brothers chose different paths."

"That they did." He thought back to their childhood years, putting on costumes in preparation for the day they would be able to play out their dreams for real. "We're looking for ways to serve our country."

"You could have done that on the police force."

"My father died."

She slowed to fall in pace alongside him. Not touching, just there. More present in the moment than most people who got right up in somebody's face. "That must have been an awful time for you."

"He didn't get to complete his term." There was something so damn sad about unfinished business—his father's term, his old fiancée's diploma never picked up.

An engagement never fulfilled with vows.

"Your mother served out his term, and very well I might add. Life has a way of working things out, even the bad things, given time."

"You're right." He needed to remember that more often and concentrate on his own reasons for taking on this office rather than doing it for anyone else. Interesting how Ashley focused him with a few words.

And hell, what was he doing selfishly spilling his guts when he was standing under the stars with a beautiful woman? She turned attention to others so artfully he wondered how many missed the chance to uncover fascinating things about her.

He tipped her chin. "What about you?"

"What about me what?"

"Your Halloween costumes." He walked alongside her, smiling down and trying to envision her as a kid, probably skinny with hair that weighed more than she did. And a heart bigger than all of that combined. "What did you pick, and I want a list."

"A pirate, a zebra, a hobo, a ninja, Cleopatra—the fake snake was tons of fun." She clicked off the years on her fingers. "A doctor, oh, and once I was a pack of French fries. Starr was a hot dog and Claire insisted she was a gourmet quiche, but we all knew it was a pecan pie with fake bacon bits sewn on."

"Wow, your foster mom organized that for all her kids?" Did Ashley realize she was walking closer to him?

Her arm skimmed his.

Her leg brushed his with every step.

Was she trying to seduce him, for God's sake?

"Aunt Libby had this huge box full of old costumes and clothes. She was constantly adding items to it throughout the year—picking up additions on clearance or from yard sales." She looked up at him, her brown eyes the perfect backdrop to reflect the stars overhead. "Actually, we didn't only use it for Halloween. We played dress-up year round."

"I'd enjoy seeing pictures of that."

Her smile faded. "If they survived the fire."

He slid an arm around her shoulders and tucked her to his side, holding her closer when she didn't object. "Tell me more about the dress-up games."

"We made quite a theatrical troop with our play acting. We could be anything, say anything and leave the world behind once those costumes were in place. Looking back, I can see how she must have been using some play therapy for a group of wounded girls."

"She sounds like an amazing lady."

"She was. I miss her a lot." Ashley stared up at him with far-too-insightful starlit eyes. "The way you must miss your father."

He tried to clear his throat but the lump swelled to fist-size and wouldn't dislodge.

Ashley slipped her arm under his jacket and around his waist. "That's why you're in politics then, to feel closer to him?"

Her touch seemed to deflate the lump and he found himself able to push words free again. "That's why I started, yes, and then I found out along the way why it was so important to him. It's not about power. And sure the chance to make a difference at a grass-roots level is…mind-blowing. But there's more to it."

"And that would be?"

"Honestly, this has gotten to be such a dirty business no sane person would even want to enter a race. Between the sound-bite hungry press and cut-throat opponents, no one can possibly lead a life clean or perfect enough to undergo that level of scrutiny. There will be blood in the water at some point and sharks will circle."

"Okay, you're really depressing me here, so how about getting to the point soon."

He chuckled low, the crash of waves stealing the sand from under his feet. "Right. Gotta work on paring down my stump-speech skills. My point? I can't let fear keep me out of the race."

"Good people have to step up to the plate, too."

"Thanks." He gave her a one-armed hug.

"For what?"

"For calling me 'good people.'" And damned if that simple hug hadn't pressed her breast against his side, which had him thinking decidedly un-good-guy thoughts about seducing her right here. Right now. Behind the nearest sand dune.

She stopped, dropping her shoes onto the sand,

then taking his and tossing them aside, as well. She clasped both of his hands in hers. "You've been worried about our engagement fib."

He stayed silent for three swooshes of the waves.

She squeezed his fingers. "Doing the wrong thing for all the right reasons is tough to reconcile. I know. I've been wrestling with the same issue."

"What conclusion did you arrive at?"

"Good people are also fallible humans. Sometimes we deserve a break, even if it's only a temporary reprieve."

He skimmed his knuckles over the ivory clear and soft skin of her face, over her chin, down her neck. She gazed up at him, her eyes so deep and darkening as her pupils expanded.

If he let himself, he could fall…right…in.

He kissed her. He had to. The past couple of days they'd been dancing around this moment and he knew the solid reasons why he should wait to pursue the attraction, give her time, romance her more. But here, tonight, under the stars, he wanted her and he could feel that she wanted him, too, from the way she wriggled to get closer. He couldn't sense even the least bit of hesitation in her response.

Her breathy sigh into his mouth reminded him of other times she'd gasped out her pleasure. This usually shy woman certainly tossed away her inhibitions when it came to the sensual.

She gripped his lapels, her fists tugging tighter, pulling him closer as she pressed herself to him. Her lips parted, her tongue meeting his every bit as aggressively as he sought hers. She tasted of citrus from her lime water earlier, more potent than any alcohol. Her soft breasts molded temptingly against his chest and his hands itched to stroke her without the barrier of clothes or possible interruption.

As much as he ached to have her here, out in the open with the sky and waves all around them, he knew that wasn't practical. "We should take this inside before we lose control."

"And before someone with a telephoto lens gets an up-close and personal of the total you."

"Not an image I want recorded for posterity."

Laughing, she clasped his hand and dashed toward his white clapboard carriage house. She kept the hem of her dress hitched in one fist, a mesmerizing dichotomy in her formal gown and bare feet.

Matthew tugged at her hand. "Our shoes."

She smiled back at him, her eyes full of total desire. "To hell with our shoes."

Staring back at her, he knew he wouldn't say no to Ashley in full tilt temptress mode. He just wished he could be sure his conscience would fare better against the harsh morning light than their shoes would against the elements.

Eight

Ashley gripped Matthew's hand as he led her past sprawling oak trees to his two-story carriage house. The quaint white home with gray-blue shutters gleamed like a beacon with the security lights strategically placed. Sand clung to her skin, rasping along her hyper-revved nerves as she raced by fragrant azaleas up the stone steps after him.

He swung the gray door wide and hauled her into the pitch dark hallway. Before she could blink, he'd slammed the door closed and pressed her against the wood panel for a kiss that sent her blood crashing through her veins like out-of-control waves during a hurricane. His hands were planted on either side of her head as he seduced her with nothing more than his mouth on hers. The taste of lingering ocean spray mingled with the lemon from his water earlier. Her shawl shimmered down her arms to pool around her feet.

Her foot stroked along the back of his calf, her sandy feet rasping against the fine fabric of his trousers. She grasped at his back, stroking and gripping and stroking more, lower, urging him closer until his body sealed flush against hers. And oh yes, she could feel how much he wanted her, too. She rocked against the hard length of him, searching, aching for release.

Matthew tore his mouth from hers and nipped along her jaw until he reached her ear where he buried his face in her hair, his five-o'clock shadow gently abrading her skin. Her eyes adjusting to the dark, she could see the straining tendons in his neck. His breath flamed over her in hot bursts.

"Ashley, we need to slow this down a notch if I'm going to make it to the bedroom, or at least to the sofa."

She didn't want to stop, even for the short stretch of hardwood it would take to reach the leather couch a few feet away in the moonlit living room. "Why move then? As long as you've got protection in your pocket, I'm more than happy with right here, right now."

His low growl of approval sent a shiver of excitement up her spine.

He tugged his wallet free. "I've been carrying protection since that first night with you. I knew full well the chemistry between us could combust again without warning."

Matthew plucked out a condom and pitched his wallet over his shoulder. The thud of leather against wood snapped what little restraint she had left.

In a flurry of motion she barely registered since he'd started kissing her again, she grappled with his belt while he bunched the hem of her clingy cream dress in his fists, higher, higher still until he reached her waist. With one impatient hand he gripped the thin scrap of her satin panties—and how she delighted in the fact that when she'd shopped for underwear, she hadn't selected so much as a single piece of practical cotton.

She managed to open his fly and encircle him with a languorous glide of her fingers along his hot hard arousal. His jaw flexed. His grip twisted on her panties until they…snapped.

Cool air swooshed along her overheated flesh in an excruciating contrast. "Now," she gasped against his mouth. "To hell with foreplay."

"If you insist," he groaned between gritted teeth.

She couldn't resist watching every intimate detail as he rolled the sheathe into place. Matthew hitched an arm under her bottom and lifted her against the door until the heat of him nudged perfectly between her legs. Inch by delicious inch, he lowered her as he filled her. She hooked her legs around his waist and pressed him the rest of the way home.

Tremors began quaking through her before he even moved and she realized their every touch in the days prior had been foreplay leading to this. He eased away. Then thrust into her with a thick abandon that sent her over the edge without warning.

Her head flung back against the door as she cried out with each wave cresting through her. Her heels dug deeper into his buttocks. Matthew moved faster, taking the waves higher. His shout of completion spurred a final wash of pleasure, and her body went limp.

They stood locked together silently for…well, she wasn't sure how long. Then he released her and her feet slid to the floor. She started to sag, her muscles too weak with satisfaction to hold her, and he scooped her into his arms.

"I've got you, Ashley. Just relax."

She hummed her approval against his chest. She would figure out how to talk again later.

On his way through the small foyer, he paused for her to flick one of the light switches, bathing the room in a low glow. As he strode into the living room, she lounged sated against his chest and took a moment to learn more about Matthew from his surroundings. Deep burgundy leather chairs and a sofa filled the airy room, angled for a perfect view of both the ocean and the wide-screened television. Striped wool hooked rugs scattered along tile into an open-area dining room and high-tech kitchen.

And dead center across the room—a narrow hallway that undoubtedly led to the bedrooms.

He stopped beside the sofa. "Do you want to stay here or head back there?"

"There, please." She wanted to learn more about him beyond his political standings, affinity for leather furniture and childhood love of cop costumes.

"Lucky for me, that's exactly where I want to be, too. Actually, anywhere you are without your clothes sounds perfect to me."

Even as she told herself to savor the sensations of the here and now, she couldn't help fearing the out-of-control waves of emotion Matthew stirred could drown her in the end. If so, tonight would be all she could afford to risk.

This could all be simpler than he'd predicted.

Matthew carried Ashley back toward his bed-room, wondering if he'd overthought this whole situation. They got along well and the chemistry hadn't been a one-time fluke. Why not ride the wave? Friendship with rocking hot sex could be an awesome, uncomplicated alternative to spending the rest of their lives alone or locked in some relationship where emotions ruled their lives to the exclusion of all else.

He grazed a quick kiss along her passion-swollen lips before easing her onto his bed. Yeah, he liked the look of her there. And he would enjoy it even more once he peeled her clothes from her sweet body.

Apparently Ashley had the same idea, because she arched up from the bed to kiss him with an ardent intent that made it clear she was ready for round two. He draped his jacket over the chair without ever breaking contact with her mouth. She tugged his tie with frantic fingers, loosening until finally the length slid free from his collar. She flicked the silk over her shoulder and set to work on the buttons down the front of his shirt until she glided her cool finger inside along his bare skin.

Matthew kissed aside one shoulder strap of her dress. With the dress's built in bra and her panties out on the foyer floor, she was perilously close to total exposure.

He smiled in anticipation against her flowery scented skin. "At least we're going to make it to a bed this time."

She shoved his pants down and away. He kicked them to the side. "I liked the hall."

"Me, too." He liked *her* anywhere. "But this time we're going to take it slower."

Matthew brushed away and down both straps of her gown, guiding it over her breasts, teasing along her hips until it slithered to her feet. He couldn't resist stilling for a moment to take her in. It seemed like longer than a handful of days since he'd had the pleasure of seeing her naked.

He remembered her being hot. He dreamed of her sexiness. But he'd forgotten or hadn't taken the time to notice some of the more intimate details of her body—such as the enticing mole on her hip that he now traced with his thumb to better imprint it in his memory. Countless other nuances of Ashley burned themselves into his brain.

Then she flattened her hand to his chest and brought a close to his ability to think. Time to feel. To touch. He traced her collarbone with his tongue, working kisses and nips lower to her tempting curves until his mouth closed over the peak of one breast, drawing it tighter, then shifting his attention to the other equally sweet swell, in need of more, more of her, sooner than he'd expected after their mind-blowing encounter in the hall. She arched against him and then they were both tumbling onto the bed.

She slid her hands down his back and cupped his taut buttocks, digging in her fingers, urging him closer. "Now, Matthew."

He clasped her wrists and gently eased them to the side. "Slower this time, remember?"

"Forget about slower. We have all flipping night for slower." She wriggled temptingly under him.

He trailed kisses between her breasts, shifting his hold on her wrists to link fingers with her. He nipped along her rib cage, working his way south.

He blew air against her stomach, lower, lower still until she gasped.

"Matthew?"

"FTW," he mumbled against her.

"What?"

He glanced up the length of her creamy white body and grinned. "FTW. For the win, lady. I'm going for the win."

Ashley swept her hand through the frothy hot tub waters, reclining back into the warmth of Matthew's naked strength serving as the perfect "arm chair." His Jacuzzi was built into the bathroom with a skylight overhead, which offered the aura of being outside without the loss of privacy.

After making love again in his bedroom, he'd shown her the oversize bathroom that had been an add-on to the carriage house. Just as she'd sunk into the full tub, he'd returned with champagne and strawberries—and joined her. The added bulk of his body eased the water just over the tips of her breasts, the gentle swoosh a warm temptation.

As much as she wanted to relax into the moment,

sipping her drink, enjoying the burst of fruit on her taste buds as Matthew fed her, her stomach kept tightening with nerves. Things with Matthew were getting more complicated by the second.

Damn it, she should be happy. She'd fantasized over what it would be like with this man. He wasn't hotfooting toward the door like after their first night together. So why did his ring suddenly feel so utterly heavy on her finger?

Matthew's hands landed on her shoulders and he began a soothing massage. "I'm sorry you're so tense. I hate to think this campaign put those kinks in your muscles."

"I'm managing." She sipped from the fluted crystal, the fine vintage tickling her nose as surely as the bristly hair on Matthew's chest teased her back.

"You're more than managing." He rested his chin on her head while continuing to knead her kinked muscles. "But you don't care for the spotlight?"

Just what she needed, reminders of Brent Davis's concerns that she could actually hurt Matthew's chances of beating that Martin Stewart. She stayed silent, finishing her drink and splaying her fingers through the rose-scented bubbles.

Steam saturated her senses. The mirror may have fogged a while ago, but she still carried in her memory the reflected image of the two of them together in the gray-and-white marble tub.

His firm caress continued its seductive magic. "Not much longer and hopefully things will settle out."

She couldn't imagine how. Every scenario that played out in her mind—continuing this charade or walking away—spelled frustration.

Perhaps her best solution would be to avoid the whole subject altogether tonight and focus on the sensations of the here and now. "That feels amazing."

His thumbs worked their way up her neck. "This Jacuzzi has eased a lot of tense muscles after working out with my brothers."

"I was talking about your hands, but yeah, the hot tub is awesome, too."

He circled the pressure points along her jaw. "I'm glad to hear you like my touch."

"Very much." Too much. This had been easier when he'd been the unattainable fantasy of a woman convinced he would never look twice at her.

She tapped her left shoulder, the one still slightly raised and blurted, "I had scoliosis as a girl."

His massaging fingers tensed for a second, an understated indication he had heard her.

"I'm lucky Aunt Libby aggressively addressed the problem with my spine early." She knew that now, although she'd hated the brace as a child. "For the most part it doesn't affect the way I live anymore. Although I shy away from higher heels and standing for too long without moving can give me a headache."

"Well, as I understand it, mega-high heels aren't good for anybody's back and standing still for an hour is highly overrated."

His easy acceptance of the subject released more tension inside her than the massaging tub jets ever could. "No way did I just hear what I thought I heard."

"What did I say?"

"A man actually dissed high heels for women?" She glanced over her shoulder and crinkled her nose at him. "No freaking way. I thought the whole male species stopped for a woman's legs extended by spike heels."

He cocked one eyebrow at her. "How un-PC of you. You make us sound very shallow."

"You said it. Not me."

"Ouch. Low blow, but well played. Perhaps you should stand in for me during the debates." He slipped his arms around her, just below her breasts. "Certainly everybody has physical traits that they're attracted to."

"Like legs?"

His hands slid up to cup her, his thumbs brushing against her nipples. "Or breasts." His head dipped to her ear. "Or the soft feel of your skin." He nuzzled her neck. "And there's your amazing hair."

"You're quite a smooth talker."

"I'm only being honest." His hands stilled again, clasped over her stomach. "Why do you have such trouble accepting compliments?"

He'd been so understanding about the subject thus far, she allowed herself the risk of sharing more about the other hurts, the emotional kind, that the birth defect had brought her over the years. "Left-over issues from the scoliosis I imagine."

"You're blessedly healthy." His eyes blazed with an unmistakable intensity and reminder of how much worse things could have been.

"Yes, and I'm grateful for the amazing doctors who helped me over the years." She hesitated. "But you didn't see me before. Achieving this posture wasn't easy. Some people—my biological parents—didn't want the financial and time-consuming strain I brought."

Matthew's muscles turned to Sheetrock against her back. She looked over her shoulder to find his eyes were equally as hard.

"They didn't deserve you." His words were gentle, but his body still rigid.

With indignation. Fury even. She read it all there in his eyes so gemstone sharp they could cut. He was angry *for her.* People had been sympathetic, helpful, but she couldn't recall anyone being flat-out mad for that ill-treated little girl she'd been.

Matthew touched her soul and wiped away years of pain. "Thank you."

"No need to thank me, I'm just stating a fact." He held her gaze. "And while I'm on the subject, you're undoubtedly a tough lady."

That felt good to hear, as well, especially after Brent's scathing assessment of her character.

"I had to be. Children can be cruel to a kid who doesn't look like the rest of them." Even adults— her biological parents—could be horribly unaccepting of their daughter's twisted gait.

Matthew was right. They hadn't deserved her. How mind-blowing that she'd never before considered that they simply weren't cut out for parenthood.

Muscles she hadn't even realized were still tensed eased at the new level of understanding. She'd talked about this with Aunt Libby and her sisters often over the years. Interesting—and a bit scary—that it had taken just one conversation with this man to help her see things with a different perspective.

Matthew skimmed a knuckle down her spine. "You wore a brace all the time?"

"Until college, then I only had to wear it at night." She cast another quick glance over her shoulder. "That's why I'm so addicted to silky fabrics now. They feel all the more fabulous on my skin."

"You're obviously a sensualist." His hands glided back around her with a touch as light as any fabric.

"I'm an accountant."

"So? People who like numbers can't like sensations and even adventurous sex?"

"When you put it that way…" And touched her that way.

"You're perfect the way you are." His thumbs grazed the undersides of her breasts while he dipped his head to tease along her collarbone. "All of that in the past made you into the sexy, smart woman you are today."

His arousal throbbed an agreement against the base of her spine. She slid her hands under the churning water to caress his powerful legs, wriggling in his lap, her pulse already pounding in her ears as loudly as the blasts of water through the Jacuzzi jets.

He cupped her waist and lifted her slightly, urging her to turn around until she knelt, her damp legs on either side of his. She leaned forward until the core of her pressed to the hard and ready length of him. Her breasts teased his chest as she leaned forward to capture a kiss.

Tonight wasn't over yet and she was determined to make the most of it.

She arched up until the heat of him nestled against her, then she slid down, slowly taking him inside her, tantalizingly so, torturously so. "FTW, Matthew. For the win."

Nine

"FTW, brother."

His brother's ill-chosen words echoing in his ears, Matthew choked midway through his golf swing and shanked the ball into a water hazard near the clubhouse. Wading birds swooped upward and out of the way.

Matthew scowled over his shoulder at his middle brother who knew the no-speaking rule. "Thanks, Sebastian."

He'd been looking forward to this afternoon of golf with his brothers, even if the event also happened to be a benefit tournament. However, if he kept playing like this, the foursome on the fairway behind them would have to stop for lunch before they could move ahead.

"No problem, bro. Always happy to cheer you on." Their lawyer sibling did have impeccable timing. "Nice slice, by the way."

The other two Landis brothers stood by the golf cart applauding with grins as smug as the one on the gator's face as the reptile slid through the salt marsh. Nope, not gonna wade in after that ball. He would take the drop for a penalty stroke.

Matthew pointed his titanium driver at the youngest, Jonah, first and then at Kyle, the next to oldest. "Your turns are coming up soon enough, and I feel a coughing fit coming on."

They'd all grown up competing with each other and nothing had changed now. He couldn't fault them for it, and of course Sebastian had no way of knowing just what a kick in the gut his FTW would apply. He and Ashley had both won in a major way throughout the night.

Matthew reached into the tiny trash can on the side of his cart and scooped out a handful of the grass seed mixed with sand. He leaned down to pack it into the divot he'd chunked out of the course when his swing had gone awry.

Thoughts of Ashley tended to send his brain off-kilter in much the same manner. He leaned on his club, images of her facing him in the hot tub threatening what little concentration he had left. They hadn't gotten much sleep, but he wouldn't change a minute of their night together.

He glanced at his watch, wondering how much longer until she would finish her meeting with her sisters to review insurance paperwork. Claire and Starr had driven down from Charleston to spend the day with her, which left him free to attend this benefit golf tournament *and* hang with his brothers. They were just finishing up the ninth hole, so he would be home before supper.

Sebastian clapped him on the back with a solid thud, the two of them the closest in height and build. "Are we going to play or are you going to laze around for the rest of the afternoon staring at your watch?"

The sun beat down unrelentingly on his head. Matthew shrugged his shoulders under his golf shirt, flexed his hand inside the leather glove, but still tension kinked through him. "Just gauging the course."

Jonah chuckled low, his attention only half with them as he watched some college-aged girl in a designer sun visor driving the course's drink cart around. "Yeah, right. We saw you say goodbye to your fiancée earlier," he said, no doubt referring to the kiss still scorching Matthew's veins. "What's up with her, dude? Why didn't you bring her by before? You wouldn't let us get away with that."

He hated lying to his family, but… Now he had this notion of letting things keep going as they were with Ashley. See where it led.

Keep enjoying what they did have.

Sebastian elbowed Jonah and pointed to the cluster of reporters gathering around the oceanside clubhouse in the distance. "Shut your trap. There's media everywhere."

Jonah pulled his gaze off the bleached blond coed in the drink cart with obvious reluctance and checked out the press gathering. "Yeah, right." He shoved a hand through his unruly curls in need of a hair cut. "Gotta keep up the good family name."

Kyle swished through practice swings with lanky grace. The workout fiend was always in motion, keeping in shape for his military career. "Damn, bro, thanks to you we can't do anything together anymore without it turning into a photo-op."

Matthew dropped a new ball on the ground. "I figured leaking this outing of ours would take some heat off Ashley for the day."

Kyle shaded his eyes against the harsh summer sun as he peered off in the direction of the press. "Giving them something else to talk about?"

"Pretty much." He swung… Watched… The ball landed on the green. "It's not like we haven't been dealing with this kind of coverage for most of our lives. I figured you could handle the heat."

Matthew climbed into his golf cart, Sebastian settling in beside him while their other brothers drove along behind. He guided the vehicle past rolling dunes with sea oats blowing in the muggy breeze.

Sebastian reached for his soda can in the holder as their clubs rattled in back. "So this woman's really gotten to you, then."

"I'm engaged to her." That in and of itself was a step he'd never expected to take again.

"Ah, come on. Be real around me, at least."

"Who says I'm not being real?" There had been more than a few moments with Ashley where he'd forgotten they were playing roles.

"You're actually going to marry her?" His brother peered over his Armani sunglasses.

"I didn't say that." Yeah, he was quibbling but this wasn't a conversation he was comfortable with. Not after a night that had jumbled all his carefully made plans. "I simply said we're engaged. She's a special, honest person who doesn't deserve how things went down."

"Bro, you are so toast." Sebastian shook his head, humor fading from his face as he replaced his drink in the holder. "Just be careful. Don't rush into anything until you're certain."

Hell. He should have seen where this was going given Sebastian's recent separation from his wife. They'd married too young, grown in different directions and it was tearing them both apart. Now that Matthew looked closer, he could see that his brother had lost weight in recent months, his angular face almost gaunt. He'd gone so long without a haircut, he would soon be sporting Jonah's length.

And he still wore his platinum wedding band.

Sebastian served as a great big reminder for how badly two well-meaning people could hurt each other in the end. Matthew hated that he couldn't do a damn thing to make this right for his younger brother.

He clapped his hand against Sebastian's shoulder. "I hear you and I'm sorry for the hell you're going through."

"I hear you, too, and I'm not trying to interfere, only adding my two cents from the hard knocks side of the romance world."

Matthew gripped the steering wheel as they whirred past a pelican perched on a wood pole. Damn it all, he'd been so caught up in his campaigning, he hadn't been there for his brother the way that he should have during what was undoubtedly the most painful time of his life. And how was that for a kick-in-the ass wake-up call about ill-advised marriages born of out-of-control emotions? "How much longer until the divorce is final?"

"This fall," Sebastian answered, his voice flat.

"A lot could happen between now and then." Look how quickly his life had been turned upside down.

"Too much already happened between now and then. We both simply want to move on without sacrificing any more blood in the process."

"I'm sorry, damn sorry. I really hoped you two could beat the odds."

"Me, too, bro. Me, too." Sebastian nudged his sunglasses firmly in place and looked away.

Message received loud and clear. Back off.

Silence stretched between them, broken only by the ever-present rustling of creatures in the underbrush that remained after the golf course had been hewn out of the wild area.

Finally, Sebastian's face spread into a smile, a little forced, but obviously where he wanted the tone to go. "Enough of this heart-and-guts bull. Let's get back to the game and I'll show you who's going to blow the odds to hell and back."

Matthew stopped the cart and retrieved a club from his leather bag in back. "I'm starting to think Mom has it right."

Kyle loped alongside them. "What do you mean?"

"The way she picked a friend to marry the second go round rather than signing on for all that rollercoaster emotional crap. Maybe we should all learn the lesson from her."

Jonah stopped short, a hank of curls falling over his forehead. "Are you flipping blind? Mom's absolutely crazy about the general."

"Yeah, yeah." Matthew waved aside his youngest brother's comment. "I know they're—God forgive me for saying this—hot for each other. Remember, I was there with you guys when we accidentally walked in on them in bed together."

Matthew shuddered right along with his brothers. What a day that had been catching their sainted mother *in flagrante delicto* with her longtime friend-turned-lover, a man she had since married.

Even their playboy brother Jonah looked rattled by just the mention of that brain-stunner of an event. "I really would have preferred to go through life believing we were all four immaculately conceived."

Sebastian made a referee T with his hands. "Okay, let's not go there again, even in our mind. But I think Jonah has a point," he continued in his naturally lawyerly logical tone, "Mom isn't just attracted to him, she really loves the general."

Matthew forced his ever-racing brain to slow and think back to his mom's Christmas wedding to Hank Renshaw. Sure the event had been romantically impulsive, but could there have been something more in his mother's eyes then? And now, as well? He thought of all the times her face lit up when her cell phone rang with the distinctive ringtone she'd programmed for only the general's calls.

Aside from successful, high-power political careers, his mom and her new husband shared a lot of views in common and didn't hesitate to take an hour from their busy schedules to sit on the porch swing and talk over glasses of wine.

Now that he looked at it from more of an analytical perspective, it seemed obvious. His mother and General Hank Renshaw were totally in love with each other.

How could he have been so self-delusional? Because he'd wanted reality to fit his need for low-key commitment—while still holding on to Ashley. Problem was, now he didn't have a solution to the mess he'd made of his and Ashley's lives. Although he did know one thing for certain.

No way in hell could he live without a repeat of what they'd shared the night before.

Back in the main house, Ashley stared out the guest bedroom window over the ocean, not too different a view than the one she'd grown up with at Aunt Libby's. Lordy, but she'd never needed the woman's support more than now when she faced the toughest decision of her life.

Even the ocean view and the soothing décor of the

guest room's delft-blue flowers accented with airy stripes did little to lower her stress level. Spending the afternoon with her foster sisters crunching the numbers and detailing the massive amount of work required to get Beachcombers up and running as a business again had been tougher than she'd expected. Once she rebuilt the place, it would be time to move on with her life—apart from Matthew. Even the thought of that hurt more than she'd expected.

However, continuing with this charade hurt, too. How long could she keep falling into bed—and tubs—with him without making a decision about their future one way or another?

Fantasizing about the man had been easy. Being with him was far more complicated and exciting. And scary. Why couldn't he have been a regular, everyday kind of guy, with a regular everyday sort of life?

She stared down at her engagement ring and practiced pulling it off her finger. Her hand felt so blasted bare. She clenched her fist to resist the urge to put the solitaire back in place and to hell with the consequences to her heart.

Ashley held the diamond up for the sun to glint off the facets. So many angles and nuances could be seen depending on which way she looked at the stone. And wasn't that much like her life? She had an important choice to make and her decision changed depending on which way she viewed the situation.

The air conditioner cranked on, swooshing a teasing gust over her neck almost as tantalizing as a lover's kiss. Then stronger, warmer.

She shivered, reflexively closing her fingers around the ring.

Matthew's lips pressed firmer against her skin. "Hello, beautiful."

She tried to force herself to relax as she turned in his arms. "I didn't hear you come in."

He skimmed his knuckles over her forehead. "You were certainly caught up thinking about something important. Did things go all right with your sisters?"

She blinked quickly as she shifted mental gears. God, she hadn't even been thinking about Beachcombers, which should totally have been her focus. "Everything went fine. There are lots of positives to focus on. The fire investigators tracked the problem to old wiring failing. Nothing we're liable for, so our insurance payment will come through smoothly. We can start contacting contractors right away."

He pressed a firm kiss to her mouth before hugging her. "That's great to hear. I'm glad for all three of you."

With his heartbeat under her ear and his musky scent all around her, the queen-size bed only five feet away seemed too enticing. "Let's go out to the living room. I know we're adults and all, but it doesn't seem right for your mother to find us in here together."

He winced. "Banish that thought here and now." Matthew backed a step but stroked her arms. "Don't worry, though. She just left, so you can relax."

"I can't do that." The ring seemed to gain weight in her grasp. "Relax, I mean."

He looked behind him and back again. "Are your sisters still here somewhere?"

"They left a half hour ago." She gathered up her words and let them roll free before she could stop herself. She unfurled her fingers, the engagement ring cupped in her palm. "Actually, I can't do this anymore."

Any hint of a smile faded from his face. "Do what precisely?"

Ashley raised her hand holding the solitaire, her hand already shaking at the thought of giving it back. Aside from her own reservations, she couldn't ignore fears of the opponent gaining momentum from her decision.

She would do her best to persuade Starr to step forward. Perhaps that would even encourage others who might have received the same treatment to open up.

Regardless, she couldn't be a party to perpetuating a lie, even as much as breaking things off with Matthew tore her apart inside. "Pretend to be engaged. Lying to the press has been difficult enough. Lying to my *sisters* this afternoon was hell. They probably already suspect anyway."

"Well, as a matter of fact—" he clasped both of her hands in his "—I was thinking about that myself while golfing with my brothers."

Her stomach twisted. So this was it. They would break things off and she would be back in Charleston with real memories to replace the fantasies. Except reality had been so much more amazing than any make-believe. "And your thoughts led you to what conclusion?"

His grip tightened on her arms. "What do you say we give it a try for real? No more pretending."

She couldn't have heard what she thought. Her stomach clenched tighter than his hold on her. "I think you're going to need to repeat that because I'm certain I couldn't have heard you correctly."

He lifted her left hand and thumbed the bare spot. "Let's keep the ring in place and get to know each other better, hang out—"

"Have sex?"

"I sure as hell hope so."

Matthew's resurrected grin left her in no doubt of how much he wanted her. Except she needed more than that now. She deserved more. "While you were golfing with your brothers, you decided we need to hang out more and have sex?"

"I'm not expressing myself well, which is damned odd considering I'm used to crafting the right sound bite—which should tell you something about how you screw with my head." His smile went from charming to wicked in a flash of perfect teeth. "How about I try this again. Let's get to know each other better, build a, uh…" He gestured for the word, his gaze scanning the boat-speckled horizon as if answers bobbed on the gleaming waters.

"Relationship. The word is *relationship,* Matthew." It was tough for her to consider, too, but at least she could say the word without becoming tongue-tied.

"Yeah, right. That." He skimmed a finger along his collar, which would have been understandable if he hadn't been wearing a freaking Polo shirt with the top two buttons undone.

"Sounds to me like you're describing sex buddies and sex buddies don't exchange rings." How odd that a few weeks ago, sex buddies would have actually sounded like a fun fantasy come true. Except now this ring screwed up everything because it taunted her with the deeper sentiments that she wanted—deserved—from life someday.

"What do you expect from me?" Matthew stared down at her, frustration sparking in his gem-green eyes. "Do you want me to say I love you? I've been in love before and it takes a while. I haven't known you long enough to be sure about something like that. But I can say that I think I could love you someday. So why break things off when there's that possibility out there?"

Could love her *someday?* Talk about a rousing endorsement.

Then her mind hitched on one phrase to the exclusion of everything else he'd said. "You've been in love before?"

He went stone still.

"Matthew? Who was it?" She couldn't resist asking, too darn curious about the woman who had managed to steal his heart. "The press has linked you to plenty of women over the years and certainly speculated about more than a few of them recently, but nothing serious ever seemed to come of those liaisons. I think that's part of the reason they've gone so snap happy over our fake engagement."

"You're probably correct," he conceded, although still neatly dodging her question.

Her curiosity only heightened. She wasn't sure why it should matter so much when she was determined to break things off. She should be running for the door before her will faltered.

Still, she had to ask. "Then who is the woman? I think even my pretend-fiancée status gives me the right to ask."

He started to reach for his collar again before dropping his arm to his side as he stepped around her to peer out the window. "Someone I knew in college—Dana." He stuffed his fists into his pockets, his jaw hard. "Dana and I became engaged unexpectedly fast and before I could introduce her to the family, she died."

Her heart squeezed inside her chest with sympathy, and an impending sense of how he'd never been hers from the beginning.

"I'm so sorry." She tentatively touched his shoulder, unable to resist offering comfort for those long-ago hurts. She knew well from her parents' abandonment how long those emotional aches could persist. "It must have been horrible to lose her."

"It was," he said simply, but the two words carried more pain than any lengthy monologue could have. His muscles tensed under her touch.

"What happened?" she asked gently.

"She—Dana—had a heart defect, something rare that had gone undetected." He scrubbed his hand over his face, his jaw flexing. Pain pulsed from him as palpably as if he'd shouted the words.

"You really loved Dana." Part of her ached to comfort him. Another part, a new stronger piece of herself asserted she deserved that same intense love. She couldn't accept being a second-best sex buddy.

Ashley stepped away from Matthew. She carefully placed her fairy-tale diamond and all the precious multi-faceted dreams it had held on to the bedside table. "I'm sorry, Matthew, this is just how it has to end—"

The phone jangled by her engagement ring, jolting her back a step.

Matthew hesitated, his eyes holding hers while the ringing continued. She waved him toward the call. She should call her sisters for a ride. They shouldn't be too far away since they'd dropped her off less than an hour ago.

His eyes still narrowed and locked on her, he crossed to pick up the receiver. "Landis residence."

She started to reach for her cell when something fierce in Matthew's expression as he took the call made her hesitate.

No more than four thudding heartbeats later, he scowled and reached for the television remote resting beside the lamp. "Right, got it, Brent. I'm tuning in now."

He thumbed the remote, activating the flat-screen television mounted on the wall. What could the press have come up with on them this time? Pictures of them would be embarrassing but useless. Still she could see from Matthew's frown this wasn't happy news.

The TV screen blazed to life with a newsflash that was already in progress. A photo-inset box appeared in the upper right-hand corner behind the newscaster's head, complete with a picture of Matthew at the golf course…

With his arm around a blond hottie plastered to his side.

Ten

"So do we shoot him outright or do we torture him first?" Her expression fierce, Starr leaned her elbows on her restaurant table across from Ashley and Claire.

Ashley tried to shake free the numbed sensation still dogging her even two hours after the call from Matthew's campaign manager. There had barely been time for Matthew to turn to Ashley and state, "The photos aren't what you think," before his family had begun pouring into the house for a troubleshooting session.

Sure he'd had an explanation about the water girl

at the golf course throwing herself at him, which left him instinctively steadying her at an inopportune time since the press packed the parking lot. His brothers affirmed he didn't know her—although unlucky for Matthew, his brothers had been in search of food at that particular moment.

He'd been so busy trying to convince her, yet the whole water-girl incident felt like nothing to her in comparison to his revelation about Dana. Ashley believed there was nothing to those golf-course photos.

Her problem boiled down to trust on a larger scale. The need to trust he could ever have deep feelings for another woman again. The belief that he could someday fall for *her*.

Her sisters had called almost immediately and turned around to come back to Hilton Head. Claire had told her—in a tone that brooked no argument—that they were on their way. Ashley had been more than grateful for the opportunity to escape the mayhem of campaign central working damage control.

Which was how she ended up in a dark back corner of an out-of-the-way seafood restaurant, wearing sunglasses and a ball cap.

Ashley scratched under the hat. She didn't want her life "spun" anymore.

Starr dragged the bread basket over from the middle of the table, the pregnant woman's appetite apparently insatiable. "So? Quick death or torture?"

Claire unfolded and refolded her napkin precisely. "To think, the press missed the real story when they actually bought into that engagement story hook, line and sinker."

Ashley snatched the perfectly creased napkin from her sister's hands. "Who says it isn't real? I never gave you any indication otherwise."

"Oh come on, we know you." Claire patted Ashley's hand, still bare of the engagement ring. "You're too much like me. You wouldn't get engaged to someone you didn't know well."

"You've never done anything impulsive in the romance department?" She waited to see how her sister would dodge that question since they all knew Claire had gotten pregnant in a one-night stand with a friend who was now her head-over-heels-in-love husband and father to their beautiful baby girl.

Claire raised a perfectly arched blond eyebrow. "Somebody's not playing nice today." She reached to the empty table next to them and snagged a new napkin. "But you're forgiven because of the stress."

Ashley struggled to shrug off the defensiveness. These were her sisters. She couldn't lie to them anymore. Perhaps it was time she also stopped lying to herself.

She rubbed the bare spot where the engagement ring had rested. "It doesn't matter now anyway. Matthew and I are over."

Or rather Matthew had been trying to bring up the possibility of staying together and she'd cut him off short.

Claire studied her with a gentle concern reminiscent of Aunt Libby's maternal care. "Is this about the suggestive photos?"

"The ones of me and him, or the ones of her and him?" Ashley crinkled her nose. "The one of him at the golf course actually doesn't worry me beyond what damage it could do to his campaign. I'm certain the picture was a setup."

And oddly enough, she was sure. She trusted him with physical faithfulness. Totally. He'd never been anything but honest with her, even when it hurt. She'd heard clearly enough in his voice how much he'd loved that woman from long ago, a real romance that concerned her far more than any manufactured one on the evening news.

Starr sagged back in her seat, tearing into another piece of bread while the other guests and televisions buzzed loudly enough to afford them privacy to talk.

"I guess this means we don't get to enjoy torturing your hunky senatorial candidate."

Ashley allowed herself a half smile. "I would appreciate it if you took a pass on that this go-round."

Claire patted her hand, her nail tapping the spot where the ring used to nestle waiting for a wedding band to complete the set. "Now your schedule is free and clear again."

Ashley tugged the sunglasses off. To hell with anonymity. She wanted to see life clearly now more than ever. "Don't worry, I will uphold my end of the obligations with reopening Beachcombers."

Claire and Starr exchanged a loaded look before Claire tugged a folder from her overlarge purse. "We were actually getting ready to turn around and come back when the news story broke."

"Turn around? Why?" When they still hesitated so long a waitress managed to work her way past with a steaming platter of crab legs, Ashley pressed harder, "Please, don't hold anything back. I've been up-front with you and I'm going to be hurt if you aren't equally open with me."

Claire twisted her napkin in a totally un-Claire disregard for order, which relayed just how nervous she must be. "We weren't lying about anything earlier. We simply omitted some thoughts we've been having about the whole rebuilding process."

Starr shoved away the now nearly empty bread basket. "What do you plan to do with your future, after the election—if you and Matthew don't stay together?"

"I imagined we'll be busy renovating Beach-combers." The possibility of taking him up on his offer still felt so alien she hadn't thought that far ahead. She needed to get her head together and in the present. She looked from sister to sister. "What are you both keeping from me? Was there something wrong with the insurance adjustment after all?"

"No, nothing like that," Claire rushed to reassure her.

Ashley relaxed back in her chair. "Okay, then. I appreciate all the times you helped me and protected me and built me up over the years." She injected strength in her words to match the steel in her spine. "But I'm not that shy, insecure little kid anymore. Could you please stop treating me like a child and welcome me into your grown-ups club?"

Starr covered Ashley's hand with hers. "We love you. It's hard not to worry."

"Thank you." She squeezed Starr's hand and reached for Claire's, as well. "I love you both, too. So tell me. What's with all the secret looks? Come on, Claire? Spill it."

"We're just wondering if we should look into options other than reopening Beachcombers."

Claire's words hovered over the table between them, heavy and unexpected.

Ashley finally got her brain off stun long enough to speak. "You mean level Aunt Libby's house?"

"No, not that." Starr waved aside that possibility, thank God. "We could use the insurance money to restore the place to its former glory. Then sell it. Let a family live and grow and flourish there."

Claire angled forward. "We could split the proceeds three ways and it will still give us each the chance to pursue any career dreams we want. I can open my own catering business with more flexible hours for the baby."

Ashley turned to Starr. "And you feel the same way about this?"

"Yes, sweetie. I do. I've always wanted to go back to art school and study abroad. Sure, my husband can afford it, but I appreciate the chance to finance it myself. You have your degree and this would give you a nice financial cushion. But we don't want you to feel like you don't have a home."

Their plan made sense. They both had husbands, homes, children and unique career dreams of their own. And she had…

A wonderfully unconventional family who loved her and a quirky old lady who'd taught her to value herself. None of that would change because of owning or selling a particular house.

Ashley squeezed her sisters' hands. "We have a bond, the three of us, that goes beyond any house. The memories Aunt Libby gave us are a far stronger link than any home could ever be. And I think she would like the notion of a family being brought up in her home."

Across the restaurant, one of the patrons reached to turn up the volume on one of the televisions. Starr's eyes widening gave her the first hint that she'd better check it out.

Ashley pivoted in her chair for a better view of the screen. A local news announcement had interrupted the sporting event. "Senatorial candidate Matthew Landis's campaign has just announced he will be making a statement to the press outside his headquarters."

What could he be planning to say? She'd left the family gathering before a consensus had been reached. No doubt if they didn't act soon, his opponent would beat him to the punch and no telling what he would concoct. Damn shame nobody ever seemed interested in posting compromising photos of Martin Stewart. But then Matthew was the forerunner right now, so tearing him down made for better news and a tighter race—which generated more public interest.

Where did she fit into all of this?

She looked at her sisters and thought of how even logical Claire had begun following her heart. Ashley stared at the pictures of Matthew on the television screen—one of him with her, then the one from the golf course, followed by an image of him alone.

From the moment she'd seen that image of him with the blonde, she'd known he wasn't seeing anyone else. Aside from the fact he'd been with her nearly every second of every day, she knew him to be an honorable man. He'd even been willing to put his campaign, his life's dream, in jeopardy to make things right for her.

How come she'd been so comfortable trusting him, but unable to trust in herself? She wanted to be a part of his life. He'd told her he wanted to be a part of hers and then shared something intensely personal and painful about his past. That indicated a willingness to take things to a deeper level than before and she should be brave enough to explore the possibility.

Life wasn't going to get less complicated if she walked away from him. In fact, already her heart was telling her turning her back on the feelings develop-ing between them would lead to complications that would hurt her for the rest of her life.

He'd supported her through a scandal that was

every bit as much her own fault as his. He deserved her support now. She was ready to fight for her place in the forefront of Matthew Landis's life.

Ashley pushed back her chair and stood, gathering her purse. "My dear sisters, I agree. Renovate and sell Beachcombers. It's time, time for a lot of things." She gathered her purse and her resolve. "I'm going to Matthew's press conference to be with him."

Where she now knew she belonged, beside the man she loved.

Matthew stood in the foyer of his campaign headquarters, gathering his thoughts. In less than ninety seconds, he would step outside and address the media about his plummeting poll numbers.

His staff stayed in the main office, their conversations a controlled low buzz as they gave him the space he needed to collect himself before stepping outside. He blocked out the noise from television monitors and kept his eyes off all the posters packing the walls.

He had speech notes tucked in his pocket, words that could end his political career, but unavoidable. He had to stop this press war that was tearing Ashley apart, and if that meant he lost the election then so be it. A man had to make a stand for what mattered most.

He hadn't been able to do anything for Dana, but

he damn well could fall on his sword for Ashley. He couldn't live with himself if he ruined her life to save a career.

In losing Ashley, he'd blown the biggest opportunity of his life, way bigger than any senate seat.

He would find another way to change the freaking world. He had the resources and the drive. Ashley had shown him there were other effective approaches to life than just his bullheaded full speed ahead manner.

Matthew checked his watch again. Thirty seconds. He reached for the knob to step out and join Brent on the porch.

A hand fell on his shoulder. Matthew jolted. Damn. He'd been so preoccupied he hadn't even heard anyone approach.

He pivoted to find… "Ashley? What are you doing here?"

Her brown eyes gleamed with a wide intensity, totally focused on him in a way that lured him, distracted him, at the worst possible moment.

"I came in through the back. Your mother met me and let me in." She gripped his lapels, energy pulsing from her, her long hair rising in a staticky halo around her. "Matthew, what are you planning to say to those reporters?"

"The truth. That I've let them dictate my decisions in a way that has hurt others. That if I'm going to be an effective senator for my constituents, I have to be willing to take the flack that might come my way from the press." He resisted the urge to gather her against him even as he ached to skim his hands along her sweet curves under her lemon-yellow sundress. "I'm going to say whatever it takes to protect you *and* set you free."

She slipped her hand through the crook of his arm. "I'm going with you."

"Like hell." He scowled.

She scowled right back. "Just try and stop me."

Before he could blink, she'd ducked under his other arm and slipped out the front door, straight toward the press conference. Hell, she was determined. And hot.

And headed for trouble.

He bolted after her, almost slamming into Brent, who was attempting to hide the panicked look on his face that appeared whenever things weren't following his perfectly scripted agenda. The instant spent working his way around his campaign manager cost Matthew the precious time needed to catch Ashley before she took her place in front of the podium.

Complete with a microphone and a captive media audience.

"Good afternoon, ladies and gentlemen of the press. I know you expected to hear from Congressman

Landis today, but I have to confess to being a bit pushy in wanting to get my two cents in first for the record."

She flashed the gentle smile of hers combined with her shy way of glancing through her lashes at the crowd. How odd that he'd never before noticed her ramrod straight steely spine under that gorgeous mass of red hair. Those years in a back brace had honed strength in her nobody was going to cow, not even the most sharklike members of the media.

"I imagine we've gathered to talk about revealing photos."

Her bluntness stunned everyone still. For all of three heartbeats and then photographers started snapping away again.

"Oh, but wait, we already discussed those pictures of me."

A giggle started in the back, slowly working its way to the front until everyone relaxed and joined in. Interesting how everyone seemed to be perspiring from the summer heat—except for cool, collected Ashley.

"I appreciate that you're all here. You offer a valuable service in getting the message out. Today, I simply want to make sure the message is factually correct so we're not wasting time with messy legalities later."

Whoa, she had the spine set on mega-strong today.

Brent shook his head slowly. "My God, she's got the press eating out of the palm of her hand. I've never seen anything like her."

Matthew turned back to stare at Ashley bathed in the beauty of her glowing self-confidence that radiated stronger than even the South Carolina sun. "Me, either."

Ashley nodded to the crowd from the podium. "Now, I happen to believe that a photo of a popular candidate, in his golf clothes, on the golf course, standing by a golf-course employee isn't particularly scandal worthy. But that's easier for me to say because I know Matthew and I trust him. I realize that trust takes time."

He didn't doubt the surety in her words and wondered why he'd ever thought she couldn't handle whatever life threw at her. Ashley was a helluva lot stronger than he'd ever given her credit for.

She was absolutely incredible.

Her tone shifted subtly from congenial to factual. "That's what a campaign is all about, taking the time to get to know the candidate. Learning to trust him to see to our best interests in the senate. I, for one, would like to hear more about Matthew's strategy for guiding our country rather than about photos that divert your attention from getting to know the smart, dynamic leadership style of Matthew Landis."

Listening to her talk, Matthew felt a kick in his gut he'd never expected to experience again, one far stronger than anything he remembered experiencing before but recognized all the same. *He loved this woman.*

She glanced his way with a steady smile that sent a fresh surge of emotion through him. "If you're ready to speak now, Matthew, I would especially like to hear more about your innovative plans to sponsor legislation targeted at helping to strengthen benefits in our foster-care system."

He wanted to talk to Ashley, tell her he loved her and yeah, he wanted her, too, but it was definitely about more than being sex buddies. However, the things he had to say to her were private and the sooner he dispensed with the press, the sooner he could get Ashley all to himself.

Matthew collected his thoughts and stepped toward the microphone. He could present that particular talking point of Ashley's proposed speech blindfolded with his hands behind his back. And after he finished the press conference, he had an entirely different discussion in mind. Except the dialogue with Ashley wouldn't be as easy to deliver and the outcome odds were shaky at best.

But he wouldn't let the opportunity of a lifetime pass him by.

* * *

Ashley applauded the end of Matthew's speech with a mix of pride and trepidation. While they'd averted a campaign catastrophe today, would she be able to turn things around for them after she'd all but pitched his ring in his face earlier?

If she trusted the look in his eyes when he smiled at her, then they weren't anywhere near over. Lucky for her, she'd learned to trust him— and more importantly, she'd learned to trust in herself.

Brent ducked his head close to her ear. "You took a real risk out there, Ashley."

"He's worth it." She soaked in the broad set of Matthew's shoulders, the honest connection in his eyes when he spoke with individual voters.

Brent extended his hand. "I'm sorry for underestimating you. I should be a better judge of character than that by now."

"Apology accepted." She clasped his palm and shook firmly. "You were only looking out for Matthew, which I appreciate."

Matthew waved farewell to the crowd and joined her, leading her and Brent back inside headquarters where the televisions already blared with reports of the media conference. "Hey, Brent, get your own lady. This one's taken."

Ashley elbowed Matthew in the side. "Did you ever consider you're the one who's taken?"

"Good point." Matthew scooped her into his arms as he'd done a week ago when he'd saved her life.

She may have squeaked in surprise, but she didn't even bother protesting and simply settled in for the ride while his campaign staff cheered them on. How far she and Matthew had come in just a week since he'd carried her from the flaming Beachcombers.

He stepped into his office and kicked the door closed. Keeping her arms around his neck, she slid her feet to the floor, leaning into him, urging his face down to meet hers. How could she have ever thought she would be able to turn her back on this, on him?

Matthew nuzzled her ear. "You were…"

"Amazing?" She angled back to grin up at him.

"Absolutely," he confirmed without hesitation. "I can't believe I was worried about protecting you from the press. I should have turned you loose on them right from the start."

She wouldn't have credited herself with the ability to field them that first day when they'd captured revealing pictures of her. But the past week spent learning about herself, learning about real love, she'd discovered there were things out there far more important than worrying what others thought of her. "I'm just glad to have been of help. I believe in you and your message."

"Thank you. That means more to me than I think you realize. I'm sorry about the way we left things earlier." He clasped both of her hands in his. "I want to talk to you about Dana."

"It's okay." She brushed her fingers over his mouth. "I understand."

"I need to say this." He clasped her wrist and lowered her hand. "I should have said it the right way earlier, but I don't have much practice speaking about the past. In fact, I don't have any experience with it at all."

"You haven't told *anyone* about Dana?"

He certainly hadn't mentioned that earlier and the admission touched her heart in a new and unexpected way. He'd chosen her over anyone else when it came to sharing such an important part of his past. What a time to realize that Matthew *had* put her first, even before his own relatives.

"Since my family hadn't met her and she didn't have any family to meet me, nobody knew how serious things had gotten. Nobody until you, now."

No way could she miss the importance of him sharing this with her and how that linked them. "Thank you for choosing me to be the one you told."

She only wished she'd been less defensive earlier when he'd tried to discuss it with her.

He cupped her face in his hands, his green eyes glinting with intensity. "I want you to understand that the past doesn't, in any way, detract from what I feel for you." He tapped her lips, paused to stroke a slow, sensual circle. "And just to clarify in case there's any doubt about how I feel for you, I love you, Ashley Carson. I. Love. You."

The magic words. Even in her fantasies she hadn't dared go there, but then perhaps that was good. Reality definitely beat any dream relationship in a landslide victory. "I know you do, but it's still awesome to hear you say it." She nipped his thumb. "And quite convenient since I happen to love you, too."

His ragged sigh shared just how much her words meant to him, a strong man so determined to take on the world full speed ahead.

Matthew slipped his hand into his pocket and pulled it back out to reveal... Her engagement ring rested in his palm. "I'll understand if you would rather have a different one to mark our new beginning, but either way, I want our engagement to be real this time."

She placed her hand over his, over the diamond and the real promise it now held. "This is exactly the one I want. I wouldn't change a thing about our past because it brought us to this perfect moment. Yes, I'll marry you."

He pressed a hard, quick kiss to her lips before pulling back with a smile. "I'm not going to give you time to change your mind, you know."

Matthew slid the solitaire back in place.

She closed her fist, locking the ring on tight. "Nobody's going to pry it off my hand again."

"You're a mighty force to be reckoned with."

And she'd only just begun finding her footing.

Ashley looped her arms around his neck, arching up on her toes for another kiss she knew would lead her to the perfect end to a perfect day. "I'm more than ready to make this relationship real."

Epilogue

November: Election Night

"Latest polling reports are in," the widescreen plasma television blared in the family great room at the Landis compound.

Ashley held her breath as the second before the announcement seemed to stretch out with a slow-motion quality. Sitting with Matthew on the sofa, she gripped his hand, their family and friends around them. Five months ago, she never could have imagined how her life would change because of one impulsive decision to take a risk with the man of her dreams.

But here she was after months of campaigning, totally loving Matthew and finding she also fully enjoyed the new world he'd opened for her.

She'd once thought herself a background, live-in-the-shadows kind of person. Now she'd discovered the rush of being at the epicenter of reaching out to others. And when she needed to recharge? She had an even larger new family to embrace, a family who'd all come to share in this moment.

Her sisters and their husbands blended right in with the Landis brothers and General Renshaw's adult children. The general and Ginger had been an unexpected blessing in her life, taking her on as one of their own. Nobody could replace Aunt Libby, but Lordy, it felt good to experience the warmth and acceptance of parental love again.

Ashley squeezed Matthew's strong hand as the television announcer continued, "With ninety-one percent of the precincts reporting, the numbers indicate a clear victory for…"

She forced herself to breathe, keep her focus on Matthew and the TV rather than the hubbub behind them from the small media crew that had been allowed into the Landis compound to report about this moment.

"…the new senator from South Carolina, Matthew Landis," the announcer concluded.

The already crowded room overflowed with cheers. Matthew gathered Ashley into a tight hug. As much as she wanted to stay right there and revel, she knew there were others in the room who deserved to celebrate with him.

She kissed him quickly, intensely, before pulling back. "Congratulations, Senator Landis."

He nuzzled her ear, the gentle rasp of his whiskers sending a shiver of excitement mingling with the surge of joy. "Thank you, Mrs. Landis."

And what an added rush to hear her new name.

They'd quietly eloped two weeks ago, unable to wait any longer to make it official. While the immediate family already knew, she and Matthew would tell the rest of the world during his acceptance speech. They hadn't wanted their marriage to be tied up with the election outcome. The vows they'd spoken were all about them and not any political agenda.

After a final searing kiss, they eased apart and the rest of their huge wonderful family surrounded them in hugs and congrats. Ashley leaned into his muscular side since Matthew seemed determined to keep his arm around her waist.

Cameras continued to flash while streamers unfurled in the air. Hats, bunting and posters instantly redecorated the house with Senator Landis paraphernalia. A champagne bottle popped some-where in the distance, and thankfully Ginger seemed to have the first interview well in hand so Matthew could enjoy more celebratory time with the family.

Kyle clapped him on the shoulder. "Don't be getting the big head now, brother. I can still whoop your butt in golf any day."

"Of course you can." Matthew grinned good-naturedly. "Golfing is like a college degree for you Air Force guys."

Laughing and nodding along in agreement, Jonah passed Sebastian folded cash.

Matthew slugged his youngest brother in the arm, laughing. "Jonah, bro, you bet against me?"

Jonah slugged right back. "Dude, we were only betting on the spread of your landslide."

Ashley patted her brother-in-law's cheek. "You're forgiven then."

Matthew toyed with Ashley's ponytail streaming down her back from the gold clasp. "So tell me then, guys, who bet for the largest win?"

Sebastian—the most reserved of the group—offered up one of his rare smiles as he pocketed the cash. "We'll carry that secret to our grave."

Ashley basked in the moment as the general and Ginger beamed with parental pride. It didn't even bother her that the small hand-picked media group in the back recorded each embrace and high five and hug. She had nothing to hide and total confidence in the love she and Matthew had found.

As the media's attention swapped from Ginger to the general for a comment, Ashley turned to Matthew. "When will we be heading to campaign headquarters to give your acceptance speech?"

"Soon enough." He skimmed his lips over her temple, the warm scent of his aftershave teasing her senses. "First, I want to have a minute alone with you before we leave."

She flattened her hand to his chest, the cotton of his button-down shirt offering a tormenting barrier to the muscles beneath. "I think everyone would understand us stealing a moment to freshen up."

Matthew took her hand and led her through the throng with amazing speed. As they made their way toward the hall, her sisters each gave her another quick hug before exchanging secretive looks. Ashley started to quiz them, then Matthew distracted her with another kiss and before she knew it they were inside the bedroom she'd used when first staying in this home.

He kicked the door closed behind them, gathering her to his chest and sealing his mouth to hers for the kind of tongue-tangling, soul-searching kisses they wouldn't have dared exchange in front of any camera.

Matthew eased away only to rest his forehead on

hers. "I want to thank you for making all of this possible."

"You would have won with or without me." She cupped his handsome face in her hands.

"Since I've had enough of debates for a while, I'm not going to argue your point." He turned his head to press a lingering kiss in each of her palms. "But I want you to understand how much more this moment means because you're in my life, how much more connected I feel to what I'll be doing because of the insights you've given me."

His compliment touched her as deeply as any intimate caress they'd exchanged. "That's a lovely thing to say. Thank you."

"I want to give you something in return."

"You already have." This whole experience had helped her mine for depths inside herself she'd never known she possessed. "I have you, our family, our future."

"But I want you to have a home."

"Home will be where we're together."

"While I agree with you on that one, I also know how much you're giving up by splitting our lives between D.C. and here." He reached to the end table and picked up a folder she hadn't even noticed when they'd entered.

Probably because whenever he touched her she didn't notice much of anything else.

Matthew passed her an official-looking document.

Ashley frowned, studying the crisp paper in her hand, her mind scrambling to make sense of the words she saw but couldn't bring herself to comprehend, to believe. "This is the deed to Beachcombers, to Aunt Libby's mansion."

"Yes it is," he answered with a smug smile.

"But it already sold." An event she had accepted even though a piece of her heart still ached over that farewell. Except now that she stared at the name on the deed… No wonder her foster sisters had exchanged that knowing look a few moments ago.

"It sold to you. Sebastian took care of the purchasing process so as to mask my name from any of the transactions, and then I transferred the title to you." He thumbed a tear from her cheek she hadn't even known she'd shed. "We'll obviously spend a large portion of time in D.C., but we have to keep an official residence in South Carolina. So I thought we could make Aunt Libby's house in Charleston our official South Carolina residence."

She clasped the deed to her heart. "Are you sure? What about your family home here?"

"Absolutely sure." His green eyes glinted with unmistakable certainty. "Charleston is plenty close enough to Hilton Head for family visits. And you'll be near your sisters. The carriage house here will be too small once we start having kids."

Children. Hers and Matthew's. "I like the sound of that very much. Thank you. Those two simple words don't seem like enough, but there aren't words for how much this means to me."

Already she could envision all the ways she would want to shape the place into a home for them. Basic repairs had been completed and she wanted to stay true to the original décor of the traditional Southern mansion. But also with central AC, a state-of-the-art kitchen and adjoining rooms for her sisters to visit with their families.

Noise floated from the floor below, reminding her their alone time would be short tonight. A doorbell rang, no doubt more staff stopping by to congratulate the new senator. Fireworks popped in the distance, dogs barked in response. A light strobed right through the shades on the window as another news van pulled up outside.

Yet Matthew never once looked away from her face, his whole attention totally focused on her. "I'm glad you're happy about this. I want us to have our own place. The family compound idea worked well for a bachelor blowing in and out of town, but you and I deserve some privacy to explore the vast benefits of married life." His eyes took on an altogether different gleam, decidedly wicked.

"You're totally not a bachelor anymore." She relaxed into the arms of the man who'd stolen her heart and given her his own in return.

He raised her ring finger to his mouth and kissed the spot where her engagement ring and wedding band rested side by side. "Lucky for me, I went for the win."

* * * * *

Don't miss the next Landis brother story, when we get to learn all about Sebastian, available in December from Mills & Boon® Desire™.

She came to take his company… but would she lose her heart instead?

New York Times bestselling author

DIANA PALMER

True Colours

As a pregnant teenager, Cy Harden's family had driven her out of town. Now Meredith Ashe runs a multi-national corporation – and she's back to take over Harden Properties.

Meredith plans to let Cy think she's the same naive girl he abandoned years ago. But when Meredith falls for Cy again, even her carefully made plans can't protect her.

Available 7th August 2009

Rich, successful and gorgeous...

These Australian men clearly need wives!

Featuring:

THE WEALTHY AUSTRALIAN'S PROPOSAL
by Margaret Way

THE BILLIONAIRE CLAIMS HIS WIFE
by Amy Andrews

INHERITED BY THE BILLIONAIRE
by Jennie Adams

Available 21st August 2009

2 FREE

STORIES AND A SURPRISE GIFT!

We would like to take this opportunity to thank you for reading this Mills & Boon® book by offering you the chance to take TWO more specially selected titles from the Desire™ 2-in-1 series absolutely FREE! We're also making this offer to introduce you to the benefits of the Mills & Boon® Book Club™—

- ★ FREE home delivery
- ★ FREE gifts and competitions
- ★ FREE monthly Newsletter
- ★ Exclusive Mills & Boon Book Club offers
- ★ Books available before they're in the shops

Accepting these FREE books and gift places you under no obligation to buy, you may cancel at any time, even after receiving your free shipment. Simply complete your details below and return the entire page to the address below. You don't even need a stamp!

YES! Please send me 2 free Desire stories in a 2-in-1 volume and a surprise gift. I understand that unless you hear from me, I will receive 2 superb new 2-in-1 books every month for just £5.25 each, postage and packing free. I am under no obligation to purchase any books and may cancel my subscription at any time. The free books and gift will be mine to keep in any case.

D9ZED

Ms/Mrs/Miss/Mr ....Initials ....

BLOCK CAPITALS PLEASE

Surname ....

Address ....

....

....Postcode...................................

Send this whole page to:
UK: FREEPOST CN81, Croydon, CR9 3WZ

Offer valid in UK only and is not available to current Mills & Boon Book Club subscribers to this series. Overseas and Eire please write for details and readers in Southern Africa write to Box 3010, Pinegowie, 2123, RSA. We reserve the right to refuse an application and applicants must be aged 18 years or over. Only one application per household. Terms and prices subject to change without notice. Offer expires 30th September 2009. As a result of this application, you may receive offers from Harlequin Mills & Boon and other carefully selected companies. If you would prefer not to share in this opportunity please write to The Data Manager, PO Box 676, Richmond, TW9 1WU.

Mills & Boon® is a registered trademark owned by Harlequin Mills & Boon Limited.
Desire™ is being used as a trademark. The Mills & Boon® Book Club™ is being used as a trademark.